First published 2023

Text copyright © Athena M. Bliss
Cover design and illustrations copyright © Athena M. Bliss
Typesetting by Marluxia Bliss
Audio book recorded by Marluxia Bliss

A record of this book has been made available through the National Library of Aotearoa New Zealand.

The author would like to express their gratitude to the Margaret King Spencer Writers Encouragement Trust.

ISBN 978-1-7386012-0-2

www.athenabliss.com

Fair Muse, whose beauty graces every line

Whose inspiration sets my quill ablaze,

For in your grace my pen hath found its might

I dedicate this work,

to you,

my source of endless awe and praise.

No verse, no prose, could capture your true light,

yet still I strive to honor you with words.

For guiding me through dark and stormy nights,

I thank you, dear friend.

Forever yours.

And to my husband too, I GUESS >:/

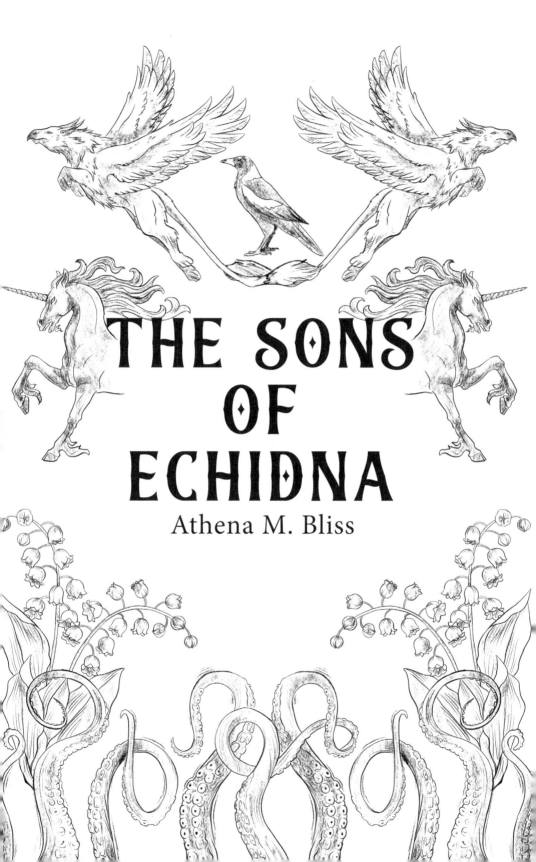

THE SONS OF ECHIDNA

Athena M. Bliss

A MISPLACED MOMENT

Lucy had failed.

She wasn't strong enough, she wasn't the chosen one.

She was just some girl, and she was in well over her head.

***

A cannonball tore through the manor's wall, hitting an antique Florentine mirror. It shattered on impact, showering Lucy with a hail of glass. Panic flared in her chest, her head in tense stalemate with her heart. Revenge or freedom? Should she abandon all she had worked for and run in a shameful twist of self preservation, or should she stay and finish what she had started?

Eleanore was just beyond the collapsed wall. Lucy could still feel the woman's life strings dancing on her fingertips; one pull and the bitch would be no more. Even without a vessel to put the stolen life in, just knowing Eleanore was dead would be worth it.

Hatred clouded her judgment, all reason suffocated by bitter memories as Lucy dashed towards the crumbling mound of rubble that separated her from her goal.

As always, the Gods had other plans.

The next fraction of a second played out in slow motion. Another projectile exploded through the brick and plaster, the smell of gunpowder filled the parlor room. Then the impact, sudden and brutal, hot iron momentarily pinning Lucy against the wall, shattering her hip and femur.

Searing pain blinded her as bone shards pierced her skin from the inside, stopped only by the leather armor that was supposed to protect her. Then to add insult to injury the wall behind her collapsed, abruptly ending the quest for revenge.

Lucy heard the crack of her spine breaking as a ton of rubble crushed her against the marble tile, dust filling her lungs.

Well, fuck.

She laughed through the coughing fit. She should have listened to Death. They had said months and apparently they had meant it.

A shadow blocked the warmth of the setting sun as a pair of feet appeared, walking towards her. Lucy could barely see through the steady stream of blood running down her face, but Death's neon pink sandals and toe nails painted with bright rainbow polish cut through the growing darkness.

"Speak of the Devil…" Lucy wheezed, struggling to take in a full breath.

She was too far gone for fear now, but even if she hadn't been in agony she couldn't make herself feel terrified of the white-haired, flowery dressed being that approached her now, a sympathetic smile on their face that made their cheeks bump the bottom of their heart-shaped, pink sunglasses.

"*Saa*...forgive me. I rarely enter uninvited, but since your house is lacking its doors now I took it as granted," Death offered cheerfully, kneeling beside Lucy.

"We might be here a while, suffocating is a slow process. But if I'm not mistaken, you have something that might speed things along."

The earring. Her last one. Cyanide.

Her trembling fingers reached for her earlobe, feeling for the tiny pearl. Lucy didn't want to die, but she would have been stupid to think that she would make it out of this alive. A quick tug and the closure released. All she had to do was bite down and the pain would end.

Not yet.

A magpie landed clumsily on her arm, snatching the earring from Lucy's bruised fingers.

This moment is mine. You gave it to me.

"Halcyon," Death frowned in protest. "It's her time. You can't interfere."

The magpie rounded on Death with a playful squark, snapping his beak at the neon plastic rings that covered every one of Death's fingers.

I am not interfering. I'm simply taking what is mine. The girl gave me a moment of her time. I chose the moment of her death.

"*Saa*, it's still her moment. You can't just remove it." Death folded their arms across their chest as the magpie flew up, holding the earring in his black beak. The bird squawked, mimicking a laugh.

I can and I am. It belongs to me now. Besides, I'm not removing it.

I'm just misplacing it.

"That will create a paradox. Humans can't survive such disruption."

No, they can't. Let's see if a lab-made Goddess can.

CHAPTER ONE

LUCY

I've dealt with the worst of humanity. I've survived the unthinkable.

I've been abused and abandoned. I have given all I had and received the bare minimum in return.

Nothing can scare me anymore. I've worked in retail.

Lucy clutched a small suitcase as her taxi stopped outside a dirt track leading into a dense forest. Mellow sunlight filtered through the canopy of budding spring foliage, casting golden hues over the path. She put on a brave face, hiding behind a strained smile, but panic still knotted her stomach.

"You sure you want me to drop you here, miss?" the driver asked, turning around. "Ain't nothing around here for miles. This track leads nowhere. I would know—lived 'round here all my life."

"Yes, thank you. Someone will be meeting me at the end." She shot him a look, a frown knitting her brow, then re-checked the creased paper on which she'd written the directions dictated to her over the phone. This was the right place.

Reaching inside her faded brown leather handbag, Lucy counted out the fare, leaving only a handful of change   not enough for a return trip. Not that she had anywhere to go back to.

Sometimes throwing yourself into the void with reckless abandon was the only way forward.

She pushed the car door open. It creaked in protest, cautioning her not to leave, but she ignored it and watched the taxi make a U-turn and leave only a cloud of dust.

The tree-shaded path led her through bush that crept along its sides, twisted, finger-like branches snagging on Lucy's skirt and untamed chestnut-and-bleach waves. She brushed them off, focusing on the birds' distant singing— a pleasant change from the constant hum of Houston.

Inhaling the raw, earthy scent of rain-soaked ground, she could almost taste the faint aroma of wild lavender. Healing. Soothing, but not enough to ease her worries. She brought up possible scenarios of things going wrong. Who knew what was hiding among ancient tree trunks layered with velvety coverings of moss.

Serial killers, bears...handsome fae lords from the countless novels on her bookshelf? She scoffed. This was Texas; it was *definitely* serial killers.

On the bright side, if I die here, I won't have to worry about bills.

Dwelling on that strangely comforting thought, Lucy found herself at the end of the path with a wrought iron gate guarding the road ahead. It towered above her, threatening to crumble into a rusty pile of dust if she dared to move it. She peered through the twisted vines consuming the metal bars, but the thick foliage obscured the building behind it.

"Hi, I'm Lucy. Here for the job..." she whispered as she squeezed through the tight gap in the gate. "Hello! A pleasure to meet you. I'm Lucille." Another forced smile tensed her face; it all seemed so easy in practice. "Greetings. I'm—I'm—"

She stopped in her tracks as the house came into view. Shadowy and vast, the old building stretched across a large estate of overgrown gardens. It was nestled in the valley of the surrounding mountains, crowned by a thick wall of forest that created a verdant halo over the manor.

The peeling plaster revealed red brick like bloody wounds through pale skin. But it wasn't the crumbling walls, broken glass in the windows, or missing parts of the roof that worried Lucy. A house of this size—so grand and imposing—should be bustling with life. Servants, gardeners, and pets, yet there it stood—derelict and seemingly abandoned.

Perfect. I came all this way for nothing.

Lucy braced herself for the long walk back to the city when the movement of a curtain caught her eye. There was someone home after all. Perhaps she had been too hasty, giving into the embrace of anxiety rather than reason. Who could blame her? Lucy's bank account was now in the red, and choosing her employment was a luxury she didn't have.

Approaching the front door, she examined the ornate knocker. It was a heavy cast-iron ouroboros piece: a snake-like creature circled and biting its tail—a curious mix of menacing and garish.

"Come on. It's this or the streets." She flexed her fingers, reaching for it.

Just before her hand could touch the cold metal, the howls of dogs startled her. Canine bodies slammed into the weathered wood, bowing it as the rusty hinges creaked under pressure. Lucy stumbled backwards, ready to flee if the door gave in.

"Back! Back away, you mongrels! Where are your manners?" A hoarse voice barked from behind the door. To Lucy's surprise, the dogs obeyed quickly; the sound of claws scrambling on tile faded away, training outweighing protective instincts.

"Back to your father, and don't let me see you until dinner. Don't need you scaring away another one." Two heavy-sounding locks thudded and a man swung open one of the double doors.

The light beaming in lit up an immaculately pressed white shirt with a well-worn brown vest and dark trousers. He was tall with cheekbones jutting out painfully against the skin of his face. Lucy could see fresh stains on his loose sleeves and a powdering of flour over the dark fabric in hand-print shapes. Black, sleek hair barely reached the sculpted jawline.

His age was difficult to pinpoint—young enough not to have any wrinkles, but heavy bags under his eye aged him with the look of a constantly tired parent. He might have been handsome if he didn't look so close to dying.

The butler offered his gloved hand to her in a greeting and stepped aside.

"Please, come in." He adjusted the eye-patch over his right eye and motioned to her bag. "May I take your things?"

"Oh, yes! Of course! I'm Lucy, by the way. Here for the job?" She smiled awkwardly, shaking his hand before handing over her suitcase. "We spoke on the phone."

"Yes. Call me Klein." His mouth curved up slightly at the corners as he gestured for her to follow.

Nodding a polite 'thank you', she proceeded into the house, the sudden drop in temperature sending goosebumps up her bare arms. Inside, she fell silent, her eyes darting around at the rotting splendor. The entry hall was rich with tarnished décor. Statues, paintings and crystal light fixtures, all dilapidated from either neglect or lack of funds—perhaps both. It must have been beautiful once, before mold and mildew had devoured the wallpaper.

"Woah. Are you guys house-flippers or something?" Lucy asked in awe as he shut the door behind her, still gaping at the room. She had never seen anything like it in real life.

Klein didn't answer.

She cleared her throat and followed him.

The manor's interior gave the same impression as the exterior; a once-grand and opulently decorated home, well overdue for a deep clean and a declutter. Old portraits of long-dead ancestors looked down through a layer of spider webs that covered their faces like veils.

Damp air thick on her tongue, Lucy examined brass fittings and mold gathered in sporadic waves across the furnishings. No matter where she looked, the decay of time had left its mark; rotting window frames and loose floorboards that creaked with each step.

Is it safe for children to live here?

"So you said this was a nannying position..."

"We can discuss your employment over breakfast." Klein joined the one-sided conversation at last. "The family will be meeting you shortly. Please, take a seat." He motioned towards dusty glass doors leading to the dining room.

Lucy blinked in awe as she approached a long table set up in silver for a banquet of fifty guests or so. Again, a second look revealed a different truth. Most of the place settings were unused, covered in a layer of dust. The silver was tarnished and begging for a good polish. The only signs of actual partaking of food were at the far end, where the tablecloth looked relatively clean and the cutlery freshly scrubbed.

Klein waited for her to sit down before resuming his duties, setting up plates of poached eggs and bacon still sizzling with flavorful fat. Lucy chose a seat near the head of the table and lowered herself timidly onto a creaky antique chair to begin the awkward wait.

Time dragged on, holding its breath in anticipation. Lucy closed her eyes and imagined a wise old lady of the house coming down the grand staircase and offering her a lazy, well-paid job. Perhaps this would be the lucky break Lucy had tried to manifest unsuccessfully for years. No more micromanaging tyrants and useless co-workers. No more dealing with weirdos and creeps through the night shifts.

No more struggling.

Just thinking about it soothed her, but before her daydream could come to a satisfying conclusion, Lucy heard footsteps.

"Morning," she smiled at the boy sitting down opposite her. He looked young. Maybe twelve at the most. Black slicked-back curls hung around an arrogant face. He barely spared a glance for her, either far too invested in the book his nose was glued to, or he didn't think she was worth his time.

"I'm Lucy," she beamed, hoping to make a good first impression.

Nothing.

He didn't seem interested. Perhaps strangers at the dining table weren't that uncommon. They must have a big staff turnaround.

Red flag. An annoying sting of anxiety pestered her like a determined mosquito.

The boy poured himself a cup of black coffee and turned a page of the book.

"So…um…what're you reading?"

A glance over the leather-bound tome. This time with a hint of annoyance. "None of your business—Ouch!" His face slammed into the book.

"Manners, you little brat." A young man who had just delivered a firm slap to the back of the young boy's head smiled. He had the same olive skin and piercing, icy blue eyes as the other, but they couldn't be less alike. "My, my. What do we have here?" he purred. "A guest!"

Lucy shrugged, unsure of how to respond. She didn't even know where to look. He wore a heavy silk robe over his bare body, a richly embroidered hem dragging behind. Each step he took seemed determined to make a memorable first impression. Strutting like a peacock he approached the table, his waist-length lavender hair in a loose braid resting over bare shoulder. He flexed fingers decorated with a few dainty rings and tapped his chin.

"Father has a type, doesn't he?" His voice snapped Lucy out of her daze. "But where are my manners? Forgive me. I'm Leander, though my friends call me Lai. The brat here is my brother Ryan. Pay him no mind. I don't."

A long pause followed as Lai waited for some kind of response. It took a slight nod from him for Lucy to remember her basic etiquette.

"Oh! Sorry. I'm Lucille. Lucy. It's good to meet you."

"A beautiful name befitting its owner."

"You have a beautiful house," Lucy blurted out, unsure how to respond to the compliment.

Lai cocked his head and smiled.

"Why, thank you. If you're into the whole Addams Family aesthetic, I guess it can be called beautiful. Personally, I find it grim. If it was up to me, I'd level the whole thing and build something a little more…modern." He sat down and pulled over a tray of freshly baked pastries, picking up a custard danish with a pair of dainty silver tongs and fully submerging it in his coffee. Lucy saw Ryan grimace.

"Help yourself. No reason to wait for anyone." Lai pushed the coffee pot towards her. "Try and eat something before my father gets here. I bet you'll lose your appetite fairly quickly when you meet him." Lai rolled his eyes.

Lucy looked up from his revolting coffee cup, questions written all over her face.

"Oh, you'll see. And don't say I didn't warn you. Daddy is old fashioned. Very old fashioned," Lai laughed, sipping on his thick, custardy coffee. "Try not to let it get to you. Nod politely, don't speak unless spoken to, and promptly ignore anything he says. It's what I do, and it's worked well for me so far."

As good advice as any. But he is *the guy's son.*

Lucy had used the same method to survive years of retail work; it couldn't be that bad. Old-fashioned managers that treated their workers like livestock were the norm. Dinosaurs like that didn't scare her. They may have a position of some authority, but she knew how the game was played. In the end, they all had to ask her for help. This man would be just like them, she was sure.

"I hope I fit in." She smiled at Lai as she poured herself some coffee.

"Oh, you will, I don't doubt it. It's not like we have volunteers lining out of the door. Only had one before you; the poor guy didn't last the night."

"Why?" Lucy blinked at him, ignoring the increasingly loud voice of doubt at the back of her mind.

'Didn't have the stomach for it, I guess." Lai shrugged. "This job is not for the faint of heart."

Alarm bells were definitely ringing now. The description had sounded like a nanny position. Start with cleaning, make sure the kids are dressed, and feed the pets. Easy enough, right?

"I'm sorry, but what do you mean by that?" Lucy inquired, hoping not to sound clueless. "Is there something I need to know?"

Lai paused, then clicked his tongue. It felt like he had a lot to tell but chose not to, quickly changing the subject. "So, you look normal. Fairly presentable. Anyone going to notice if you go missing?"

Very funny. He's winding me up.

"My mother knows. She's expecting a follow-up call to see how the interview went in about an hour." Lucy glanced at her phone, double-checking her pocket for the pepper spray that she carried in case of emergency.

No one would call. Only her friend Xim was aware of her career move, and she had promised to give Lucy some space after their fight.

"There's no signal here; I wouldn't bother." Lai noticed her glance down. "So let's hear more about you, honeybuns. How old are you?" He placed his feet on the table and leaned back, the old chair creaking beneath his weight.

"Those don't belong on the table." Lucy gave Lai a pointed look. "I'm twenty-five. How old are *you?*"

"Rude question to ask. Just look at me, not a day over eighteen." He shrugged, not even attempting to disguise the obvious lie.

Lucy rolled her eyes.

"Fine. How about you give me some real information. What do I need to do here? You don't look like you need a babysitter."

Klein snorted as he listened in on the conversation, ignoring a dagger-like glare from Lai. "A bit of everything," the butler explained vaguely. "Maintenance work, cooking, caring for children and animals." Lucy noticed the change in intonation at 'children' along with a long look at the lavender-haired man.

"I can do that. Children and animals are just about the same thing."

"Don't let Father hear you say that. He loves his animals way more than his kids. Speak of the devil—" Lai sat up straight and fixed up the revealing robe. "Remember: old fashioned," he added in a whisper as he pretended to focus on a piece of bacon.

The atmosphere changed immediately when the head of the household entered the dining room. The air thickened with tension, making it hard to swallow. She'd expected an older gentleman with a distinguished look in a crisp suit with a newspaper under his arm, but the man who emerged looked nothing like that.

He looked rough. *Rough* might have been an understatement. His bronze skin was covered in scars, each telling a tale of an adventure, and if an old battle wound didn't mark his flesh, a faded tattoo decorated it.

Like Klein and Lai, it was difficult to decipher his age. He had the deep frown lines of someone who had seen half a century pass, yet the muscle definition of a man still in his prime.

He carried himself with a posture of effortless power. Tall, with dark, messy curls falling across his broad shoulders. His faded linen shirt was marked with soot and singed holes.

"Settle, girls..." he ordered. For a moment, Lucy thought he was talking to her before she noticed his pets: six massive dogs.

They were a strange breed, one she had never seen before, with black, coiled fur that looked scorched. Their bright orange eyes glowed like lumps of coal in a winter's hearth.

The hounds obeyed without hesitation, laying down around their master's chair, but Lucy couldn't take her eyes away from them. Their breath was visible even in the relatively mild temperature. One of them let a drop of drool fall from their loose jowls, the fluid hissing as it hit the cold marble floor. In their presence, the room felt a few degrees warmer.

"Ummm...that's an interesting breed."

"Do not speak unless spoken to." His eyes snapped to Lucy's face at the sound of her voice, noticing her for the first time.

Biting the inside of her cheek, Lucy met his frigid gaze. She wanted to shrink into a tiny ball of regret, but Klein's firm hand on her shoulder as he wheeled a breakfast trolley past gently reassured her.

"What is your name, girl?" Her new boss watched her, with a twitch of his scarred lip showing quick-forming disdain.

I hate him already.

"Lucille, sir," she said, her throat suddenly sandpaper dry.

"I am Aristos Galanos; Aris to those that matter. You will call me 'sir', and you'll be working for me." He picked up the juiciest piece of bacon on the platter and fed it to one of his dogs. The biggest bitch licked her master's fingers, begging for more. She didn't have to wait long.

"The house has a strict code of conduct you will follow. Any deviation can be catastrophic for you and anyone living here. Klein will explain all of them to you, and I expect absolute obedience." Another piece of bacon left the silver tray and was quickly devoured by a happy hound.

"Yes, sir." She wanted to roll her eyes, her inherent dislike of authority bubbling close to the surface, but a bright red flash of a negative bank balance cooled her temper. Right now, she needed the job more than her pride.

"You'll be paid monthly and possibly receive days off."

"I—Possibly?"

"As you can tell, we are quite isolated. I'd rather not waste the time I'm paying for on your childish whimsy. I need someone dedicated to the role; this position will require your undivided attention."

Deep breath. In and out.

The scenario playing out in front of her was strange but all too familiar.

"What about my pay? How much will I be getting?"

Aris blinked slowly, uninterested in continuing that particular line of question. "It's rude to discuss money in front of others. Haven't you been taught that? Your pay will be adequate."

"How much per hour is adequate?"

The question went unanswered as the head of the family got up from his seat and examined her like a prize cow at auction.

"How old are you?"

As Lucy tried to fashion a response, a shiver ran down her spine, unsettling her rapidly fraying nerves. Aris leaned in closer, triggering a deep primal response, making every hair on her arms stand erect with his predatory stalking.

"She's twenty-five, not too bad," Lai volunteered.

"Did I ask for your *charming* insight?" Aris frowned, his lips pressing into a thin line. "A little past your prime. Unmarried. What's wrong with you?"

Indignation flared in her bones. "Excuse me?!"

"I'm asking if you have any physical abnormalities. Perhaps hysterical tendencies?"

Lucy felt her eye twitch, the irritation seeping to the surface.

Hysterical tendencies? What is this—the nineteenth century? Is it even legal to ask those questions?

"I'm healthy, thank you very much."

He gave his son a look, and Lucy watched the little exchange. Lai simply shrugged, his face full of amusement and impish delight.

Aris sighed. "Lai will find you a room, and Klein will provide orientation. You start your duties tomorrow morning." He waved his hand, dismissing any further questions.

The interview was over.

CHAPTER TWO

KLEIN

Klein's hands flitted from folded to stuffed in his pockets to folded again. Nothing felt natural. He pressed his fingertips together in an unintentionally menacing gesture, which he quickly dismantled.

Don't get your hopes up. She won't stay.

He tried to relax his posture, only to look more stiff and cloddish. How could one girl throw his entire equilibrium askew? Another failed candidate. She was just that. Was it even worth getting to know her?

A few days and she'd leave. Things would go back to normal.

"Ready for your orientation?"

Lucy nodded, but looked as though her mind was elsewhere.

"Are you sure?" He leaned in, trying to catch her full attention.

Familiar insecurity wormed its way inside. He was always the invisible one; he was used to it by now.

"Oh! Yeah, sorry!" She laughed it off. "Just need some fresh air. It was quite an introduction. Mind if we start outside?"

Klein couldn't see a reason not to. He nodded and motioned for her to follow.

"Yes, if you can ignore his sandpaper personality the man isn't that bad, I swear. You'll hardly see him if that is of any consolation."

Stained glass double doors led from the dining room into the garden. Despite the unkempt shabbiness and overabundance of weeds, the garden had its charm. Topiaries that had once been perfectly manicured stood overgrown with wild vines that used them to creep closer to the light, while the morning sun warmed the cobblestone paths and encouraged the wildlife to enjoy its rays out in the open. Lizards with reflective scales basked around the rim of a bird bath that held only a splash of greenish water.

Embarrassment warmed his cheeks. The gardens were hardly anything to be proud of. With most of his time spent maintaining the house, the great outdoors were greatly neglected. Only one small patch of flowerbeds got any of his attention, a collection of herbs. For medicinal use and pleasure.

"As you can see, it needs a cleansing fire." Klein motioned to the wild hedges and overgrown planters. "I keep meaning to tackle it, but honestly, I wouldn't know where to start. I am but one man and this is a job for a dozen."

"It's beautiful. I honestly prefer it wild." She offered an encouraging smile. "I don't like trimmed lawns. They're bad for the environment."

Lucy knelt beside a patch of grass that was slowly reclaiming the footpath, reaching out to stroke the petals of a lily of the valley that was peeking out of the shade. Picking one stem covered in tiny white blooms, she placed the flower in her breast pocket.

Klein strolled alongside her in comfortable silence. He didn't want to interrupt the idyllic moment with the burden of business just yet. In all honesty, he didn't want the morning to end. It felt good just to talk to someone, a fresh face, a face that studied everything with innocent child-like curiosity.

That was until a gecko Lucy was examining was snatched up and devoured right in front of her. She screamed, stumbling back and pointing at the peacock, the lizard's bright tail still sticking from inside its beak.

"Ah." Klein stepped forward, standing in between her and the bird. "Meet Barbara. Lai's pet and problem." Should he mention the years-old feud now, between Lai and the bird? A bird bred especially for him and who now blamed its existence on the man, terrorizing him any chance it got?

No. She would find out eventually. At the expense of Lai's dignity, no doubt.

Lucy looked a little shaken but nodded, turning away from a gruesome sight. Klein didn't want her to be traumatized further by that dreadful creature so he steered deeper into the garden. Away from any more unpleasant encounters. He was used to the bizarre ecosystem formed by the family's eclectic collection but to anyone new the dynamic might be startling.

"That's a weird-looking mermaid." Lucy's voice snapped Klein out of a daze; she seemed ready to change the topic. He froze for a moment but joined her by a marble statue of a woman with two snake tails.

This is somehow worse.

"That's Echidna, the 'Mother of All Monsters'. All of the great beasts of myth can be traced back to her bloodline. Well– all the beasts within the greater Mediterranean region. Let's not give her too much credit."

What was that?

Klein chastised himself. Why not tell her everything else? He could've just passed it on as a random statue. He could already imagine Lai's groans when he would eventually find out.

"Never heard of her. Are you sure she's not from Starbucks?" Lucy scrunched up her nose, as if trying to remember something. "Not the prettiest of statues, I gotta be honest."

Klein tapped his fingers against the weathered stone, watching her.

"She's the patron of this family. Or matron, I guess. The Galanos clan trace their bloodline back to her."

Stop it. Stop. She didn't even ask. You will either compromise the family or sound like a nut job. Klein wasn't sure which one was worse.

Lucy snorted; that little noise felt like relief. She didn't believe him and had no further questions. The less she knew, the better she'd sleep.

"Shall we start with the house rules?" Klein watched her wander off in search of something new to look at, his heart skipping a beat. A few more minutes and he would have volunteered more secrets. "I wouldn't call them rules per se. More like stringent guidelines." He followed Lucy, unsure if she was paying attention.

"I'm listening." She smiled at him; his concern must have been obvious.

"Firstly, you are not to visit certain places without supervision. The west wing is out of bounds except for Aris's office and chambers. That marble pavilion you may see in the distance? It's for family only. Oh and the forest? That's especially off-limits."

Lucy glanced over to the pavilion, a miniature replica of a Greek temple complete with Doric columns, a grin forming on her face.

"You know it's hard to resist things when you're told they're forbidden, right?"

Klein had no response to that; he knew the temptation all too well.

"I mean it. The forest may look inviting but you must never enter alone."

Lucy scrunched her nose, considering the rule. "What's in there?"

"Not something you need to concern yourself with."

"Yeah, that makes it sound like I should be very concerned. What are you hiding?" She frowned.

"Nothing."

"Come on, don't start this friendship with a lie."

Their relationship had started with a lie long before this conversation. From the newspaper ad, from the phone call, from the greeting at the door.

"Klein..." Lucy sighed. "I listen to serial killer and horror podcasts so I can sleep. If you tell me there is something creepy in that forest, I'll be there all night looking for it."

"...Fine. It's full of–" He paused, trying to think of something that might scare someone her age. "…Spiders."

Idiot. She's not five!… Yet the answer had the desired effect. And it wasn't exactly a lie.

Lucy took a deep breath and turned away, poorly hiding a smile. "Say no more."

Klein looked back at the old warped trunks in the distance, spotting a shadow darting in between them. Even if he could tell Lucy the truth, all he could offer were personal theories. There were few things he knew for sure. The forest was there to keep intruders out and to keep the family in. No one ever returned from it and whatever was lurking in the woods was… big.

"Anyway," he quickly changed the subject. "Rule number two. Do not open doors if you don't know what's on the other side. Rule number three—invite no one in and make no deals." He gave Lucy a look, reminding her to take mental notes.

"I hope you know how weird and shady that sounds. You're taking this haunted mansion thing a bit too far. Fine… Knock before entering and shoo all unsolicited salesmen. Is that what you meant?"

Klein narrowed his eye; an oversimplification, but close enough. Lucy looked smart; she wouldn't do anything stupid. However, he knew she wasn't taking him seriously– 'Make no deals' was a fundamental rule if you considered the squatters the house was riddled with. Then again, he had thought that the other house inhabitants were smart enough to stay away from dodgy deals and had been disappointed on more than one occasion. Worst of all, Klein felt that he had been beyond bargaining with the Fae, and yet he had found himself in debt to a particularly nasty pest.

"Rule number four–and you're distracted again, aren't you?" He let his arms drop, sighing heavily. Lucy's eyes were drawn to marble columns. "You want to see the pavilion."

She nodded. Klein hesitated, torn; on the one hand, the tour might earn him a few brownie points with the newcomer, but on the other, this would end badly for both if Aris saw them. The head of the family was not one to hold his temper in check.

"We have to be quick, alright? In and out." He looked around to make sure no one would spot them breaking the first rule already and led her to the miniature temple, nestled among climbing rose bushes.

"I know you think it's something exciting." Klein stepped inside, beckoning her to follow. "Sorry to disappoint; it's just an old tomb."

He watched Lucy examine the tombstone carved out with sirens and scenes of sailing. She couldn't read the inscription in a foreign language, but she didn't need to. The glass sarcophagus built into the floor revealed the interred.

"Oh..." Lucy gasped, covering her mouth. Inside it laid a woman. She looked like death had claimed her only yesterday. Her olive skin and long, sun-bleached hair mirrored Lucy's perfectly, but the glass was covered in lichen, and the headstone was old and weathered.

Klein was about to answer the question before she could even voice it, but the sound of footsteps made him freeze. He knew that heavy, confident stride, with the sounds of dogs accompanying it.

"What the fuck do you think you're doing?" Aris growled, grabbing Klein by the upper arm, dragging him away from the tomb.

Of course you wouldn't trust me alone with her. I'm the only one she can be safe around.

"Please, it's my fault–" Klein explained quickly, knowing well enough the physical disadvantage he was at but eager to protect Lucy from Aris's wrath.

"Silence! Take a walk, girl. Don't stray too far. I'll decide what to do with you later."

"I asked to see." Lucy clenched her fists, wanting to clear up the confusion, but Klein shook his head, warning her against arguing. He knew that escalating this fight would not end well. It was better to give it time to settle.

"Just go enjoy the gardens, okay?" He offered her an encouraging smile that must have done little to reassure her with Aris standing there, seething. "Please."

The fuse was burning, and the longer she lingered, the more likely she was to get hurt. "Go." He saw her hesitation, but she finally listened and, with a slight nod, left the pavilion, glaring at Aris.

Klein stared at the man, wincing at the depth of the grave he had dug, hoping Lucy wouldn't hear the fallout of his poor judgment. The last thing he wanted was to sour her first day with violence.

"Have you lost your mind?" Aris demanded as he circled around Klein like a hunter stalking its prey. "Are we going to have a problem? Is a pair of tits enough to cloud your judgment?"

"No, sir." Klein's jaw stiffened with repulsion at the implication.

He tried to argue but Aris waved away any attempt at a protest. "We need her. I need her. But I don't need her *that* much."

Yes you do. You are out of options. You've tried everything and you are getting desperate.

"Next time she slips, it's on you. I won't have that kind of liability roaming the estate. I mean it, Klein. One more mistake, and you will be the one to put her down. She can't leave."

"I understand."

"Do you? Need I remind you what is at stake here? I will not be the weak link that lets the dynasty die. Play along…"

The crushing weight of expectations sunk Klein's shoulders. He had been playing along. For far too long.

"…this job is a hard sell–"

A single hand gesture and Klein knew his explanation would fall on deaf ears, but he sensed something else. Something aside from anger.

Klein could smell it and so could the anxious dogs.

The head of the pack stank of fear.

CHAPTER THREE

LUCY

Lucy took a path west, her mind still lingering at the pavilion. She felt terrible for getting Klein in trouble on her first day here; perhaps she could make it up to him later somehow?

She heard no commotion or anything that suggested that the argument had turned physical, which was a slight relief.

And even after that display, she couldn't help but enjoy the garden.

Despite the knot twisting in her stomach, she still loved the wild, overgrown paths and garden beds that bloomed with fragrant flowers. It was a shame that the brute of a man had put a dampener on it.

She strolled hidden paths with only pale marble statues for company, their empty eyes watching her with sorrowful understanding. Any other day she would have found the garden of ghost-like figures unnerving, but not today. Today their presence comforted her.

Lucy passed a statue of a fierce goddess holding a bow, hand outstretched to anyone needing help. Feeling a bit silly, she accepted the gesture only to find the hand warm to the touch. Its unexpected warmth soothed her. For a moment she startled, before realizing the stone was warmed by the sun; she gave an embarrassed laugh that felt irreverent in front of the warrior.

A tinge of pain stabbed near Lucy's heart. Holding the statue's hand like that had made her think of how much she missed Xim. Her best friend had tried everything she could think of to keep Lucy safe in her home with her, but Lucy's ego had made up its own mind. She couldn't keep sleeping on the couch while Xim's parents whispered about her in the next room.

The Farrowatchers were wealthy, successful, and educated, while she...well, she was an impostor, a gate-crasher who knew she wasn't as welcome as they pretended she was. Not that she was ungrateful. They took her in after her parents passed, and provided her with everything a girl needed. Still, Lucy never felt she was good enough for them, or for their daughter.

Letting go of delicate carved fingers Lucy continued, following the path past a small family chapel. She peered through its windows, but the darkness inside kept all of its secrets. Disappointed, she walked until the cobblestones turned into a dirt track, and the garden rose up to escape its borders as it turned into thick scrub.

Lucy hesitated. Aris had told her not to stray too far, but her curiosity–and her pride– strangled all reason. The mosquito voice of doubt buzzed at the base of her skull as she stepped off the path and into the overgrowth; she laughed off her anxiety. The forest was still some distance away.

The thin track–more of a goat path than anything else–wound for what felt like quarter of a mile through the tall grass before finally starting to thin as she reached the end. Lucy had no idea what she had expected to find there, but what she did stole her breath away; she gasped in awe as the light bounced off of a mirror-like lake, rimmed with pale pebbles around its shore. But it wasn't the body of water that stopped her in her tracks; an enormous ship, three-masted and fully rigged, rested on the surface, a dozen cannons reflecting light from the gun deck.

Lucy felt so tiny at that moment, dwarfed by the sleeping giant. She cautiously approached the water's edge, examining every little detail of the magnificent ship; the hand-carved designs, intricate rigging, and gilded letters painstakingly picked out along her side.

Artemis.

She couldn't understand how the ship had come to be there, bobbing in the lake like a giants' bath toy. There was no ocean for miles, but Lucy inhaled a lungful of fresh, salt-scented air. It brought back memories of summers on the coast, of happier times. She dipped her fingers in the water and licked them, her taste buds immediately overwhelmed by brine and seaweed.

"Salt lake. This family has way too much money." Lucy sighed in defeat as she kicked off her shoes and socks, carefully storing them on the stones out of the waters' reach. She laid down to bask in the warm morning sun, her feet in the water, the backs of her calves licked by the gentle waves. She watched the clouds float above her and enjoyed the soft caresses. For the first time in a long, long time, her thoughts didn't want to carry her away. She was there and now. Aware of every sensation. The water, the sand, the sun on her skin and something wet and powerful wrapped around her ankle.

What?

She didn't see the subtle movement below the surface. In the blink of an eye, the water tension broke, and a thick tentacle hauled her into the cold. Her scream was abruptly silenced by the icy water filling her lungs.

She had no time to think; her hand instinctively grasped for the keys in her pocket, grabbing them out in a well-practiced grip for the walks to her car after a late shift. She wrapped her fingers around the improvised weapon, stabbing blindly at the tentacle pulling her under; the water churned as the monster loosened its hold, and Lucy dashed up towards the surface.

The sun promised her safety, and with a desperate gasp, Lucy breached; the *thing* had towed her far from shore. Frantically she splashed towards the dock. She wasn't a strong swimmer, shoulders and chest aching as her primal instincts forced each clumsy stroke.

Just a little more. Almost there.

Lucy saw him between gasps; Aris stood on the edge of the pier as she fought for her life. She felt a flood of relief and tried to shout, but her lungs were full of seawater, and she barely managed a gurgle. He was there to help.

Wasn't he?

He watched Lucy, his face impassive as a tentacle rose from the water just behind her.

She made one desperate attempt to pull herself from the water, elbows trembling beneath her weight; she reached for Aris, expecting help.

"Take a deep breath," he smirked as he kicked her into the water. Lucy fell back with a cry, dragged into darkness as the monster wrapped around her waist.

That bastard!

No, she wouldn't give him the satisfaction.

Even with her life on the line, Lucy hesitated. Her dark secret. The power that only left misery in its wake. She didn't know what it was or how to use it, it just happened and she needed it to happen now.

She sunk her nails into the tentacle and pulled. Not at the flesh but at life. The soul, the memories– the monsters' energy drained from its tentacles and into her mind, feeding her aching lungs and exhausted muscles.

One by one golden threads she could see only in her mind unraveled in Lucy's grasp, light and life seeping from them. Lucy imagined yanking them with all her strength and to her relief the tentacle released her, the creature retreating back into the depths. The few seconds of oxygen Lucy had left were barely enough to get to the surface before she blacked out.

***

She woke up to vomit in her throat and pressure on her chest. She flailed to shove off the boot that was crushing under her breastbone, furious that she had lived through the lake only to be suffocated on land. Her fingers dug into the leather, but the man was stronger, pushing the hard sole under her ribs.

Then it all came up, her body purging swallowed water, her lungs burning with salt. Lucy bent over and coughed up the last of it, panic pushed aside by rage.

"You watched me die!" She wiped her mouth, forcing herself to focus on Aris.

"You are not dead," he answered, almost wistful.

"What the fuck was that?" She demanded as she struggled to her feet, shaking knees barely supporting her weight. In response, a thick tentacle rose from the water; Lucy scrabbled back from the shore as fast as her exhausted legs could carry her, but the tendril didn't seem interested in her, holding itself out to Aris, Lucy's keys jammed deep into its flesh.

"I couldn't care less if she ate you. It's your own damn fault; I told you not to wander." Aris frowned as he reached for the injured arm.

"She is old and harmless. You are the monster that hurt her."

He carefully removed the keys and threw them at Lucy's feet.

They were sticky with blood.

"Have you fucking lost it?" She demanded, outraged. "I almost died, and you're standing there petting that– that thing– like it's one of your fucking dogs!" Lucy picked up the keychain and clutched it to her chest, her entire body trembling, not sure if it was from anger or the cold.

She felt the weight of the keys in her palms, grounding her from the insanity around her. Her apartment belonged to a stranger now, her car had been written off months ago, and the little locker key from her past job was just as useless. None of the keys unlocked any doors.

Carrying them felt like little more than habit. A life-saving habit.

"Go back, girl, before I lose my temper." Aris let go of the tentacle, watching it retreat into the water. "You're scaring Martha."

Martha. Of course. That's an appropriate name for a Kraken.

"I'm not going anywhere except my room to change, then you and I are gonna talk," Lucy spat, jabbing her finger at Aris. "If I'm gonna stay—"

"You aren't. You will pack your things and leave."

Lucy froze, a wave of fresh nausea flooding her gut. She couldn't go back. She couldn't face Xim as a failure. She'd promised her. Lucy promised she would make something of her life. She would earn the money, she would have a fresh start. Returning now, empty handed and begging for a place to stay, was a fate worse than death. Aris may as well have let the monster eat her.

"Joke's on you, asshole. I haven't even unpacked." Anger refueled Lucy's weary body as she turned and stormed towards the house.

Aris didn't so much as spare her a glance, watching the lake water settle into a mirror-smooth finish.

CHAPTER FOUR

LUCY

She ran into the house, bitter tears blinding her.

"Fucking assho–ahhh!" Lucy cried out in panic, arms flailing as she tripped over something, the sudden fall leaving her no time to react as she scrabbled for something to grab onto. A split second before impact a pair of strong hands caught her, saving her from the merciless floor.

"You tripped me!" Lucy twisted sharply to face her savior, a familiar face framed with lavender hair.

"Yes, but I've also caught you. Why must you focus on the negatives?" Lai gave her a cocky grin as he helped Lucy back to her feet.

She wanted to punch him in his smug face.

"Your father threw me out and being murdered wasn't in the contract. I almost got eaten by a giant fucking squid!"

"Was there a contract?" Lai raised an eyebrow, determined to keep winding her up.

"Shut up." She shoved him, but to her surprise found the young man unyielding. She tried to push him again with both hands. "Jesus, how heavy are you?"

"Okay, now you're just being rude," Lai huffed. "Get inside, now. You're filthy and not in any state to leave anyway."

He was right, of course; Lucy sniffed like a scolded child. Looking down, she noticed rips in her tights, bruised knees and a trail of wet, muddy footsteps.

"I need to go. I'm sorry, but this is too much."

I have to stay. I have no options left.

Lai paused, an odd expression on his face. "You can't leave."

Her blood turned to ice in her veins. Lucy wanted to ask why, but she knew the answer. She had seen too much; the strange hounds, the giant squid, the... she didn't want to think the words, but they formed in her mind unbidden: *Magic.* Her mind raced with questions and half baked solutions.

Whoever those people were, she was now their hostage; she suddenly doubted Aris had meant for her to leave *in one piece.* Maybe Lai had been sent to intercept her; she doubted the head of the family wanted to deal with her personally. He was watching her now, testing her reaction; the only bright spot of hope was that he didn't seem to want to kill her, just to see how she handled the development. She had to be smart if she wanted to live or ever see her friend again. She had seen enough documentaries to know that screaming and begging would only get her killed.

Trust. She had to earn their trust before attempting to escape. One thing was clear — the job was a ruse. They had darker plans for her.

"You don't want to leave," he added, pushing her up to his door and into his little sanctuary.

Lucy didn't have much time to reflect on her own thoughts, her senses assaulted by the room she found herself in.

It looked like a dragon's hoard; she stared around, overwhelmed by the sheer volume of visual noise. Trinkets, souvenirs, and keepsakes covered every available inch of wall space, creeping up the door and window frames and all the way to the high ceiling—the ceiling decorated with rolls upon rolls of layered silk, stretching from the central chandelier and falling like colorful waterfalls around the Turkish-style floor bed.

At least, Lucy assumed it was a bed; she couldn't see anything past a mountain made of dozens of cushions, forming a plush nest. All of it was crowned by a headboard made out of a full peacock tail, each feather dipped in gold.

"Was a mad man imprisoned here with a Bedazzler?" She pointed to the table and a desk completely covered in rhinestones. Lai puffed out his chest, seemingly flattered.

With great reluctance, Lucy strolled the cluttered bedroom, examining shelves full of curiosities. Most of it seemed like meaningless trash, but each piece was carefully displayed; Lai must have valued the memories attached to it all. Her hand traced over dusty seashells, porcelain figurines and a collection of paper cups. Jewelry boxes overflowed with beads, bracelets, and rings, from tacky costume trinkets to heavy gold pieces tarnished with time.

Time seemed irrelevant to Lai's reverence of the junk he'd hoarded.

Comic books were layered with centuries old manuscripts and plastic tables were given the same treatment as intricately carved wooden ones, laden with keepsakes from every era. Lucy flipped through a clip full of tickets. The first faded slip read:

To the Exhibition of the Works of Industry of all nations, 1851

The last one in the clip looked a lot more familiar. *The Burning Man* admission. Her mind tried to connect the dots but it managed only one line, from the *I don't know* dot to the *I have no idea* dot.

"I'll run you a bath," Lai announced, opening a door hidden by a silk curtain that led to a comparatively plain bathroom.

"Excuse me?" Lucy raised an eyebrow, taken aback by Lai's boldness. "Look, I know you're trying to be friendly, but this is all a

46

bit much. I should probably be calling the cops." She glanced back towards the exit, noticing Lai rummaging in a dresser.

For a moment Lucy regretted that outburst. She probably should not have threatened the strange man with the police. Her hand dove down to her pocket, looking for her pepper spray as she extended it in front of herself, ready to press down.

Finger on the trigger, Lucy watched him turn back with a towel and a change of clothes. A simple set of linen pajamas. Nothing unsavory aside from the look on his face.

"Truly terrifying." Lai clicked his tongue and pushed her hand down. Lucy didn't resist, embarrassed more than anything.

Damn it, Lucy! Stop freaking out. Pretend to be his friend. Do what they ask and look for an exit. Besides...they don't know your secret.

Perhaps they should. Perhaps they might back down a little then.

"Can you blame me?"

"No, of course not." Lai walked over to the bathtub and turned on the water, adding a few drops of pleasantly smelling oil to it. "You should be afraid, I'd be worried if you weren't. In honesty...I'd be afraid if you weren't. I'd be stuck with someone much scarier than my father," he smiled.

He has no idea.

Lucy placed the pepper spray on a nearby table and pulled off her soaking jacket.

"Why else should I be afraid? Aside from the obvious monsters — your father and his pets."

"That's plenty, don't you think? Although the old lady that gave you a nice slimy hug isn't a monster. Can't say the same for my father. He's a dick. I'm not going to defend him."

Lucy watched him light up a candle. She didn't want to get into that bathtub, but what was she going to do instead? Grab her things and walk back alone on a highway back to town? She didn't think she'd even live as far as the front door if she tried. Regardless of her decision, her chances of getting murdered were about the same.

"Wait. What do you mean, *stuck* with him?" A sudden realization hit her. "Are you a prisoner too?"

"Prisoner?" Lai raised perfectly shaped brows. "No. I am—" he paused, his hands summoning up the right words. "Grounded."

Any threat of danger Lucy felt might come from him fizzled out into nothing. "Grounded? How old are you?" She tried her best not to laugh.

"Oh this question again. You are so rude." Lai rolled his eyes, uncorking another glass bottle and pouring its contents into the water. The room instantly filled with a familiar scent, just like the lily of the valley flower in the garden. "Father deemed me a threat to the family's secrecy and security. I honestly can't blame him. I'm a loose fucking cannon."

Another prisoner. The sudden kinship felt almost comforting. Lucy was getting sore from tensing constantly, waiting for something terrible to happen. She didn't know if she could trust him but she felt she did not need to distrust him

"I don't know what to do," she said quietly, allowing a little vulnerability to seep through.

"Never used a bath before?"

Lucy smiled, but it felt forced. "I can't go back."

"Then don't."

"It's been made perfectly clear that I'm unwelcome here. Besides, even if I wanted to stay, your dad is way too much of an ass for me to stomach."

"Oh I agree, absolutely. This place is a shithole and the company is less than desirable, except me. I'm a fucking delight." He winked. "This place sucks...but so does the town. So does the world. This place at least is a little special. You'll see."

Lucy watched him, trying to get a read on the man. He sat on the edge of the tub, mixing the water with his finger tips. Beautiful and serene. The silk robes draped over his smooth skin and the lavender hair almost made him look like a siren, luring her into the water.

"You know. When they make a doco about my murder, people will be yelling at the screen, calling me an idiot," she sighed.

"Don't worry. My mug shot will convince them they'd do the same." He flicked his hair with a dramatic flare.

"You're insufferable." Lucy grabbed the clothes and the towel, locking the door firmly behind her once she had chased Lai out and letting the hot water melt away her anger, leaving only a clear mind and plans of escape. They hadn't tied her up or locked her in a dungeon. That was a bonus. Perhaps they did need help; that would allow her certain freedoms she could use to her advantage.

***

Now warm and mellow, she scrubbed herself with the towel and changed into dry clothing, moving her personal belongings from her wet pockets. The lily of the valley had somehow survived the vigorous dunking in the lake, albeit missing a few of its bells; she tucked it into her hair.

Back inside the lights were dimmer, and a bottle of lemonade and a plate of treats waited for her by the bed.

"What's this?"

"Not sure where you come from, but I call it chocolate." Lai passed her the bottle and made room among the cushions. "Still sealed, don't worry."

"Don't be a smartass," Lucy frowned as she sat down, succumbing to the weight of weary limbs. Despite her guarded manner she was thankful for his little gesture. She had considered the possibility of it

being laced with something but she needed to look like she trusted him, so she ate one. Then another. Chocolate made everything better.

Sitting down on the floor beside her, Lai grabbed one as well. She noticed that he positioned himself lower, perhaps to appear less threatening. They sat in silence for a while, each with their own thoughts. Lucy contemplated her situation. The shame of going back to failure almost overpowered her commonsense. Was she truly considering staying?

"I doubt I can change your father's mind."

"Trust me. Father will change his own mind. All you need to do is give him time. I know the man. What could you have possibly done to offend him so?"

It had been nagging at her, that very question. Wandering the pavilion couldn't really justify nearly killing her, could it? And as undignified as it had been he did save her, sort of. She hadn't pulled herself out of the lake and forced the water out of her lungs. It was contrary, confusing. He had pushed her back in, then…

"…I think he saw me–"

How could she explain the horrid gift she was burdened with? No– not a gift; a curse. Every time she had used it, her life had become just a little bit worse.

A painful memory flooded back, still as vivid as if it had happened yesterday and not nearly twenty years ago. A fun bike ride that had ended with ripped jeans and bloodied knees. She could remember sitting on the lawn in front of a large brick house, crying her eyes out.

Then a quiet *meow*. Her beloved kitten rubbed against Lucy's thigh, concerned by her humans pain. Like any child would, she scooped up the animal that brought so much comfort. Ten minutes passed, and Lucy had felt better, but the cat wouldn't leave. The young girl lifted up the animal only to find it stiff. The warmth was all gone, and the kitten dropped to the ground without making a sound. Lucy remembered her scream as she hovered above the dead cat, her parents rushing out to see what was wrong. Later that night, as she tossed and turned, she discovered that her bloody and scraped knees were perfectly healed as if she had never skinned them at all.

The memory still filled Lucy with guilt and shame that lingered for hours. She needed to change the subject before it made her cry in front of Lai.

"He saw me break a rule I got told about five minutes earlier and then injured a literal monster when it tried to eat me."

Lai pressed his lips together but Lucy couldn't tell if it was to hide annoyance or a smile.

"Don't." She shook her head. "He was super pissed. You don't get it; I need this job. I have nowhere but a cardboard box on the street to go back to. And... I think I might have freaked him out." Lucy hugged one of the velvet cushions to her chest, scared. Not a feeling she was fond of. For years she had only herself to rely on, and the loss of control felt suffocating.

"Once again, I doubt it." Lai leaned in closer, studying her guilt-filled face. "Wait, is there something you're not telling me? What do you mean, you 'freaked him out'?"

Lucy felt the need to finally share her burden overwhelm her common sense. No one else would ever believe her on the outside. No one ever did. Not even her parents. She could faintly remember them arguing over it. She even had to spend a few nights at the Farrowatcher labs as men in white coats studied her, whispering something to her father. Not that it brought any answers. In fact, no one had ever mentioned it again.

Lai gently nudged Lucy with the tips of his fingers. "I want to help you, but I need to know what you're worried about."

It took Lucy a minute to gather enough courage to share her secret. Maybe it was a bad idea; after all she had just met him. But something about him felt genuine in his desire to help. A fellow prisoner in a place that could hold the answers to all her questions. The word popped back into her head; *Magic*. Was the risk worth it? What did she possibly have left to lose? Nothing, but if someone here could lift her curse...

"Just promise you won't freak out, okay? It's weird."

"I truly doubt you can weird me out."

Lai nodded his promise as she sat up and reached over to a flower arrangement on the bedside table, pulling out a dried up, yellowed flower. Then she took the lily from her hair. Lucy closed her eyes, focusing on the stems against her fingertips. In her mind's eye, they were laced with light like veins, one dim and dying, the other pulsing with life. Mentally she pinched the glowing veins and forced the light into the dying flower, shoving more and more energy into it until the living plant was dead and the dying one was as fresh as if it had just been picked. Trance-like, she offered the renewed flower to Lai.

"Oh, hell no!" Lai gasped in horror, pushing the flower away.

"You promised!" Lucy protested, snapping out of her daze and dropping the flowers onto the bed, cheeks red.

"It's not a trick; it's real magic...Shit okay, that changes things." Lai held up his hands, which were breaking out in painful hives. "I'm allergic to magic. It's impressive! Count me amazed, but I can't be near it." He rushed over to a tall cabinet and, after a few seconds of frantic rummaging, scooped a couple of antihistamines from a bottle.

Lucy's shoulders sagged. Should she apologize? A little part of her felt good about the reaction. She'd made him scared. A man who wasn't bothered living next to a Kraken infested lake was looking at her like a threat. "Anything I can do?"

"Yes," Lai nodded, chasing his medication down with a glass of water. "Tell me where you learned to do that. There's no magic left. It's gone. Used up." He looked at her in a mix of excitement tempered with dread.

"What do you mean 'there's no magic left'?"

"Exactly that. Like fossil fuels. All burned up on frivolous bullshit."
He checked his hands again. "Okay, think of magic as energy. There
are two types. One type is harmless; everyone is born with it; it's what
makes humans...human. Like a soul, I guess. There's a tiny drop in
everyone. Then there's a kind that you can harvest. Like oil. Except
we got greedy, and we burned through it all; the only oil-magic left is
in artifacts and stuff. Now you–you have way more than just a soul's
worth. That I can stomach, but hit me with a dose big enough, and I
react badly. So where did you get yours?"

"The life-swapping thing? I've always had it. Ever since I was a
little girl, I didn't know what it was."

It wasn't just a curse.

It was magic.

Lucy got up, excitement building up inside her. She could barely
hear Lai's offer. He cleared his throat and she glanced at him as he
repeated it.

"Shall we find out?"

CHAPTER FIVE

LAI

As night began to fall, Lai led Lucy down to the library. Before today, he could not have even imagined taking a girl to a place like that; a certain animated movie had set high expectations for a library reveal at a manor house. Lai knew better than to expect a gasp of awe. The library was just as bad as the rest of the place. No one besides Ryan used it, haunting the shelves like a sulky ghost, so just like everything else in the house the library had fallen into disrepair.

The dim light from the hallway lamps did not reach the room. There were no candles, and the antique gas lanterns were covered in thick layers of spiderwebs. Books that had once been carefully shelved now cluttered every available flat surface. Priceless manuscripts and ancient rolls littered the mosaic floor, crumbling into dust with the passing of time and the lack of care. The typical dusty scent of old books was overpowered by an irritating mildew odor.

Lai lifted his robe's hem, stepping over piles of ripped out book pages, the dust thick enough to crunch under his bare feet. He hated these filthy rooms. How they looked, how they smelled... If money wasn't a factor he'd be out of there in a heartbeat, but he had expensive tastes and no one to bankroll them.

"Give me a moment," he muttered as he opened a corner cabinet, rummaging through dried-up fountain pens and moldy papers. "No candles. Okay. Plan B." Lai walked over to the window and pulled open the heavy drapes with a dramatic cloud of dust, but the moonless sky offered no light, still too early for the moon to rise. "Promise me you won't freak out?"

"Absolutely not." Lucy shook her head. "If you are about to pull something weird, I will freak out. I guarantee it."

Fair enough. Lai clicked his tongue, reconsidering it. The poor thing had been through a lot already and the day wasn't over yet. Still... he needed some light. Of course he could have gone back and brought a lamp or two, but he loved getting to scratch the itch of revenge. She had startled him with her magic, it was only fair he repaid the favor.

"Gaia, initiate day protocol," he ordered.

Lai felt Lucy's gaze on his back. He knew exactly the look she was giving him. In all fairness, he did look like a mad man, barking orders at the sky. Then something shifted. The tree line in the distance began to glow. The sun rose over the horizon, rapidly gaining altitude and stopping dead on the midday mark in the sky.

"What the holy fuck..." Lucy's jaw dropped as she placed both hands on the window as if seeking a screen flicker. "This is a TV, right?" She felt around the window frame, searching for hidden wires.

Never gets old. Wish I had more people to shock, though.

With a roll of his eyes, Lai pulled the latch. A gust of fresh air hit Lucy's face. Nothing seemed out of the ordinary, just a garden filled with the confused singing of birds awoken from their slumber.

"What the fuck, Lai," Lucy demanded, voice trembling. "I thought you were allergic to magic?"

"It isn't magic." He shrugged. "It's technology. G.A.I.A. Geo-dynamic Artificial Intelligence Architect. It's our private little haven. Outside of time, outside of space. Park it anywhere or any*when* you want and connect to the desired world." He glanced at her, an eyebrow raised. "Gaia keeps the sanctuary protected, and we can control most of her functions, like time of day and weather. Of course, it's better to leave the default setting on and let the seasons play out." Lai tapped his chin. "Magic is rare and wild. Technology is a lot more reliable."

"But how?" Lucy stared at the garden, gob-smacked.

Lai pulled a face, embarrassed. "Do I look like the kind of guy who can explain the inner mechanisms of pocket dimensions? I don't even know how magnets work."

She looked at him, deep in thought. "I believe that. If it makes you feel better, I never really understood how they work either. Have you ever had an allergic reaction to them?"

"If you've finished freaking out over day and night cycles, we can start looking." Lai laughed as she teased him. "Let's not linger here too long; father hates when we mess with Gaia, it wreaks havoc on the wildlife."

"No, I'm not done," Lucy grabbed his robe. "You can't just dump all that on me and expect me to accept it. I've been dealing with crazy all day like a good little girl. Not this time. I want more information so that I don't go insane." She jabbed her finger into Lai's chest.

He rubbed the spot she had poked. Lucy had a point and he sensed the incoming meltdown. He had to admit, he'd experienced similar turmoil learning about Gaia, or most technology for that matter. The manor might be a family home but the family died out a while ago. Hunted to extinction.

He didn't belong there anymore than Lucy did. She was trapped in a new world, he was trapped in a strange time.

"You get two questions then. I'm feeling generous tonight," he offered with a dismissive shrug.

"Where did Gaia come from? Is it like alien tech?"

Of course she would ask questions he had no answers to.

"I don't know. We've just moved in one day; someone else set this up. Many generations of our family have used this house and this land. One day someone must've put the protective barrier around it, made it mobile."

"Was I drugged at breakfast this morning?" she asked, shoulders slumped in defeat.

"No, drugs are expensive. If I had any I'd take them myself, not waste them on you." Lai glanced at Lucy and walked over to the bookshelf, focusing on what they had come here for.

"What-"

"Uh uh–two questions only. If you want me to answer more, I'll be expecting something in return," he winked suggestively, knowing well enough that should stop her asking.

It worked like a charm. Lucy pressed her lips in a pout but didn't push further. In all truth Lai had no answers. He knew what Gaia was but neither him nor anyone else in the family actually knew how it worked. It just did and for them, it was good enough. The weather stayed constant, gently ticking over each season. The time matched their clocks most days. And there was security. Gaia, blended seamlessly with a chosen location, keeping curious people out and keeping all the secrets in.

Together they examined the bookshelves for anything related to magic. Lucy tried to read spines, written in forgotten languages, while

Lai went by the pictures on the covers. Old, water-damaged tomes, books with spines that disintegrated with a light touch, priceless annotated first editions and worn collections of handwritten journals; if it might have any information about magic, then it joined the pile in the middle of the room.

"Alright, let's see what we've got." Lai sat down cross-legged and passed over the first book to Lucy. The book had a woodcut image of a woman in a pointed hat leaned over a cauldron on the cover.

"It says *'A Feminine Touch to Beer Brewing'*." Lucy gave him a look.

"How was I supposed to know? There's a witch on it," Lai huffed, tossing the book aside. "Well, what about this one?"

"No idea, can't read it," Lucy turned the book upside down, but it didn't make any more sense that way either. "Wait, why are you asking me?"

He shrunk, fingers twisting a page corner. She had shared an intimate secret with him, it was only fair he told her his. Not that it was a secret at all. More like an embarrassing fault. "I can't."

"Can't what?"

"Read."

"Wait, you can't read?"

"I know the letters, and I understand the concept, but when I look at the page, it just turns into a jumble of nonsense. Trust me, I've tried," he muttered, looking away.

Thankfully, Lucy dropped the topic.

Another hour passed with little to show for it but a pile of rejected books and mounting frustration. It was an old library in a creepy ass mansion. Of course it should have books about magic! Was that much to ask for?

"You know what?" Lai dusted off his robe. "Let's bring in the experts. These are useless." He tore out a few yellowed blank pages from the books and grabbed a pen from the desk, placing them in front of Lucy. "Make it sound like a formal dinner invitation. Let's say Sunday after next at six."

"What the hell are you talking about?"

Lai pushed the paper towards her. "We're going to invite some of my family's more scholarly associates over so we can ask them for answers; we're never going to find anything like this."

"Scholarly associates?"

He blew a strand of hair away from his face. She had his number. He had other ideas brewing but this might shed some light on her powers. "Okay, maybe they aren't scholars. Family friends. Aren't many out there but they might know."

"And you want me to write to them?" She looked at him, wide-eyed.

"I can text one of them but the other two are rather old fashioned. Why are you questioning me? I'm trying to help!"

Myself.

Lucy took the paper from him with a great deal of apprehension.

"Don't mention my name. Write one to a man named Al; he will, of course, bring his sister, but that can't be helped," Lai added through his teeth. "Al doesn't know magic, but he is an 'anti-mage' of sorts. Magic doesn't work around him, he might know what it is."

Pausing for a second, Lai considered the other candidates. There were many. Gods and acquaintances from countless worlds. Any of them would be more help than his current guest list, but this wasn't just about Lucy.

"Okay, one to Glyph. He's my godfather and knows everything." Lai bit his lip, a whisper of reason begging him not to continue. "… Then the last one to Eleanore. She's father's ex. She's a bit rough, but she has seen everything. In more than one world. Make it sound formal, and don't forget to tell Klein, so he can make preparations."

The old fountain pen needed some encouragement to start working again before Lucy carefully wrote out each letter. Her penmanship wasn't great and the stubborn, sticky ink smeared in a couple of places.

"Perfect. I'll make sure the letters get where they need to." Lai waved them dry and folded each one. "Be a darling and clean this up, would you?"

Lucy gave him a withering look, but it was technically her job– if she still had a job. With the patience of a saint, she picked up the scattered books, placing them one by one back on the shelf.

"Oh, look, Lai– it's her again." She lifted a dusty tome with a carving of Echidna etched into the thick leather binding. "Klein told me how your family's got that ridiculous story going..." she turned to him, attempting a joke that died on her tongue at the cold expression on his face.

Klein did WHAT?

"Oh, did he now?" Lai smiled, but it didn't reach his eyes; pale, icy eyes that carried a hint of malice. He saw his reflection in a glass door of a bookcase and with the next blink, resumed his usual carefree countenance. Klein was always bad at keeping his mouth shut. Oh well. The cat was out of the bag.

"Yeah. He just mentioned something about the bloodline." Lucy put the book back.

"We preserve it and keep it pure. Some say with questionable methods." Lai focused on Lucy, watching her every move. He didn't care for his father's methods or plans. "Not allowed to let it pass into the general population either. We aren't special, though." He pointed to the carved family crests decorating the ceiling. "There are lots of families like us, or at least there used to be. Who knows where they are now. There, that's us." He motioned to an image of a tree with hands for branches and snakes instead of roots. "Next belongs to Daughters of Babylon, and that one is the Lords of Byzantine. The two firebirds are the Sirin Sisterhood." He paused, looking at the dozens of designs, each with millennia of history behind them. "Most of them are now extinct. Exterminated by a family of hunters. We don't want to do this, but we also don't want to be the weak link that ends the dynasty." He smiled at her with thinly veiled grief.

"What do you mean? Do what?" Lucy backed away, her fists clenching. "You know how that sounds, right?"

"Yeah, I do. Let me rephrase it. It's a legacy we carry on. A curse some call it. A lot like what you have." He reached over and touched her hand, his skin cold against her, a stark contrast. Lai couldn't blame her for flinching.

"You have magic too?"

Something like that.

"No more questions, remember? Let's get you settled; it's getting late." He walked over to the window and shut the curtains. "Gaia, goodnight."

The sun plunged back below the horizon, and the room drowned in darkness.

CHAPTER SIX

LAI

"Keep up, sunshine." Lai bounced up the old wooden staircase, his silk robe flowing dramatically behind him.

He waited for Lucy on the last step, bare toes curling over the cold marble floor.

Too cheerful, you are overcompensating for almost losing it in the library.

Tone.

It.

Down.

"Let's find a room for you near mine— in case you ever need anything."

Now that sounded almost perfect. A model of decorum and tranquility.

"What would I need?" Lucy asked, her intonation indicating she was catching onto his plan far too quickly.

"Maybe you'll get scared of the ghosts."

"Are there ghosts?"

"...No."

A lie. He knew that the house was full of residual hauntings. Antique wood stored moments in time, memories that played like an old movie projector. Faded figures, soft voices and gentle footsteps were all common occurrences. "Do you want a friend or not?" Lai laughed, shaking his head. "Here, this room is a few doors down from mine. Let's see if it's empty." He took a dainty bronze key from a nail hammered into the door frame and slid it inside the lock. One click and the door opened with a screech of rusted hinges.

The smell. It hit in a wave of sickeningly sweet musk. Lucy took a few steps back, looking a tad green around the gills. Lai himself was unaffected. He recognized the stench–he was used to it.

"Must be a dead rat or something. Wait here. I'll open the windows."

Lucy nodded. He didn't need to tell her twice.

Acting like a knight to the rescue, Lai lit a small brass lantern and braved the room. Thick clouds of dust rose to greet him, disturbed by the hem of the long robe.

Choking on the stale air, he reached the windows shrouded in heavy velvet drapes, throwing them open. Once fresh air entered the room for the first time in at least a century, he turned to examine its condition. Wooden floors, a threadbare rug, mahogany bureau desk, a wardrobe and a daybed.

The bed.

"Oh, fuck."

"What is it?" Lucy's footsteps approached the door.

"Wait there, it's a huge, dead–" Lai rushed to the bed and covered partially mummified human remains with faded sheets. "–rat."

Damn it Klein! How hard is it to look after this place?

Quick body disposal. Piece of cake. He had done this before. Yes, they had been fresh and weren't flaking everywhere, but how different could this be? It was time to put his hair up. "Sorry....no proper burial tonight," he muttered, undoing his braid and rearranging his messy hair into a high ponytail.

The inside of his nose burned as Lai peeled the corpse away from the ruined bedding, rolling it to one side. The dried tendons snapped easily as he folded the room's previous occupant into a tight parcel.

He made a makeshift body bag out of a lace-trimmed sheet and, with a strained groan, heaved it from the bed.

The window! An obvious solution to the problem. All he needed was to carry the bundle a few yards. Unfortunately for Lai, the Irony Gods were watching, and they were in the mood for entertainment.

Giving himself a quick countdown, he swung the flimsy bag towards the window, failing to consider the age and condition of the sheets. The loud ripping of fabric filled the room, followed by the rather musical sound of bones bouncing off the walls and floor.

"Wow, okay. I see how it is." Lai looked up at the heavens with an accusatory glare. It wouldn't be the first time a higher power had ruined his perfectly executed plan. At least this time, the stakes were low enough to ignore the insult. Still, it felt personal.

"You need help?" Lucy called out from just outside the door. "You know, I'm not scared of rats." She peeked in, taking a moment to take in the scene. "Ummm. It must've been a giant rat." She entered the room, nose covered with her sleeve.

"Five feet at least." Lai frantically picked up an armful of bones, tossing them out of the window. He struggled to read her expression. Most folks would have freaked out at this point.

"Store your Halloween decorations here?" She picked up the skull, its hair and the dried up scalp still attached, and passed it over to him.

"Yeah, I didn't know we had these. Usually, it's just plastic pumpkins and bats. Gonna step up our game this year." Lai used the skull like a puppet on his hand. "Trick or treat?!" He gave a nervous laugh and launched the mystery head outside.

"You must think I'm an idiot."

I do.

"I don't." Lai swallowed heavily.

"I can tell it's an old body."

"You can?"

"You have less than twenty seconds to find a good reason for it being here or I'm out."

Lai blinked, fidgeting with a tie of his robe.

Give her the truth, you don't have time for a convincing lie.

"In all honesty? This place stood abandoned for a century before we moved in and there are hundreds of rooms. No one knows what's in most of them and no one cares to find out. I'm sorry, I don't want you to be scared."

Lai watched her take a deep breath, like an ocean receding before unleashing a deadly wave.

"I'm not scared. I'm fucking terrified but I need this job. I worked Black Friday sales. The dead don't scare me, It's the living that I'm wary of." Lucy paused, her hands trembling. "Okay I'm lying. The dead do scare me, but I'm exhausted, emotionally and physically; after my tangle with a Kraken and the use of my power, I am blessedly numb."

Lai picked up an unattached foot and flung it out of the window, as if it would help the situation.

"..And if you try to hurt me... Well, I'm not defenseless." She pointed her hand at Lai to remind him of his allergies. "You wouldn't be my first victim, just the first human one. I can handle you."

He snorted, holding back a laugh. Imagining her killing anyone was hard. "It's a deal! I'll warn others that you are a force to be reckoned with."

As she examined her new lodgings, Lucy paused over the ruined mattress. She looked over at Lai, her eyebrow raised. He knew what she was thinking.

Why are you looking at me? You expect me to clean this up?

"I'll find a new one." He sighed walking over, rolling up the old-fashioned feather bed and dragging it to the window before sending it to the garden below. A loud thump was followed by curses; the angry muttering sounded like Klein. Something about ungrateful kids.

"Is there a bathroom?" She placed her bag on the floor by the desk.

"Umm—no. Plumbing doesn't extend this far into the house. Neither does electricity or gas, for that matter."

"I'm sorry, what?" She picked up her bag again; it seemed she was willing to tolerate Krakens and murderous bosses but the lack of plumbing was a deal breaker. Lai knew they were going to be friends at that moment. Their priorities aligned perfectly.

"It's an old house." Lai shrugged. "There are toilets down the hallway, and you can use my room to wash and charge your phone."

"So you live with a supercomputer but have no electricity?"

"We do have it wired to the middle of the manor, but if you know any electricians that will service pocket dimensions, then pass on my number. I'd love to have lights everywhere else." Lai shrugged. "Not that we need it. I do enjoy my luxuries, but everyone else is used to living without the basic amenities."

Lucy groaned, fingers pinching the bridge of her nose. "I guess it's something I can get used to. I'll go and find Klein for now. This room needs airing out."

"Can't disagree with you on that," Lai smiled, wiping his filthy hands on the remains of a pillowcase. "I'll drag over one of my mattresses...guess I don't need six of them."

"But your highness, you might feel the pea if there are less than six."

He squinted at her, barely hiding a smile. "I'm about to revoke your bathtub privileges."

**

As the newcomer disappeared downstairs, Lai strolled across the hallway to the west wing. His father was undoubtedly in his office, in just as much of a huff as Lucy.

Naturally, he was correct. The head of the household sat at his desk, flipping through an old journal, turning the fragile pages a little too fast. His father was rattled, no doubt aware of Lucy's magic. Lai had to pause and enjoy this rare sight.

"Must you inflict your presence on me?" Aris looked up, his irritated gaze joined by a dozen glowing eyes. The hounds stared at Lai with innocent curiosity.

Lai cooed, almost floating inside and parking his ass on the old oak desk, to his father's great displeasure. "We need to have a little chat, papa dearest."

The lines on Aris' face deepened, filling with dread.

"'Those that fail to learn from history are doomed to repeat it.'" Lai quoted, picking up a polished silver paperweight and examined his distorted reflection in it. "I think Churchill said that? Anyway; this isn't going to be any different, you know."

"What are you on about?"

"I'm saying that you can't keep repeating the same mistakes and expect a different result. Let's face it. Your kids do not turn out great. This family is doomed. Why keep trying?"

"I beg your pardon?" Fury ignited on his father's face but was quickly doused when Lai gestured to himself as exhibit A.

"She is not for me," Aris answered with a snarl. "I am getting older and my progeny have been a disappointment. You have contributed nothing to this family; since the only thing of value you have to offer is your blood, you will be used for breeding."

It was Lai's turn to stare at Aris with mouth agape and indignation trembling his breath.

"I refuse!" A tirade of resistance built up, ready to be unleashed when a loud bang on the table reminded Lai of his place in the food chain.

"Must I jog your memory about the situation this family is in?" Aris growled, clenching his fists. "You live a lifestyle unsustainable with our finances. So if you want to keep playing a princess, I suggest you either find a rich prince or get with the program. You've wasted your inheritance, compromised the bloodline and—" Aris pointed his shaking finger.

"Crashed your car? Drank the sacred rum? Opened Pandora's jar? Released the Wrath demon? Pushed that kid into the gorilla enclosure? Wrecked the time-line?" Lai finished for him with a roll of his eyes as his father glared. Aris wasn't wrong but to be fair, a lot of those were accidents.

"The rules were that I must produce an offspring. I did." Lai pointed to the shelf where an egg about the size of a football sat. Rough scales decorated its rounded sides, with stick-on rhinestones and a healthy dousing of glitter.

"It wasn't funny then; It's not funny now," Aris growled. "My hounds bring more value in their breeding than you do."

Covering his bare thigh with a layer of silk, Lai sighed, shifting from the table to the chair.

"Look, the marriage scams were fun. We can keep going with insurance fraud. It is getting harder, but you know I can make any death look natural."

"It's not enough, Leander." His father stared into the distance.

"So you're tempted by the old family business?" Lai said, each word coated with bitter venom. "Why start with one little girl? Let's do what grandpa did and keep forty of them in the cells. Fuck it, let's sell Louis. He should fetch enough to pay for what...a new roof? Your debt to the witches? Why are we still paying those harpies?"

Aris stood up, his hand raised in the air, but Lai didn't flinch. The hit never came. Instead, his father's arm dipped under the weight of the accusations, and he lowered himself back into the old leather seat.

Both men sat in heavy silence, disturbed only by the anxious shifting of dogs. Neither dared to continue the soured conversation.

"You know if you need money, you can always ask Goldfang. Your dragon sugar-daddy would be happy to help," Lai said, trying to lighten the atmosphere. His attempt seemed to work.

"You are my greatest disappointment." Aris smiled dryly as Lai puffed out his chest, proud of the accomplishment.

"Whatever you decide to do, keep in mind that she is not entirely defenseless."

"I know. I smelled it the moment she arrived. She reeks of magic. How? What are the chances of her being here?"

Lai shrugged. "Just...I know you are used to women who know how to deal with you; she is still fresh. One day Lucy will have you on a leash, but right now, she is terrified."

THE MOMENT WE MET

Lucy retraced her steps from her bedroom to the entry hall as she memorized her way around the house. Her fingers caressed the ornate railing as she stomped down the grand staircase, her mood sour as she processed her eventful day of mayhem and magic. Turning at the bottom of the stairs, she tried to remember where the dining room was.

The room was empty and still, lantern light filtering through stained glass windows that stretched to the ceiling, illuminating the dusty table. She hated to admit its beauty, but the tarnished silverware sparkled like stars in the low light.

Tap-tap.

A large magpie was pecking at one of the dessert spoons, chewing on the silver.

"Oh! Oh, go on, shoo–" Lucy flicked her hands at the bird to try to scare it back outside. The magpie didn't even flinch, fixing her with a bemused look before returning to the spoon, prying metal with a sharp, powerful beak.

"Shoo, you little bastard." Lucy took off her jacket to swat the bird. "Leave the silverware alone! If you take one, they're going to think I've done it."

The magpie stopped pecking and glanced towards Lucy.

May I have a moment of your time?

A voice echoed inside Lucy's head, making her jump; she looked behind her, but no one was there.

May I have a moment of your time?

The voice asked again. The magpie stared at her with one void-black eye.

"Holy shit–" she threw her jacket, but the bird dodged it, flapping its wings in indignation.

How rude. I've only asked for a moment of your time.

The tiny voice of reason she suffocated with a pillow of stubbornness screamed. Money and pride wasn't worth any of it.

Go back.

Go home.

"Sure, why not. What do you want?" She almost laughed, a strangled, wild giggle that threatened to break the dam of her sanity. A talking bird wanted a moment of her time.

That is all, thank you. The magpie cawed wickedly and flew out of the open window, disappearing somewhere above the house.

Lucy sighed.

She was going mad.

CHAPTER SEVEN

LUCY

Still shaken from the strange encounter, Lucy stepped outside, inhaling the cool night air. Her distracted gaze flitted between the marble statues dotted across the garden, their blank eyes followed her with suspicion, offering none of the former comfort.

She felt like a soccer ball passed between players, blocked from reaching her goals no matter how much she tried; once again she flew out of bounds only to be forced back into the cruel game, but now it had new rules.

Her brain was screaming at her for being such a passive little maid. Was her fake submission really fake? Or had she simply accepted her fate once again, letting others take charge of her life? Admittedly this place wasn't just another mindless job she could do on an autopilot, but retail only stole her time and energy. This place, this bizarre family, had stolen her freedom and her sanity.

Her soul clawed at her like a caged animal, the futility and absurdity of the situation suddenly suffocating. The only thing Lucy wanted right then and there was to have control of her life, playing by her own rules, and she wasn't about to spend another minute in shackles. Even if some part of her wanted to stay and learn more, Lucy knew she had to at least try. Try to regain her freedom.

Barefoot, she strode over the gravel path, the stones hurting her feet but the pain only fueling the panic that was quickly converted to adrenaline. The large iron gate that had first met her loomed ahead, but its resistance was only in Lucy's mind. It didn't try to stop her, its bars so wide and rusted that she could slip in between them almost effortlessly.

Lucy paused as a strange doubt wormed its way inside. She looked back at the wrought iron, the patterns among bars that looked almost like a sinister face. She could swear the metal smile had a patronizing curl, like it knew she couldn't escape.

Like it knew she wouldn't.

Well, now she had to prove that damned gate wrong.

The highway was at the end of the drive. The road home, even though she had no home to speak of. But she had Xim, and Xim wouldn't ask too many questions. She would just take her back, help her find a job, give her a couch to sleep on, all for the low, low price of Lucy's pride.

The dirt track leading up to the manor looked different in the dark. The whimsical forest that greeted her in the morning had changed its mood dramatically. The moon, freshly peeking over the tree-line, illuminated the path ahead of her, but the sickly pale glow didn't offer comfort, instead disguising dips and rocks as shadows. It wasn't too late to turn back. Lucy had nothing but the few belongings she had emptied from her soaked clothing, her phone and wallet resting heavily in her flimsy pocket.

Her phone! She fished out the gadget, thankfully waterproof. It had no signal, but the battery was still at a comfortable 70% and the flashlight worked even with condensation fogging the lens.

The glowing anchor to the real world soothed her frazzled nerves. All she had to do was get to the bottom of the track and call her friend, swallowing her pride.

Ten minutes it took her last time. Ten minutes of a leisurely walk down a worn trail from the taxi. But now, twenty minutes down the road, the end was nowhere in sight. Anxiety took over as Lucy broke into a short, stumbling run. Was she lost?

No way! There were no turn offs and she had been walking straight ahead. The path covered in pine needles didn't narrow or turn more than a few degrees, and she could make out old tire tracks underneath the rotting vegetation.

She shone her phone light ahead, desperate to hear that noise of passing trucks, see the glare of headlights from cars on the road, but the only light she could see was from her own flashlight, glittering as it reflected off the gate. The fucking gate!

With an inhuman howl Lucy grabbed onto bars, shaking the unyielding metal. Her cries of frustration were met by a bone rattling roar, a blood chilling noise that echoed in the forest that Lucy had just bolted through. She clung to the gate, her eyes darting between trees, looking for whatever creature had answered her call.

"Is someone there?" She wanted to sound brave, but her voice came out as a squeaky whisper. Besides, it was a stupid question; there was a kraken in the lake, it only made sense that there were monsters in the forest too.

She swallowed heavily. She knew that if she had stumbled upon another family pet, her chances of survival were pretty low; alone and defenseless, she didn't dare turn her back on whatever prowled in the forest, as if keeping eye contact would somehow save her.

Another growl, this time followed by a low hiss. Lucy could see the shape of the creature, a black mass, moving with surprising grace for its size. Something as big as a truck weaved in and out of the moonlight, creeping ever closer through the tangle of woods. She didn't understand how she hadn't run right into it before; it wasn't even a hundred feet away.

Trying not to breathe, Lucy felt for the gap in the gate, her hands frantically, treacherously searching for the way back to the manor. She could have sworn the bars had shrunk, perhaps to teach her a lesson.

Stupid, ugly old gate.

She looked away for just a second to see what was taking her fingers so damn long. A second was all it took; before she could turn back to the woods she felt hot, stinking breath on her shoulder.

It smelled like a corpse, musky and sickly sweet. Lucy's trembling hand raised the phone as she turned around, the flashlight flooding the darkness in front of her. She saw jaws filled with massive, sharp teeth, bear-like but far, far bigger. The stench of the creature, or perhaps its last meal, stung her nose, bringing up her own bile.

I survived the Kraken only to be eaten by this. Her last thoughts felt so cynical.

She closed her eyes in the face of the inevitable, hoping the vicious yellow fangs would only hurt for a moment. She almost thought of herself as brave, but she screamed as she was suddenly and violently jerked backwards. Someone had pulled her back through the bars and away from the gate.

"What are you doing? Do you want to die?" Klein's voice made her open her eyes. She was safe, safe on the manor side of the gate. Beyond the cast iron, the creature was nowhere to be seen.

"I was just—" Lucy swallowed her protests as she examined his expression. Every muscle in his face was tense with anger or …fear. His fingers were still digging into her shoulders, probably leaving bruises, a trade she welcomed considering she could have been ripped to shreds.

"I told you it's dangerous!" Klein loosened his steel-like grip, struggling to regain his composure.

"Oh, don't worry. I've learned that the hard way." Lucy snapped back, stewing with revulsion and blatant loathing for this place, the gratitude for her life quickly evaporating.

The long pause that followed did little to dissolve the tension. Lucy glared at the butler which he mirrored with the same intensity. He folded first, his brow relaxing into a tired arch, shoulders sinking with what seemed like relief.

"You should head back inside. I'll see you in." Klein muttered as he picked up her phone. She hadn't even noticed that she had dropped it. The screen had a spiderweb of cracks across it, the cherry on top of the cake.

CHAPTER EIGHT

KLEIN

Klein lifted the basket he'd dropped earlier after spotting the young woman in trouble and followed closely as Lucy stomped in a huff towards the house. The awkward silence made his stomach knot with worry. She had been about to run away, of that he had no doubt.

Hopefully she's changed her mind about that now.

Relief flooded him when Lucy sharply turned toward him on the front step but his elation withered at the look on her face; Klein could taste the tension that accompanied a confrontation, like arthritic joints sensing a storm.

"What happened?" He asked as he set the basket down. "I couldn't find you after you left the gardens."

"Oh, I was this close to being food for a giant squid, my new boss tried to kill me, you lot live in some sort of a simulation and there was a corpse in my bed! So, yanno. Nothing serious," Lucy scoffed at him, arms folded over her chest.

Klein felt his heart sink. It was his fault. He should have warned her, he had completely forgotten about Martha. Not that the old lady could eat Lucy, even if she tried.

"I'm sorry." He reached out his hand to her shoulder in a weak effort to comfort her but one glare from Lucy forced him back.

Silence. Klein felt her eyes scrutinize every inch of him. All he could do was stand there, an open book. Anything she wanted to know he would give her. "Please-"

He hated the weakness in his voice.

"Why did you post the ad?" Lucy demanded, in no mood for his sympathy or his comfort.

Klein fidgeted with his eye patch, nursing the answer. How could he tell her the truth? The truth he wanted to be no part of.

She rephrased the question, adding a spoonful of malice to her tone. "What did you hope to get out of this?"

Klein felt he was about to snap like a twig against the force of her questions.

"Change."

She looked at him in disbelief. "Change?"

"…and help. Someone to share this with. All the amazing things this place has, all the creatures you won't see anywhere else. Not the horrors, not the experiments," he said, contemplating his next words. He couldn't do this little world justice; he wasn't eloquent enough. How could he convince her it was all worth it?

Show her. Show her what you see.

"I know you've had the worst possible first impression. I'd be livid too if my first day went as well as yours. Just–give me your hand." He picked up a handful of crushed granite from the basket and filled Lucy's outstretched palm. "Trust me."

"Yep... that's something alright." She stared at the chunks of rock in front of her, deeply unimpressed. Then something hit her. Literally. A stone, falling from somewhere above. She looked up, probably expecting a prank, but instead she saw moving shadows. The carved stone gargoyles that decorated the parapets were inching down towards her, their movement sloth-like, careful yet determined.

Lucy held her breath as one of them scraped down the storm-water pipe and reached for the rocks in her hand. Gently scooping up a couple, it began to crunch with a delighted snort. Others soon followed, most lured by Klein's basket, but a couple were curious about Lucy herself.

"They're from the same breeder that erected the gargoyle guard at Notre Dame. Not as large or as agile as Gothic Spanish breeds, but they can handle most intruders if needed." Klein emptied the basket onto the ground, letting the gargoyles eat their fill.

"Alright, I guess this is pretty damn cool," Lucy said in an unnaturally high lilt. Klein could see her hands shaking uncontrollably; she was terrified, petting the creature eating rock crumbs from her hand. "Although I'm still sure I got drugged at breakfast. This is–"

"I know," Klein smiled, taking off his knitted cardigan and wrapping it around her shoulders. She didn't protest. "There's more. We have a couple of griffins nesting nearby and a faerie infestation I'm trying to deal with. Despite this place's history, it was rebuilt as a sanctuary. Even Martha; yes, I know, you're not a fan, but she's old. She's worn down her beak, so she can only eat mashed fish," he paused, hoping his pleas were enough. "Every creature here got hurt and needs help. Even the ones living inside the house."

Lucy stood in silence, watching the gargoyles rummage through the basket. She seemed overwhelmed; Klein couldn't fault her for that.

"...You know how every girl dreams of being taken into the world of romantic fantasy novels?" Lucy finally managed. "This is not it. Instead of a castle, I have a crumbling, moldy mansion. Instead of a handsome Fae warrior, there's a man who tried to kill me, and let me tell you right now the reverse-harem is entirely off the table." She gave a desperate laugh, eyes closed as she swayed into him.

Klein felt his heart skip a beat as Lucy pressed her forehead against his chest, grounding herself. She was shivering, but he couldn't tell if it was from cold or shock. His first instinct should've been to comfort her but instead his gaze darted across the windows in panic.

The magpie sitting in one of the second storey frames puffed up, glaring at him.

Don't be like that. We almost broke her. Not that you were of any help.

Klein glared back, still uncertain on how to reassure her. She was clearly vulnerable. He placed both hands on Lucy's shoulders, about to offer a hot drink and perhaps an escort to her room when a cold, gruff voice cut the moment short.

"Why are you so pathetic?" Aris barked, appearing behind them. Klein knew he was referring to him, his pale face flashing red as he snatched his hands back. "Girl, follow me. Let's have this talk."

Lucy gave Klein a grateful look as she pulled away. "Thank you," she mouthed quietly, following Aris inside.

CHAPTER NINE

LUCY

"It's unfortunate you had to witness that display." Aris paused on the stairs to make sure Lucy was following. He was talking about Klein. Lucy scowled at him, unimpressed. Klein had saved her life; Aris had tried to kill her. Despite her plan to dance to their tune for now, she wasn't about to give up all her fight. Besides, Klein was a perfect candidate to help her. He, himself, seemed like a prisoner. One touch and the man trembled like a leaf. Manipulating him would be easy.

"It's fine. Not as bad as the display I had to witness earlier," she huffed, unable to hold back her sharp tongue.

Damn it, Lucy, less sarcasm.

She followed Aris in silence, studying him. Broad shoulders, strong arms, and sun-scorched skin pointed to hard labor. Those scars told tales of battles. Where did he get those injuries and what was with this place and that ship? She couldn't figure out exactly how the puzzle pieces fit together, but they were all there in front of her.

"So. Are you going to tell me why you are here and who sent you?"

What? Lucy flinched when he addressed her. *Sent her? Like a spy?*

"Desperation and bad luck. I don't want to be here anymore than you want me here," she explained.

"Well, that didn't answer my question. Follow, girl."

Lucy clenched her fists. *Call me girl again, bastard.*

The hounds greeted them on top of the staircase, their stubby tails wagging so hard they looked like they were dancing. The hellish beasts greeted their master like a pack of over-excited labradors, taking away a little of Aris's sting.

"Hello, my darlings," Aris whispered, perhaps hoping Lucy wouldn't hear as he scratched his oldest hound behind her ear.

She did, and her eye-roll was almost audible. How could that man be so nice to his pets and be an insufferable asshole to everyone else? Then again...Lucy thought back to her old job. After a twelve-hour shift dealing with the worst of humanity, all she wanted was a cuddle with her old roommate's cat. Perhaps it wasn't so unbelievable after all.

Aris unlocked his office door and lit a handful of candles. "What are you waiting for, girl? Sit down."

Lucy took a deep breath so that she could verbally tear him a new asshole, but as the light flickered into life, she almost forgot the reason for being in his office.

Why did everyone in the house behave like a hoarder?

Unlike Lai's stash, though, this one seemed to hold actual scientific value rather than just emotional. Floor to ceiling shelves were crowded with journals, maps, and samples of rocks, miniature model ships and the articulated skeletons of small creatures, all covered in a thick blanket of dust.

"Is that a… baby unicorn in a jar…?" Lucy pressed her face against a glass filled with murky liquid, trying to see the creature inside.

"No. It's a goat with one horn." Aris took a seat behind a large oak desk. "I'm still working on that. Sit." He raised his voice, trying to get Lucy's attention, but only his dogs followed the command.

"Is this real?" Her attention was now on a giant skull in the corner. "Is this a dragon? Wait, are dragons real?" Lucy traced her hand along a row of long teeth, one fang made of solid gold. "Do you have dragons here? At this house?"

Aris grit his teeth. She was testing his patience. "Don't be stupid. Dragons are incredibly rare, intelligent, and would not tolerate captivity." He watched her examine rows and rows of samples, each carefully preserved and labeled, stacks of rare books piled on the floor and taxidermy covering the wall. "Are you ready to discuss your employment, or shall I wait here until you've finished gawking?"

Lucy sighed heavily and took a seat opposite him. Damn, this obedience thing was hard.

"Let's try this again. Why are you here?"

"I've answered twice now. I saw the ad; I responded because I needed money and a place to stay."

"I want you to think harder about this. No one like you comes here by mistake; someone is always pulling the strings. Who showed you the ad? Who encouraged you?" Aris opened a fresh page in a leather-bound journal, ready to write down her answers.

"My best friend's fathers?" Lucy frowned, leaning on the table. "They encouraged me because I'd been living in their spare room for the last six months. That doesn't mean anyone was manipulating me. Your collection is missing a tinfoil hat if you think that someone sent me here for some nefarious purpose."

Aris didn't look convinced. "So is that it? You're here just to work. I smelled your magic, girl. You blew your cover."

How can you smell anything past the bullshit you're spewing?

Lucy groaned as she got up and reached into her pocket, dumping her wet wallet onto his desk. "There, check it." She opened it and emptied all the cards and old receipts into a soggy mound. "See what's missing? Money. That's it. Honest money the nanny position promised to provide. If anything, you lot are the ones being fucking shady. Who here needs babysitting? Lai, a grown-ass man acting like a teenager? You?"

Lucy felt the energy shift as Aris straightened in his seat at the insult; she expected him to yell or try to hit her. But he did nothing. If anything that made her more afraid. She had already figured out the man was violent, she hadn't expected him to be delusional as well.

She had come here on her own accord. No one had sent her.

"I need names. Everyone who was around you when you found the ad." He slid a piece of paper across the table, avoiding her personal belongings cluttering his desk.

"Mr Farrowatcher, his husband Mr Farrowatcher, their daughter Xim Farrowatcher, and their little chihuahua-cross dog, Zappy." Lucy wrote the names out for him.

Aris looked at the paper. "I've heard the name Farrowatcher somewhere before, but can't put my finger on where."

"They're everywhere. My parents worked for them. They develop medicines and weapons. New technology, satellite networks. Lots of government contracts."

Who didn't know the Farrowatcher family? Their logo was on every cell phone. Cars, planes, makeup. Anywhere she looked Lucy could find her friend's name. Xim told her that the family's ambition was a curse. Lucy used to laugh at that. Who wouldn't want to be 'cursed' with so much money?

Shaking off the pesky memories, Lucy looked up at Aris again, but his eyes were glued to the journal.

"Still...Can't trust those tiny dogs..." He muttered with a straight face, speaking to his hounds, who wagged in agreement.

Does he know I'm still in the room?

"I think that's the first thing we've agreed on. That tiny bastard could not be trusted." She thought back to the time the dog had pissed in her shoe and shuddered.

A hint of a smile appeared on Aris's face but was gone the next moment.

"Take your things. I'll give you another chance only because the dogs trust you. You will start your duties tomorrow."

He nodded toward three of his girls sitting near Lucy, who stood to attention as he mentioned them; they were rewarded with brisk head rubs, their glowing tongues lolling out of their mouths in canine bliss.

That could've gone worse. Lucy wished only the dogs a goodnight, standing to leave.

"Girl, wait. Did anyone else in your family have magic?"

"I never asked them, and it's a bit too late to ask now." She glanced away, not wanting to discuss something so painful with Aris.

He didn't press for details, but his dogs sensed Lucy's pain, rubbing against her hand.

"Go on, get out. Why are you even up so late? How are you supposed to do your job with only a few hours of sleep?"

Lucy smiled, giving a dog a sneaky pat. "How do you tolerate him?"

"Out."

CHAPTER TEN

LUCY

This dream again.

The last day that felt...normal. The day before the crash.

Lucy loved and hated this recurring visit. Her brain played out the memory night after night like a broken record.

Her room. So many memories were attached to those baby pink walls covered in a patchwork of her art.

Light beamed through a crystal sun-catcher, throwing a rainbow of colors over the drawings, adding cheerful hues to the angsty black and white characters.

There was nothing unusual about that day. A warm summer's Sunday filled with that particular lazy energy known only to those with zero responsibilities.

Lucy glanced past her book towards the open bedroom door. Most nights, the dream was one of comfort, but today, her brain amplified a new part of it—the voices.

The gentle murmuring of her parents' conversation was clearer, and for the first time, she could hear another participant. Not an unfamiliar one. Her father's best friend stopped by often enough, but why could she not remember his visit that day until now?

Tip-toeing across the creaking floor, Lucy listened from the top of the stairs. What sounded like a friendly conversation a moment ago had become heated.

"Ezell, be reasonable," Mr Farrowatcher urged in a hushed tone.

Lucy heard her father pacing the room.

"I am done playing Victor's games, Henry," he said, keeping his voice down. "I'm taking my family, and we are leaving."

"We will find the missing girl; I can promise you the project hasn't been compromised. We will move operations from Mexico back home. You can't just withdraw. This is Victor's life's work."

"Henry! Enough!" Lucy could hear the frustration in her father's tone. "I saw what happened to that child. We needed two vessels for the memories alone. I told him and he didn't listen! I'm out. I'm not endangering my daughter anymore. Your husband is a mad man."

Henry didn't answer; only the sound of fingers rapping on the tabletop interrupted the poignant silence.

"I understand." Their visitor rose from his seat. "I'd do anything for my daughter too, but please. Take a day to think about it. For me?

Take your wife to the beach house. Discuss it. If you decide to go, I won't stop you."

***

"Morning, sunshine!"

Lucy yelped, startled awake. "Why are you in my bed, Lai?" She demanded with a groan, kicking him under the covers and scooting away—her heel connected with his legs with force.

"I was cold. Now I'm cold and in pain," he winced, rubbing his sore kneecap.

"You better not be trying anything."

"I wouldn't dare." He took over her warm spot, pulling the blanket up to his chin. "You aren't exactly my type."

What was his deal? Not his type? He'd had so many opportunities to try something. It wasn't like she could escape. Maybe it was her magic that kept him at bay...

"I'm glad we're on the same page." Lucy stretched, chasing away the last of her sleepy fog. "I don't want your father getting the wrong idea. I do need this job." She groaned as memories of last night flooded in. She wasn't looking forward to seeing the man who had been happy to watch a monster eat her.

"You better stay on my good side then. As my glorified babysitter, it's your job to make sure I'm happy," Lai winked. "You don't want me telling daddy..."

105

"How old are you? Do you even need a babysitter?" Lucy narrowed her eyes, hitting Lai with her pillow.

Was he serious? Would he complain to his father if she didn't play his stupid games?

"Oh, that rude question again? Of course I don't need one, but it would be fun to have one."

"Awww, some repressed childhood fantasy?" She teased.

"Yes, let's call it that. I would like to see how far you'll go to keep your job. This could be mutually beneficial."

"Not that far, so don't try it." Lucy poked him right in the middle of his forehead, establishing a firm boundary. She wasn't about to let him walk all over her. Her obedience had to be believable.

"I don't know. I get the feeling you could be into some pretty questionable stuff." Lai watched her, unable to hide a mischievous smile. It was somehow both endearing and infuriating.

"Keep this up, and you'll never find out." Tossing her blanket over his head, she got up to get dressed. "Let's go; I don't want to be late for breakfast."

They were the last to arrive. Lai waltzed in and took his usual place at the table, leaning back on his seat to show off bare thighs. He looked disappointed when no one acknowledged his shenanigans. Even Aris didn't rise to the bait, holding up his newspaper to block the view.

Lucy examined the yellowed front page; December 1991. *He has a lot to catch up on*, she thought to herself, though she didn't comment on his peculiar reading material.

"Good morning." She took an empty seat as she examined the place settings, who sat where, and what they were drinking. She noticed Aris filled his teacup from a personal flask with something that was definitely not tea.

He noted her curious glance, setting the newspaper down. She could smell the drink from her seat. Dark, sweet liquor. Most likely rum.

"I see you are not taking your duties seriously."

"Well, I haven't been told what my duties are."

"I thought it would be obvious." Aris glanced at her past his newspaper. "You are the woman of this house now."

Lucy rolled her eyes and looked at Lai for translation.

"I think father wants you to take on all of the dutiful housewife tasks." Lai was more than happy to explain, gleefully waiting for Lucy's reaction.

"Ah." She could have figured that out by herself. As long as those duties included only the house tasks, she could manage. He better not try anything else.

"I expect my children to dress appropriately for meal times." He looked over at Ryan, who didn't seem to care, still wearing pajamas with his nose planted firmly between the pages of a book. Lai raised a leg to demonstrate just how inappropriately he'd dressed that morning and scowled when no one spared him a glance.

"Understood," Lucy nodded, trying to stay on his good side. She didn't want a repeat of yesterday.

The breakfast went on in relative peace. Lucy watched the family members interact with their meals and each other, studying their dynamic. Lai made another textural monstrosity to consume; this time, it was a porridge mixed with instant coffee and a spoonful of jam. She wondered if he had any taste buds at all. He hadn't eaten anything even remotely normal yet.

Ryan was the only 'normal' one at the table–normal for a middle-aged man, not a child. Plain oats and black coffee didn't seem like something a kid would volunteer to eat. She almost expected him to light up a cigar.

The clanking of dishes caught Lucy's attention. Klein was polishing the glasses on the breakfast tray, stacking them in preparation for the next meal.

"Hey, let me do that; you sit down and eat," she offered as she got up to help, but Klein held the glass protectively to his chest and out of her reach.

"That's okay. You finish your breakfast." He offered her a polite smile.

"No, you gotta eat too," Lucy insisted.

Klein glanced at the table, his eye darting from one family member to another as if looking for help or permission.

"Sit down, girl. He eats alone," Aris said.

She glanced back at the man, who was holding his newspaper over his face.

"Why?"

When no one else volunteered any details, Lucy sank back into her seat, although Lai gave her a look that promised gossip later.

She would have to wait until they were in private again to satisfy her burning curiosity.

"Has anyone seen Louis?" Aris asked; all of the family tensed around him.

"Yes, about three days ago. I guess it would pay to check the nest again," Klein answered, ignoring Lucy as she tried to get his attention, shock all over her face.

"Who is Louis?" She asked. Her mild concern was nothing compared to the hurricane of emotion that struck as Lai explained.

Pressing a clean napkin to his lips, the lavender haired man answered in a quiet mumble.

"He's our youngest brother. Lou is six."

Surely I heard him wrong.

"What did you say?"

"We have another brother. He's pretty independent, though."

"Hold on." She needed a moment to process that. "A six-year-old child has been missing for three days, and you lot are just eating breakfast like it's not a big deal?"

Would it be appropriate to start slapping these men so early in the morning? Lucy wasn't just angry, she was panicking. Something almost ate her in that forest last night and now she'd found out that a child was loose. Alone and vulnerable.

"It's not a big deal." Klein topped up her cup of tea. "We're in a custody battle with two lovely lady griffins nesting nearby. They want a family, but unfortunately, they've killed the last known male of their kind."

"Who could blame them?" Lai snorted. "Call it what it is, Klein. They're a pair of angry, clucky lesbians who're better at looking after the kid than we are."

No shit! Anything is better than you lot!

"Yes, well. Girl, take Ryan and go collect the child." Aris put down his newspaper, physically bracing himself for a barrage of complaints from the boy. He was not disappointed; Ryan nearly choked on his coffee.

"I can go by myself–"

"I'm well aware, but she needs to learn."

Lucy glanced at Ryan, then Aris and back at the boy. "Come on, kid, let's get you changed, then you can show me that nest."

If only looks could kill.

"Kid?" Ryan managed in a strangled voice. A glare from Aris cooled him down from a boil to a furious simmer. He muttered darkly into his coffee cup.

"One of you hates being called old." She looked at Lai. "And one of you hates being called young. Very sensitive about your ages."

"You think I'm old?" A dramatic gasp escaped Lai's lips.

"Never, darling. Ryan, come before I offend someone else."

"Don't worry; it's not anything you're saying. Just your presence." Ryan finished his drink and left the table.

Lai gave Lucy an encouraging smile. "I think he likes you."

CHAPTER ELEVEN

RYAN

Ryan despised Lucy's condescending smile. His face burned when she suggested he needed help while he tied his laces. He had little patience for the games his father played. They were just fine without her. Everyone minded their business, meal times were silent, and no one called him a child.

"Let's get this over with. I don't want to waste my whole day looking for that little troll because daddy dearest decided to care all of a sudden." He secured a canvas bag over his shoulder, treating it with utmost care. Ryan knew the drill all too well. Retrieve and replace. That kept the flying beasties at bay.

"So this happens often then? Your brother getting stolen?" Lucy asked as she followed Ryan through the east part of the garden, towards a vast wildflower meadow surrounded by chalky cliffs.

"You could say that. They take whatever they can mother. Small animals, pups—anything childlike."

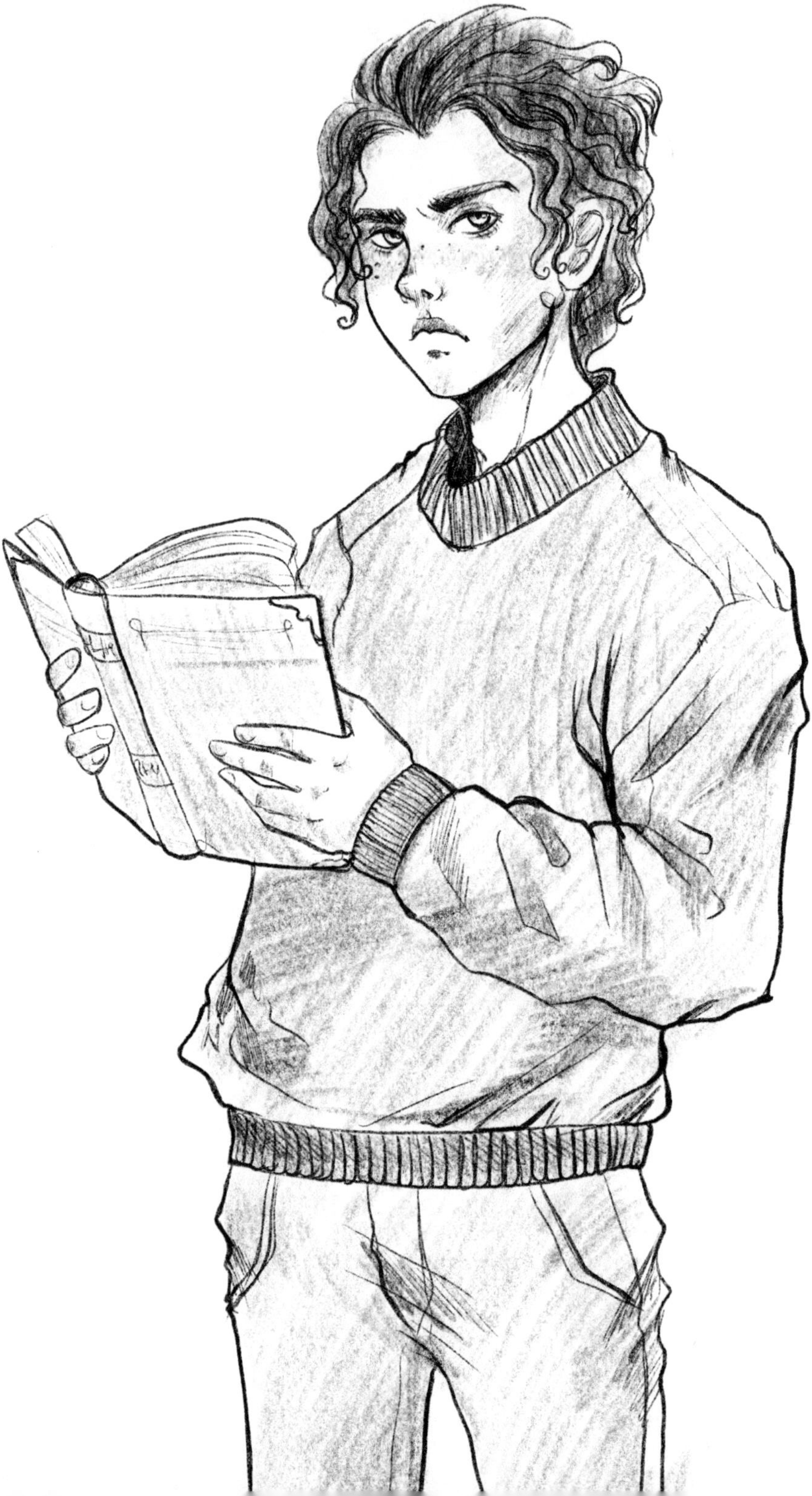

"So, how many times have they taken you?"

Will anyone notice her missing? These cliffs can be so treacherous.

Ryan took a deep breath, counted to six and exhaled. "I suppose you think you're very funny."

"I'm hilarious," Lucy laughed. "Come down dressed properly for breakfast tomorrow, and I'll stop."

Ryan paused to look at her, trying to figure out if there was a catch. He knew better than to make deals.

"I honestly doubt it, but fine."

The garden came alive around them, all manner of creatures waking up, studying the rare visitors. Ryan knew better than to linger too long but Lucy still suffered from curiosity, examining deadly butterflies as they huddled on a branch, wings raised as a warning.

"Must you?" He huffed, annoyed by the delay. He was going to add a warning but decided against it. After all, how else was she going to learn?

"Look at the flowers on this thing, they look like fairy dresses." Lucy gasped in awe, leaning towards a vine with large bell-like white petals. "Do you know what they're called?"

"I do. *Digitus Comendentis*." Ryan chuckled. "We should really keep going. Do not smell it—"

Too late. The intoxicating aroma reminiscent of spiced vanilla lured her closer. Lucy reached for the velvety petals, but before her fingers could caress the flower, the vine pushed away from the post and wrapped itself around her arm.

Crying out in shock, Lucy pulled back but the plant had her tight in its grip, every flower opening up just a little wider, showing pale fangs, ready to snap over her hand.

"Oi! Enough," Ryan stepped forward and stomped on the exposed root. The creature hissed in pain, letting go of Lucy and wrapping itself back up around the wooden post, vines tightening up in a sulk.

Lucy moved back to the middle of the path, holding her arm, a few nasty scratches on it. Ryan almost felt bad for letting it get that far, but this was for her benefit. This was a sanctuary and the creatures it housed weren't harmless.

"Here…" he passed her a little packet of tissues from his bag. "You really need to pay more attention."

Lucy nodded, looking a little less relaxed now, Ryan could see her eyes darting from one plant bed to another. She wasn't about to trust even a dandelion.

The cliffs approached quickly as they walked, a narrow, steep path leading the way up the face. Ryan would have enjoyed the warm, quiet walk, but anxious Lucy seemed determined to fill the peaceful silence.

"What's the deal with Lai and the peacock?" Lucy asked.

Ryan snorted.

"You'd have to ask Lai. His feud with the bird is none of my business," he replied, clipped and cool.

"Oh." A few minutes of blissful silence, then…

"So, would it be okay to borrow some books from you later?"

Kiss ass. Ryan rolled his eyes, not caring if she saw. "Of course," he replied coldly, humoring her. "What kind of books do you like?"

Lucy considered that, chewing on her bottom lip as she tried to think of something age-appropriate. "I like romance and adventures. I adore love triangles."

"I've never read an actual love triangle book."

"Yeah? I have a few I could–"

"That's not what I meant. I meant, *geometrically*. They're love *angles*. 'Triangle' implies that all three points are connected; a love triangle would mean Jacob and Edward were hooking up as well." Ryan couldn't help but let a little bit of his passion show; the misuse of 'love triangle' was a gripe close to his heart. "It's never a true triangle– Oh hey, careful!"

He grabbed Lucy's arm as the path took a corner; they were standing on the edge of a ravine, a narrow gap that cut straight down, deep into the earth.

"Oh, shit!" She grabbed the rock wall beside her, scrambling to get her footing and catch her breath.

"Sorry, I should've warned you. Although it would be kind of ironic." He pointed down to the bottom of the pit.

Lucy squinted to see through the dark; the sun had just reached its zenith, and its warming light reached down through the gloom, picking up flashes of white hidden in the dirt below.

Piles and piles of tiny skeletons mixed with clay from the cliff side. A few stubborn plants strained towards the sun from between infant rib cages, fertilized by long decayed flesh.

Lucy looked down, her eyebrows furrowed. "Are those...bodies?" She took a few steps back down the path, watching Ryan cautiously. "They look small. Like–"

"Children, yes," he answered; he did not look down towards them. "They're the unwanted children of my ancestors. Girls, mostly."

"What? Why?"

Ryan shrugged. "I don't know who started it. My great-grandfather used to say, 'when you have a monopoly on the breed, you don't sell the bitches'," he mocked him in a deeper voice, rasping and ugly.

"You're talking like someone would want your bloodline. This is fucking horrible." Lucy trembled in a fury.

Could he blame her? The scene drenched in death didn't shock him, but the slaughter of helpless children was sickening. Even for him.

Especially for him. A generation ago, Ryan would have been one of them, inhaling damp soil with his last gasps.

He watched Lucy, his head cocked to one side. He looked just like his father as he studied her outrage. Ryan was a little disappointed that she didn't catch on. He had given her so many clues. "It is, and they do. Don't worry, though; we haven't contributed to this gruesome collection. I know it's hard to believe that my father has four sons, but it is what it is."

"Wait–four?" She counted family members on one hand, but kept coming up one short.

"Yes, use your math." Ryan held up four fingers. "Klein-"

"What?"

"Why are you interrupting me?"

"Klein is your brother? I thought he was–well, the butler." Lucy shook her head in disbelief.

"What gave you that idea?"

"Maybe him doing absolutely everything from cooking to cleaning? Lai treats him like a servant and your father just lets it happen."

Ryan paused. She did have a point. Lai and Klein had a different mother, a woman loved deeply by the man he called father but who passed away before he was born. According to others, Klein became the glue that held the family together. It was the only version of Klein that Ryan had ever known.

Unfortunately, the womb that carried Ryan was as cold as death. Just as nurturing too. His life was merely a transaction, nothing else. Unwanted at that, rejected by both sides at first. Klein had raised him but he had his hands so full, his love and affection was carefully rationed. So Ryan sought comfort elsewhere. Books. He found his family among faded pages.

"Someone's gotta do it." He started back up the path, bored of her questions.

To Ryan's relief, she seemed to have given up on trying to make small talk. Probably far too preoccupied with all of the new information she had to digest, or maybe she was just out of breath. He could ignore her angry muttering and panting as they hiked; Ryan preferred the almost silence now that they were getting close. He knew that the griffins would be away hunting but taking stupid chances wasn't his style: less noise, less opportunity to be spotted.

"There. On that cliff." He pointed to a minivan sized nest made from thick branches and the pelts of small animals. It balanced precariously over the cliff's edge, supported by an old, dead tree. It looked like it was defying gravity.

Lucy looked up as a young child peeked over the edge. Covered in mud with a head full of wild raven curls and a smattering of dirty freckles across his nose, Louis waved at Ryan, showing his brother something clenched in his fist.

"Mamas just brought food!" The child yelled over to him, dangling a long earthworm so everyone could see. Quick as a flash, he slurped it into his mouth like a strand of spaghetti.

"Don't eat that; it's–" Lucy gasped, too late. "...Guess a little extra protein won't hurt?"

"I like it; it's like meat jelly." He held out another worm to her.

Lucy politely declined.

She scaled a few large boulders, careful of her footing. Ryan wondered if he should have warned her that the errand would involve rock climbing; perhaps Lucy would have worn something with a little more grip than her ballet flats. Holding on for dear life, she reached the nest and scooped the child from his temporary home.

Lucy slid back down, scooting across the boulders on her butt. Louis seemed to have fun at least, kicking up his legs in excitement as they dangled over the cliff.

"Let's go back, don't dawdle." Ryan opened his rucksack and gently extracted a large ostrich egg. He climbed effortlessly up the rocks to the nest and placed the Louis-substitute inside. "Should keep them busy for a while."

"If they are so good to Lou, then what's the hurry?" Lucy asked.

Ryan sighed; rather than explain, he pointed at a horse in the distance. Lucy followed his finger as her eyes lit up in excitement.

"Is that a unicorn?" She took in a big breath and Ryan braced himself for a squeal. Thankfully she managed to hold it in.

"It will have been stalking this nest for days now," Ryan explained. The pitch black unicorn turned its head at the trio, its eyes glowing red and hooves digging up the dry ground. It watched them like a tiger watched a hare, eager and hungry.

"We can't approach it. Not with Louis. That thing…it hates men. It will gore any that comes close to it. My father's ex used to own it, it was given to her as a gift. That's Madison's unicorn and no one can get close unless they want to be turned into ground beef."

Lucy pursed her lips in thought. It looked like thinking was a challenging task for her.

"Yes, you can, but not now. Not with Lou with us. Come on. I want to avoid that thing if we can. If it gets close enough, it'll try to kill him."

***

They took the same route back, Lucy holding Louis' hand the whole way.

"It happens often, huh? Maybe next time, I'll pack you an overnight bag with snacks and a drink bottle." Lucy changed the subject as the child beamed in excitement. "I hope you don't get scared up there."

"Mamas are nice!" Louis insisted. "They tell me stories."

"They don't talk." Ryan glanced at his brother.

"They do! Like this!" Louis puffed his cheeks and gave a loud bird call.

"That's not talking."

"They do talk! They tell me stories! Mamas told me about their village. They told me about their nests! They make huuuuuuuge nests with roofs and rooms!"

Lucy picked up Louis as she noticed him dragging his feet in tiredness, hoping to avoid a sibling fight. "I'll make a bag with clothes, food, and maybe even some books."

"Picture books! I can't read yet," he nodded excitedly.

"You can't?" Lucy looked at Ryan. "What the eff have y'all been doing?"

He scoffed. "I'm busy, and no one knows where he is most of the time. Lai can't read either, and he's fine."

"Do you want him to turn out like Lai?"

"Good point. I'll teach the brat. You don't need to guilt me into it."

CHAPTER TWELVE

LUCY

"Ah, back already? Good. Give me a hand with this—"

Lucy stormed towards the man and pressed her finger to his lips. The sudden physical contact startled Klein so much he dropped the fish he'd been carrying, watching it slide across the slippery, scale covered floor. It was only then Lucy noticed the state of the kitchen and the smell, but she wasn't about to let him get away with lying to her just because he was covered in fish guts.

"You didn't tell me you were part of the family!" Kleins nostrils flared as she got closer into his personal space, making him squirm.

"I—" he opened and closed his mouth, looking a lot like the fish on the table next to him. "I thought it was obvious, Lucy. It isn't a secret."

Maybe it was a little obvious.

"What about that pit?"

His eye darted towards the open door but his escape was blocked off. "Every family has skeletons in their closet…"

"One or two!! Not literal ones, usually!" Lucy wanted to scream but something about Klein made it almost impossible to direct her wrath at him. She realized she was holding him by the collar, a step too far yet he allowed it. Taking a deep breath she released her grip. "So, what are you doing with all the fish?"

"We're meal prepping for your favorite pet." Klein heaved a heavy bucket of herrings onto the table. From it he lifted one by its tail and put it through an old, metal, hand-cranked grinder. The creaky mechanism turned with a groan, mangling the fish into a pale mash.

"Ah, yes. Martha," Lucy sighed, disgust written all over her face. The miasma filling the kitchen air would make anyone feel nauseous, a perfume of fresh fish, shrimp paste, and seaweed that would linger on for days.

"I only prepare the food every couple of months or so; even I find it to be a bit too much. Grab that bucket I've filled, add water and place it into the walk-in freezer. We give it to her in popsicle form. Easier to grab and eat."

Lucy did as he asked, picking up the heavy bucket in her arms; she retched in horror as the foul soup slopped over the edge and down the front of her clothing. She tried to clean it off, only spreading the oily liquid over her shirt until she gave up in defeat.

Klein dodged a squirt of guts as another fish went into the grinder.

"I know it isn't pleasant, but trust me, there are worse jobs."

"I bet. Lai told me I'm going to be his nanny; that prospect is terrifying." She smiled at him, feeling guilty for the earlier outburst. "To be honest, I'm more worried about cooking. I can make simple meals, but I gotta confess I'm not a great cook."

Klein narrowed his eye at her. "I'm sure your resume included 'excellent cooking skills'. Don't worry, I can teach you. That being said, I don't know why I bother to cook. Father doesn't have any taste buds left; Lai mixes his food into a monstrous paste, and Ryan snacks throughout the day. I'm pretty sure he only turns up for meals to prove he's still alive," Klein sighed. "I do try, although it might not seem like it."

"Oh, I know you do," Lucy smiled. "It's just way too much work for one person."

Klein walked over to a large copper barn sink and rinsed the fish scales from his hands. "Someone's gotta do it. If I don't, they'll drown in their filth."

"Yeah, I can see that. Lucky for you, your dad decided to keep me on. I didn't think he would."

She paused for a second, studying his reaction. She had only just found out that he was the eldest, not another prisoner. That was going to make her escape harder. He was whipped into obedience it seemed, treated like a servant. "I might be crazy for staying. I can just tell Xim would be freaking out. Imagine if I told her that I'm working for a man that tried to kill me."

Lucy shook her head in disbelief. Thinking that out loud made her realize the ridiculousness of her situation, but her last manager had seemed determined to drive her into an early grave with fourteen-hour shifts and slow mental torture. At least Aris was honest in his intent.

Compared to her last job, her new boss seemed merciful.

"He didn't try to kill you. He was just introducing you to the old lady." Klein took off his stained vest and offered a clean towel to Lucy. "If it helps, I only have to cook breakfasts and dinners. The family scavenges for lunch, and if they're hungry, they can always order pizza."

"How do they order pizza?" Lucy gladly washed her hands. "Lai tried to explain this place to me. Apparently, it's difficult to get into."

This was it. This could be her way out!

Do I want a way out?

"It's not getting in that's difficult. It's getting out." Klein gave her a look, a hint of warning in his eye. "Anyway, Lai got fed up with waiting at the end of the drive and had Gaia create a pass for the driver. This place has top tier security. No government, no special forces; not even gods can access it without permission. But a pimply teenager working for Domino's has access to our top-secret location. All because my brother is too lazy to cook."

"Why am I not surprised?" She forced a smile.

"I have a few other chores to do. Think you can go and feed Martha by yourself?"

Did he just ask her that? Knowing well enough that the damned creature had almost killed her?

"Is she going to try to eat me again?"

"Martha is a geriatric squid. She can't eat anyone. I swear you are getting as dramatic as Lai," he chuckled.

Oh, he was testing her patience today. Dramatic? Lucy squinted at Klein, lips pursed in a tight pout.

"You sure you're not his long lost twin?" Klein teased. "He makes the same face when I ask him to do something."

Lucy flipped Klein off, but he accepted the gesture as a humorous one. "Someone has been watching too many soaps," she muttered.

"You've discovered my guilty pleasure." He opened the heavy metal door to the walk-in freezer. "Take a couple of those and go apologize to the old lady."

Taking the offering, she examined the two buckets filled with frozen fish paste. The stench of fresh feed still filled the kitchen, but at least they wouldn't have to do this again for a while.

"Don't get eaten."

***

Strolling towards the lake, Lucy greeted the now-familiar statues and glared at every vine crawling upon them. She wasn't exactly happy that she had to see the beast that nearly killed her, so a hasty delivery wasn't a priority.

The afternoon sun cast a golden hue across the sky, dotted with wispy clouds, and for the first time in days Lucy had a moment to herself, a moment to feel normal. Yes, she was carrying two heavy buckets of feed for a giant squid, but for just a few minutes, she was just a girl, enjoying the warm rays of the sun.

Walking out on the dock, Lucy looked over the water; the lake didn't have a single ripple in it, hiding the creature beneath. She emptied the buckets in; the frozen fish popsicles bobbed on the surface of the lake but remained untouched. Was Martha still sulking? Surely Lucy should be the one upset. She had almost drowned!

Maybe I am being a little dramatic.

Perhaps an apology would entice the deep-dwelling creature to have its lunch.

"I'm sorry about the other day!" Lucy called out, sitting down on the damp wood. She felt a bit silly apologizing to the sea monster, but if Klein was right then maybe Martha deserved it.

A few moments passed before the water tension broke, and a shy tentacle pulled the fishy ice block down into the murky depths. Lucy felt a strange elation, but all positive feelings shriveled up when she heard footsteps somewhere above her.

"Didn't learn your lesson the first time?" Aris looked surprised to see Lucy by the lake again. He stood on board his ship, watching her on the docks below. "I think Martha is still scared of you. She hasn't even touched her second bucket."

Lucy glanced up at Aris, then back at the second fish-cicle. She opened her mouth to protest but decided not to, walking to the edge of the dock. "I'm sorry I stabbed you with my keys. I thought you were going to eat me."

The same tentacle that had pulled her under earlier landed on the pier next to her, the wound from the stab healing but still visible.

Her mother always told her to treat each creature she met with respect and kindness. She made her dad stop for every turtle on the road. Every stray cat in her neighborhood eventually found a home, and spiders were captured and released. Lucy's perception of Martha shifted when she saw the wound presented to her as a child would show their mother a cut on the finger. She did the only logical thing and leaned down to kiss it gently.

"Please forgive me." The whispered apology was entirely sincere.

Aris huffed in disbelief as the lone tentacle wrapped itself around Lucy's hand, just holding it as she had with him after her injury. Then just like that, the second part of the kraken's meal bobbled on the surface then disappeared. The terrifying beast that had sunk hundreds of ships simply wanted her hand held while she ate.

Lucy did just that. She held the tentacle, her thumb rubbing small circles on it with a silly smile on her face. She couldn't help but relax, fear ebbing away.

"Hold your breath," Aris cautioned.

What? Why?

Lucy obeyed instinctively, taking in a deep breath and holding it.

Was she about to be pulled under again?

She was. Martha pulled Lucy in, less suddenly this time; the old lady just wanted a better look at her new friend. The ancient Kraken swam closer to the surface, one giant eye scanning the tiny human. Lucy used that moment of calm to stare back at the creature. She sensed no threat, just curiosity that went both ways. How many people had ever looked at one of these and lived to tell the tale?

As the air depleted in her lungs, Lucy felt the squid's arm unwind, and wasting no time, she made her way back up, gasping for breath the moment she reached the surface.

"Thanks for the warning," she meant to sound grateful, but with wet hair clinging to her face and her graceless doggy paddle in the water, she must've looked anything but.

"She is a hugger," Aris said coldly as a couple of tentacles helped Lucy climb up. "Come up here before you catch a fever."

Lucy looked up at the ship, surprised that she was offered the chance to go aboard. She was under the impression that the man hated her; why would he invite her up there? Scrambling onto the dock, she ditched her soaked shoes that had weighed her down.

The reason for his seemingly noble gesture was simple. Aris wouldn't miss a chance to show off his favorite child to anyone willing to spare him the time. Boys and their toys...

"Where are your manners, girl? You must always ask the captain for permission to come aboard before crossing the threshold."

"Um, but you...Never mind. Permission to come aboard?" Lucy resisted the urge to roll her eyes.

"Permission granted." It had obviously been a while and Aris looked pretty damn pleased to say it again.

The ship itself had seen better days. Although still otherworldly and beautiful, *Artemis* showed as many scars as her captain. The dark wood was gouged and repaired in dozens of places along the rail, with lacquer chipping from the combination of salt and sun.

He motioned for Lucy to follow him to the captain's quarters. The room was a stark contrast to his cluttered chambers on land. Plainly decorated and organized, the bedroom still smelled of exotic spices and a lingering aroma of tobacco.

Aris walked over to a solid oak wardrobe and offered her a thin cotton towel and a long linen shirt. Most likely one of his. "Can't have you sick on your first week here. Change, girl."

"Where should I change?" she asked, looking around; the room offered no privacy of any kind.

"Is this not good enough?"

Lucy blushed red and, turning her back to Aris, took off her soaked clothing, drying herself off. The shirt was long enough to wear as a dress, and she did just that, letting the fabric fall shapelessly around her body.

Bastard must be enjoying the show, I should've known better than to come up here.

Placing a disapproving frown on her face she turned around to silently confront him only to find Aris with his back to her.

He didn't pay any attention to Lucy as she changed; he seemed to focus more on the journal stacks piled up near the bed. He mindlessly flipped through the yellowed pages, muttering under his breath.

"What are those?" Lucy asked, folding wet clothes into the towel to avoid making a mess of finely woven straw mats covering the floor.

"Old logs. Nothing else," he frowned, blocking them with his body, away from prying eyes. "Must you be so nosy?"

Lucy huffed, turning her attention to the walls crowded with frames and tapestries. She was under the impression he wanted to show off, but once again Aris turned prickly the moment she had probed him for information. Perhaps he'd be more willing to talk about his boat?

"How long have you had this ship?"

"I had her built for me when I was barely eighteen. She was a gift." Aris walked up to the chart Lucy was examining and took it off the wall. "This is something you might want to learn."

Lucy held in her question of how old he was. No one in the family seemed particularly forthcoming with the information anyway. "What is it?" She examined the parchment with frayed edges. Old ink revealed no information that she could understand; a mixture of lines going up and down like miniature graphs, and descriptions along each one written in a language she couldn't read.

"We use this to train our hellhounds. A lot like what farmers use to train their herding dogs," Aris explained impatiently.

"I can't read this." Turning the parchment sideways, Lucy picked out a few words she'd seen before.

"You don't know your Latin?"

Latin? Did she want to ask his age? Not even her grandfather demanded something so antiquated.

"I was placed in Spanish class instead. Some of these words look familiar, but…" Lucy reached into her memory to try and grasp at strings of school lessons. Everything about the language, just like every memory from school, dissolved into a pool of useless trivia and algebraic formulas she was yet to use.

Aris sighed, taking the scroll away from her. "Spanish is good too, I guess; I picked up plenty of crew every time we dropped anchor in Malaga. Good men there..." He drifted off into memory but snapped out of it quickly. "This, here." He pointed to the first line on the scroll. "This is a summoning whistle. If there are shadows, any hound that we've trained will obey. Not all of them, of course, but the closest. Just like magic, the method is not as important as the intent. It does help, though."

"How exactly does it work?"

Aris pressed his lips together and whistled a sharp tone with a melodic trail off that sounded like a bird call. A few seconds later, a couple of hounds from his pack appeared from the shadows cast from the lit candle. They looked excited, waiting for a reward.

Was it too late to tell him she could barely whistle? Lucy pressed her lips together, attempting to mimic the call, but it sounded nothing like his. A mix of high pitched squeals followed by a raspberry.

The hounds cocked their heads, and so did Aris. All three stared at Lucy in confusion.

"...dang it, I think I did it wrong."

"Surprisingly so. Now try again. Split it into two parts. Copy me." He demonstrated the whistle once again, this time slower.

'Performs well under pressure.' Yet another lie on her resume.

Now with the audience, Lucy attempted the call again and again until she got the melody right.

"Close enough. The first part needs to be a lot more assertive. Hellhounds are lazy. You've got to be in charge."

Lucy tried again, her lips getting itchy.

"Now, both together. Like you mean it."

She did, willing with all she had for it to work. The shadows stirred, and another hound appeared stretching from its nap. A welcome sight despite the dog's displeased expression. Lucy grinned from ear to ear, turning to face Aris.

"Impressive. This one doesn't like doing tricks. You must've annoyed her enough."

She knelt down to pet the dog, cooing and praising the hound. It seemed like a good reward for showing up. The hound wagged her stubby tail, pushing away the other two dogs who were trying to get in on the action. "Who deserves all of the pets?" Lucy asked the dogs in front of her as she did her best to pet them all equally, all while avoiding their burning maws.

"Now you are just spoiling them." Aris uttered a short double whistle, and all three hounds stood at attention. "If you are ever in trouble get them to focus, and then it's the same whistle but twice to attack."

Lucy nodded. It sounded simple enough in theory.

"Go on then. Back to your beds, you lazy mutts." He dismissed the dogs, drowning the room with awkward silence.

Lucy decided to break it first. "Thank you for teaching me that. Was that magic?"

"No, it wasn't magic; it's just a quirk of their breed," he shrugged. "You have a lot to learn. Especially if you plan on staying here."

For a second, just a second…she actually considered it.

"I do; I'll learn everything that you want to teach me."

Aris couldn't help but laugh. "Careful making offers like that to strange men, girl."

"I meant for work!" She scooped up her wet clothes, blushing furiously.

He studied the curious woman in front of him. "What do you want to learn?"

"How to work with the animals, the Dos and Don'ts. I doubt I'll find much information on Kraken care and hellhound husbandry in books."

Aris walked over to Lucy, standing a little bit too close. Close enough she could feel the warmth radiating from his body. A familiar heat she had felt mere moments ago while stroking the dogs.

"You just have to remember that they know everything. Their senses are so much more advanced than ours," he whispered, leaning in closer.

Lucy froze, her breath catching in her throat. This was a new sensation; she was afraid but refused to move. She had a chance to step away and leave, but the danger was alluring. Did they know her plans? Did he?

"For example, I can smell your fear, and..." He chuckled, leaning away.

A dark shade of red colored her cheeks. No way he could smell anything aside from lake water. He was messing with her.

"Go home, girl. You've done enough for today. The rest of the afternoon is yours."

"Do I have to ask the captain to leave the ship as well?"

"Unfortunately, the alternative is me having to suffer your company."

Prick.

CHAPTER THIRTEEN

LUCY

Lucy rubbed her eyes, trying to shake the dream away. She glanced around, surprised Lai wasn't already in her bed, then looked at her phone and groaned. 5 a.m.

They hadn't taken her phone away. In fact, they hadn't taken anything from her, confident in their isolation. The battery was getting low but Lucy kept it on anyway; maybe someone would decide to look for her and the ping from her phone would give away her location.

Lucy regretted asking Xim to give her time, a few months to get back on her feet. It would be ages before her friend sounded the alarm.

Lucy pulled the thin blanket up to her chin, trying to go back to sleep, but a restless leg refused to let her snooze. She groped in the dark for a box of matches and lit up her candle, which cast only enough light to find her suitcase, so she could get dressed.

It was time to explore her prison.

***

The house was quiet, more than usual. Nothing growled at her from behind the closed doors and no one whispered in the corners. Even the damned bird was nowhere to be seen. Lucy found herself almost bored. She was expecting something to happen as she turned into the empty hallway but the house was deeply asleep.

Seeking adventures in this place seemed like a bad idea, especially since she still had the scratches to remind her that curiosity comes at a price, yet despite the pain, the lesson she'd learned that day had begun to fade away. To her own surprise, she soon found herself to be bored by the cold hallways, and first rays of light lured her into the garden.

Greeting the sun, she stretched her stiff body, embodying her inner cat for just a moment.

"Morning, Barb." She waved at two dark eyes staring at her from the bushes. "Alas, I am alone. Your nemesis is probably asleep."

The peacock hissed, fanning out its tail in a threatening gesture but backed away further into the vegetation when Lucy didn't rise to the challenge. She puffed out her chest, then exhaled in a laugh. Deep inside she knew that in a fight she'd lose to the strange bird, but it was fun to torment it nonetheless.

Continuing her morning stroll, Lucy stepped onto the dirt path leading into the familiar gardens. Perhaps she could chat to the statues again, since they provided some strange comfort, but her plans were rudely interrupted by a scream. Her initial reaction was to duck and return to the house immediately but the scream sounded like it belonged to a child, so all fear was choked out by the protective instinct she didn't know she had.

Lucy rushed ahead looking for the source of the scream when she saw Ryan running across the lawn with speed she never expected from the bookworm. Then she saw why. Behind him was the most majestic creature she had ever seen. The black unicorn chased down the boy with grace and splendor that didn't belong in this world. Its mane blew in the wind like black silk; a flag that promised no mercy.

Despite the deadly horn facing her, Lucy ran towards the creature, throwing her arms up in the air, hoping it would be enough to give Ryan a moment to find safety in the house. The unicorn stopped, its anger melting away instantly upon seeing Lucy.

"Woah, okay. Good pony." She slowly inched closer, placing her hand on the velvety nose. The unicorn leaned in, snorting. His entire body language shifted from murderous rage to cuddly pet. Lucy heard the doors slam in the distance. Ryan was home, safe.

Her heart pounded as the unicorn lipped her shirt. Lucy was face to face with a creature of legend and it was nothing like the fairytale books made them to be. She stroked the black fur, cautious of the horn with a coppery stain on its tip.

"Do you have a name? You are so pretty," she cooed as the unicorn nudged her affectionately. "Guess I'll ask Ryan. You know, you can't chase him like that. He is only a child."

The unicorn bowed its head in understanding but his glowing red eye was watching the house. He didn't intend to let Ryan escape again.

"I mean it." Lucy forced him to look at her. "If you promise to behave for me, I'll make sure to spend time with you?"

Lucy was unsure if the creature could understand her, and just assumed that anyone who hated men was intelligent enough. The unicorn huffed, making no promises, turning to walk away. She let him go. That was already a close call and all the adventure she needed.

***

"That better not be you, Miss Lucy." Klein looked up past his coffee mug at the young woman sneaking in. "Why on earth are you up so early?"

"No reason," she said. "Why are you awake?"

"I haven't gone to bed yet," he smiled, feeding the magpie on his shoulder. "Let me make you a drink, something to help you sleep." He got up, adding firewood to the coals inside the old iron stove.

"I might not wake up in time if I go to sleep again."

"Fair enough, a coffee then? You have a rather unpleasant job this morning. Father will be teaching you the basics of hellhound care."

Lucy sucked in a breath. Her last experience with the dogs was pleasant enough, Aris aside. They might've looked threatening, but the silly hounds were a delight most of the time. The barking and burns in her clothing after being ambushed by the pack in the hallways were a minor inconvenience. What could be so bad that Klein thought it was appropriate to issue a warning?

"Coffee would be wonderful."

Klein placed a copper kettle on the stove. "I hope you have a strong stomach."

"Strong enough, why? Is it really that bad?"

"You'll see. There's a reason he does it before breakfast."

Lucy looked suspicious. "What exactly is it?"

Klein glanced at her, a smirk curling his lips. He removed an ancient French press with a large chip in the glass down from the shelf. "Just the usual; feeding, cleaning. I think he's making a delivery as well."

"Any tips for me that might help?" Lucy asked with growing apprehension.

"Wear something you don't mind throwing away after. The smell doesn't come out." He poured her a cup of strong coffee.

"I hate to ask this, but do you have sugar and creamer? I have no clue how Ryan does it, but I can't drink it black."

Klein nodded, placing a jug of fresh cream on the table. Lucy wondered where it came from. She hadn't seen any cows around. She didn't want to know the answer.

"So, do you ever sleep?" she asked, turning the coffee into a sugary concoction that Lai would approve of, mixing the sugar cubes into a dark brew that filled the room with a pleasant aroma.

"I've got to admit, I struggle with it. I don't know why. I've tried everything to help me sleep. That's why I grow my own herbs out there." Klein glanced out of the window towards his 'garden'.

Lucy studied the bags under his eye and his tired, drawn features. He looked almost trance-like before he suddenly grabbed onto the table edge, startling himself awake. She scowled at him.

"You should go to bed. Right now. Change of the guard. I'll keep an eye on things here." She frowned, hugging her coffee. Poor man. They must have been working him to death.

"Are you going to be okay?" Klein rubbed his eye. "If you find something to do until seven, you can see father for your morning chores. I'll take care of breakfast."

"I'll find something to clean, don't worry about me. Go to bed."

After making sure he actually left, Lucy mindlessly stirred her coffee, watching the first rays of sun illuminate the horizon. She felt strange. No matter how hard she tried to keep her anger alive, the coals seemed to cool. Keeping her guard constantly was exhausting, especially since no one seemed interested in doing anything to her. Aris was a dick, yes, but the rest of the family treated her kindly enough.

Especially Klein.

Besides, she was getting to see things that no one else would in their lifetime. The glance into the mythical and magical made her feel special.

It could just be Stockholm syndrome though.

Still…

Lucy had made a promise to herself. She would do something with her life, not spend it serving others for minimum wage. She had begged for a sign, for the universe to point her in the right direction. Perhaps this was the reply she'd been waiting for.

Her call to adventure.

***

"Oh, you decided to show up at last?" Aris addressed her while facing the open window, a trickling noise filling the room as a golden stream drummed on the corrugated iron below.

"Are you really pissing out of a window?" she asked, shocked, before turning her back to give him some privacy.

"Good for the garden," he shrugged, shaking himself dry.

You're getting paid to work here, she reminded herself, taking a deep breath. Her disdain for Aris increased by the minute.

Tucking himself into musty leather pants, the man turned to face her. "I can make you empty my chamber pots if you prefer. Grab that bucket. Hope you haven't eaten yet."

Lucy hesitantly turned, picking up the bucket. "Don't worry; I haven't." She was scared she might find piss inside the tin vessel, but to her great relief, it was empty.

He whistled for his dogs to follow, leading Lucy outside and past the rubble of the east wing. Lucy glanced at the collapsed wall and what looked like cannon balls embedded in the plaster.

"So how—"

"Eleanore," Aris answered, stone faced.

He didn't elaborate further. Lucy had to assume it was a scorned lover's revenge. It was on the extreme side of post-breakup payback, but who could blame the woman? Lucy might've done the same. Gods knew the man was infuriating enough.

She followed him down the side of the house, past the now familiar garden and the back porch. She noticed the gargoyles were splayed out toward the morning sun, absorbing the warm rays. They looked like stone carvings, chipped and smoothed by centuries of rain. If she hadn't see them move that night, she would have never believed they were alive.

Near the door leading to a cellar stood a metal shed. It took a moment for Lucy to realize that the black speckle over it wasn't part of the paint. Thousands of fat black flies clung to the walls, desperately looking for any gaps.

Aris took a large curved blade from his belt as the dog's excitement grew. "Bring your bucket over, girl." He opened the door, and a wave of the sickly smell of rotting flesh came over them. Inside the cramped space hung three carcasses, suspended by metal hooks from the ceiling. They weren't human, that she could be sure of. The hooves and horns were a huge relief.

Still, more dead things. Covering her mouth, Lucy did as Aris told her.

Moving aside as she offered him the bucket, Aris let out a chuckle. "You've got to learn, girl. I'm not paying you to do it myself." He placed the blade in her hand. "See that deer that's bulging with fly larvae? Scrape the soft layer off like a kebab. The most pliant, almost dissolved flesh is for the pups. Then you can carve that boar for the older dogs."

Setting the bucket down below the deer, Lucy cut into the slimy meat.

Don't think about what you're doing. Just do it. Take it one moment at a time and just get this done, she thought to herself as the bucket slowly filled up with a mix of rot and maggots. *Almost halfway there, don't show him weakness.* She was thankful she hadn't eaten yet.

Aris pushed a little bit past her, cutting into a slightly fresher carcass and separating thick chunks of meat. "Oh, and don't forget to feed him." He tossed the brown flesh to the hissing peacock, who had just chased away the hounds for his breakfast.

Lucy chose not to question it, instead following the instruction, tasting bile rising from her stomach.

"Don't let too many maggots drop, they are full of goodness. Lift the bucket." He stood beside her, turning the carcass on a large metal hook so she could easily access the other side. "Hellhounds prefer their meat in the late stages of decomposition. They have rather delicate guts."

"Who would have thought," she muttered, trying to trick her brain into thinking this was normal, knowing full well it was not. God, she needed a shower after this.

"I know. If I were in charge of the underworld, I'd be ordering Chihuahuas or Pomeranians. Vicious little bastards who can eat rusty nails. These..." he pointed at his pack, who were chasing a butterfly, then running away from it when the wind changed direction. "They just look scary."

"Ugh, Pomeranians. My parents had one that bit my granny on the ankle one time." Lucille smirked at the memory, thankful for the conversation distracting her mind from the task at hand. "They called it Peaches."

"I'm trying to breed a three-headed one." Aris carved out breakfast for the hounds, tossing chunks of boar to the pack.

"Any luck?"

"Some. Vicious little bastard killed the other two heads and died."

"I guess no one wants a three-headed dog in the cone of shame."

"I can tell you with certainty it doesn't work." Aris unlocked the cellar doors, taking the stairs down; stairs that didn't seem to end, disappearing deep into the darkness. "Come on. Let's feed the pups, then take them to their new owner."

"Where are we going?" Lucy traced the damp wall with her fingers, measuring each step with her feet, the unevenly spaced stairs a tripping hazard.

"Underworld."

"I'm sorry?"

"Underworld," Aris repeated himself. "Seeing grandpa Hades." He chuckled, walking down with the sure stride of a man who'd taken the path many times before.

I'm sure it makes sense but I'm not going to ask.

They descended for at least ten minutes, guided only by a dim kerosene lamp. As the air turned thick with the smell of sulfur, the temperature began to rise. The heat stung their lungs, each breath requiring a monumental effort. At first, Lucy tried to count the stairs, but once she went past three hundred and the heat had turned her brain into mush, she decided to give up. What was the point anyway?

"This is more than I've worked out in the last year. Fuck…" She groaned, arms heavy from the weight of the bucket and the strain of carrying it.

Aris sighed, taking the heavy load from Lucy. "Mind your language, girl."

For a moment, she contemplated taking the bucket back. Lucy didn't want to appear weak but she had to admit, her fingers were going numb from the narrow iron handle digging into her skin.

At last, the stairs ended with a metal door. "Know how to work a lock?" Aris took a key from his pocket and offered it to her

Glaring, Lucy took the key. Of course she knew how to open a lock! With full confidence she slid the key inside but it took her almost a minute to turn the stubborn, rusted mechanism. All accompanied by the man's sighs of disapproval. At least the sounds on the other side were more encouraging.

A cacophony of delirious barks met them when the creaking door gave way. The room behind it was no bigger than her bedroom, only it was made entirely of chiseled stone with a low ceiling and soot-covered walls.

"Oh, hello, yes, it's food time," Aris cooed to a handful of pups that looked like pompoms of singed pubes. Perfectly round balls of coarse, curly hair with puffs of smoke escaping their flat faces. At the back of the pack Lucy could recognize a Welsh Corgi, although the two extra heads seemed like a new breed feature.

"Hello," she said to the dogs, lowering herself to the ground. The 'hello' was less enthusiastic mainly because Lucy struggled to breathe, feeling slightly overcooked by then. The pups were cute, but the smell of their feed along with the usual filth made for an overwhelming aroma.

Aris poured the slop into their bowls, watching the tiny hellhounds devouring it with great eagerness, rancid flesh covering their little noses.

"What's with that one?" Lucy pointed at the corgi, who had three bowls of dry kibble instead.

"Special order. Hades is planning a welcome home gift for his wife." Aris handed her a leash.

Lucy examined the delicate braided leather cord, embroidered with golden flowers that matched three collars the dog wore. It was beautiful and had a strange glow to it; the set looked otherworldly compared to plain leashes Aris was clipping onto the others.

Which neck should I attach it to?

She froze. Surely the middle was the obvious answer, right?

Then again nothing in this place was obvious. Was there a dominant head? The left one was looking up at her with a big toothy grin, panting in excitement.

"The middle one, girl."

Damn it. He had noticed.

"This way." Aris opened another door once all the dogs were fed and leashed. "How do you feel about more stairs?"

"As long as they're leading to somewhere I can breathe better, I'm fine with them," Lucy sighed, feeling beads of sweat roll down her back. Her shirt now clung to her body, wet and sticky.

"Yes, this is as hot as it gets. It's cooler when we get down to the river."

"River?"

"Yeah, part of Styx flows right under the house. Particularly convenient when we need to drop off stock."

"Isn't that the river for the dead?" She wished she had paid more attention in class.

"Yes. I do warn you, it's pretty crowded these days on the river bank."

***

Another half an hour passed, and the steps turned into a rocky path. Thankfully the air current no longer burned their lungs with each breath but instead felt surprisingly soothing. The kerosene in their lamp ran out ten minutes in but the cave was illuminated with tiny glowworms, scattered over the rocks all around them, adding to the eerie atmosphere.

Was Aris telling the truth? Could this really be the underworld?

Surely this was just an elaborate cave system. The river used for nothing more than black market transport at best. There was no such thing as...

Hell.

Aris hadn't been exaggerating; the river swarmed with thousands upon thousands of people on its banks, all yelling at the passing barge.

Young and old, children with mothers and frail elders, all waving at the vessel gliding over the black mirror-like water. The agony and desperation in their voices was heartbreaking. Countless souls, searching for a way out, unable to move on.

"They are waiting for passage to the underworld," Aris explained as Lucy stared in shock. "In the past few hundred years, the funeral rites have changed. No one is buried with fare anymore."

In a panic, Lucy looked through the endless crowd, searching for a pair of familiar faces. "Can the coins be given for passage after they were buried?"

"You are not going to find them. Millions have died since then."

Lucy felt a wave of disappointment flow through her as her heart sank into her stomach. "I don't know what you're talking about," she said, looking away, holding back tears.

Aris turned to face her, but Lucy avoided his eyes. She didn't need another judgmental stare, another mocking smirk. The silence that followed soon turned unbearable, filled only by mournful wailing of the crowd. Lucy slowly lifted her gaze up but was surprised to be met with an expression she hadn't seen before. Instead of the usual condescending frown, the slight upturn of his brows showed concern.

"I assume you are worried about your parents."

"I didn't know to leave a coin. They were Baptists."

"Haven't you read your holy book?"

"Some of it...why?"

"... and I was dead, and behold, I am alive forevermore, and I have the keys of death and of Hades." Aris quoted the passage, jingling the key chain. "It's in the Bible a dozen times."

"What?" Lucy blinked at him, numb with disbelief.

"Your lot piggybacks on ancient infrastructure without paying for the privilege. Faith sustains old gods, but these people arrive here without a fare, expecting to be ferried to their final resting place. Poor Kharon is working overtime."

"So what happens if they can't pay?"

Aris shrugged, motioning to the still water.

"I need to put a coin on their gravestones," Lucy whispered, unable to stop looking at the faces around her as they approached the water's edge.

Aris flagged down the ferryman. A tall, pale figure with a mop of messy blond hair begrudgingly stopped, but grinned as he recognized an old friend.

"Hitching a ride at last?" Kharon laughed, motioning to an empty spot on his barge.

The look Aris gave him made it abundantly clear that he heard that joke every time they met.

"Not yet. Death is yet to catch me, but I tell you he is as persistent as debt collectors. Oh, speaking of death and debt," passing on the leashes to the ferryman, Aris reached into his pocket and handed the man a few coins, motioning towards Lucy.

Every muscle in her body tensed. Was he sending her away? Paying the reaper to get rid of her? She stumbled back, only to be blocked off by a crowd of people begging to board the barge.

"Relax, girl. What are your parents' names?"

Their names? Oh! Was he paying for them to cross?

"Ezell and Sarah Howard," she stuttered out, shooting him a thankful look.

"To Elysium," Aris whispered to his old friend. "Hades owes me. Oh, and this is for the man himself. Five guards and a gift for the missus."

The ferryman nodded at Lucy, then, making sure the dogs were secure, pushed his barge away, letting the river carry it.

Lucy couldn't wipe a smile off her face, sticking close to Aris. The fear she had for her parents being trapped forever here had lifted. Aris was a piece of work, but this man clearly knew the loss of someone dear. She thought of the beautiful woman encased in glass, and her heart ached for him. She never thought she would be thankful to him, but here she was, rubbing away stray tears behind his back.

"Come on; it's never good to linger here," Aris whispered, placing one hand on her shoulder. He did look rather somber himself, and Lucy noticed he slipped the rest of his money to a woman with a handful of children clinging to her skirts.

***

Memories of her parents occupied Lucy's mind the rest of the walk. The day she got the call to tell her that her parents were dead flashed through her mind. The weeks that followed it seemed like a nightmarish blur. People she barely knew suddenly offered their condolences and help, then faded into obscurity days later, leaving her alone to grieve

The tiny silhouette of the barge in the distance made Lucy wonder if she'd be allowed one day to board it–Just for a visit.

Definitely not if she ran away.

This place was a prison and a key at the same time.

"I should've warned you," Aris muttered, climbing the steep stairs.

"No, it's alright." She followed, her muscles burning in protest, but the pain was a welcome distraction.

"I did what I could to help."

"I know; thank you."

"Maybe if you're ever on Hades's good side, you can request a visit...or just sneak in. What is that hairy bastard going to do? I trained all his guards."

"Hades is…hairy?"

"Didn't use to be..." Aris said. "Messed with a nymph, so now he is spotting very fashionable goat legs."

"Note to self, don't mess with nymphs."

"Yeah, I didn't get that memo. Still waiting for that to backfire one day." He paused for a quick rest as they reached the chamber where the dogs were kept before. He probably didn't need it but Lucy was gasping for breath.

"I'm not sure goat legs would look good on you."

"I think I'm hairy enough that a pair of hooves wouldn't be noticeable."

Lucy smirked, holding back a laugh. "Don't flatter yourself."

Silence followed as both of them sat on the top step, not exchanging a word for several minutes. This place had a strange hold on Lucy. Of all things it could be, she found it peaceful. Once the cries died down in the distance, it could almost be considered beautiful.

"Come on then. The worst part is still to come." Aris slapped his knees and got up. "Do you want me to carry you?"

Looking at the steps, Lucy contemplated the question for a moment. She had made it this far on her own, but damn she was tired. "If I say yes, do I lose any points with you?"

"You haven't earned any points yet, so you lose nothing." He shrugged.

"Then sure." She always liked to think of herself as an independent woman, but heatstroke sent her pride to the back burner.

Aris lifted her with one arm as if she was weightless, carrying her upstairs. Lucy had to admit, she was impressed with man's strength and thankful for the opportunity to rest.

The gentle sway of his stride and heat combined made her eyelids heavy. The descent and the roller-coaster of emotion by the river added to her fatigue. Lucy's head found a perfect spot on his shoulder to nap, and the rest of the journey passed in blissful ease.

***

It could have been a nice little moment if Lucy hadn't woken up to her ass being planted on the damp grass.

"Make sure you latch the shed so the dogs don't gorge themselves." The caring man she'd caught a glimpse of was left below ground, replaced by the usual cocky asshole towering above her.

Lucy muttered a faint thank you, as she closed and locked the shed. "I'm not sure about you, but I need a bath."

"Agreed. I'll see you at breakfast. Don't be late." He whistled for his dogs, which were still being terrorized by Barbara. The hounds clung to their master's legs, cautiously eyeing the strutting bird.

With the stink lingering on her skin and clothes getting to be a tad much, Lucy raced to Lai's room. Surely he wouldn't turn her away?

***

"Oh no, you don't! You don't get to use my bath smelling like that. Go and use the hose outside like the animal you are!"

"I'm already here, come on!"

"Fine! A quick shower." Lai watched her from his pillow fort with a great deal of mistrust. His face scrunched up in a disgusted grimace as he shooed Lucy on. "Quickly now, don't let the smell seep into the rugs. Ugh."

Lucy rushed towards the bathroom, tossing her clothes into the trash. She didn't want to test Lai's patience; the princess seemed delicate today. The only other bathroom she'd managed to find in the whole house was on the next floor up in the empty servant quarters; however, when she'd turned the taps on, she was rewarded with a

162

growl. Not from the pipes but something living inside them. Lucy didn't stay to find out what it was.

Strong pressure and steam felt like a blessing on her sore body.

Hot water and fragrant bath oils overpowered the sickening smell with scents of jasmine and winter rose. Lai's bathroom was filled with dozens of scrubs, shampoos and perfumes and Lucy must have used more than half of them before she felt clean. Only memories of the underworld lingered when she stepped out of the tub, enjoying the comforting hug of a soft towel.

"You are testing this friendship." Lai appeared in the doorway with a can of air freshener in his hand.

"Would it help if I told you how amazing you are?"

"It would help a little." He motioned to his closet. "Get dressed; we're late for breakfast."

Lucy rushed to the double doors opening the closet only to find another room hidden inside. No, not a room. A warehouse. Startled, she closed the doors and examined the old antique wardrobe, its back not even touching the wall, no bigger than the one in her room which was filled with old dresses and linen.

Lai didn't offer an explanation, only tapped the back of his wrist to hurry her.

It wasn't the weirdest thing she'd seen today. Lucy shrugged and stepped inside examining the racks of clothing. Thousands upon thousands of elaborate outfits from richly embroidered robes to what seemed like just strips of leather filled the space. Lucy was going to miss dinner, never mind breakfast if she kept gawking so she grabbed a few pieces from a casual rack and stepped back into the room.

Glancing at Lai, she tossed a change of clothes at him too. "For me, please?" she asked, combing her hair and twisting it into a messy bun.

"Why does everyone take issue with my midriffs?" Lai huffed, pulling his vintage 'Titanic' crop top off and changing into a plain shirt.

"Thank you." Lucy paused by the mirror to make sure she looked presentable. A plain white blouse and dark trousers seemed to do the job. "You are the best."

"I know. The sacrifices I make for you."

CHAPTER FOURTEEN

LUCY

Lucy yawned, rubbing the sleep from her eyes as she stumbled into the kitchen. Today was technically her day off, but something told her Aris wouldn't respect that luxury. The last thing she expected was for Klein to violate the sacred day.

"Miss Lucy!" he called out. "If you are not busy, can you please take the clean dog beds up to their master's room?"

"Ugh, sure..." she muttered. Of course he wouldn't know what a day off was. Klein didn't have a stop button.

"They'll be in the room next to his bedroom. Just leave the beds outside the door. He is currently out, but still... Don't linger."

A barely audible groan escaped her as she grabbed an armful of freshly laundered dog beds. She could have sworn she saw Klein wash them just a few days ago. Then again, she wouldn't put it past Aris to mandate his dog's bedding to be washed more often than his own.

"Don't give me that look. He doesn't let anyone in there. It's his private space." Klein pressed his lips into a thin line, disapproving of the little attitude she'd picked up.

"Fine, fine!" Lucy sighed; this could be an opportunity. With Aris away, she could look for a way out, snoop around yet another forbidden room. "Where did he go anyway?"

"I wouldn't know. I didn't ask," Klein shrugged, rolling a tobacco paper between his slender fingers. "He just said he was going out."

"Like through the front gate?"

Wow, Lucy. So subtle.

"Unlikely. There are other ways to leave." Klein gave her a curious, prying look. Fair enough. "Just give me a heads up if you are going to try something stupid again," he sighed as the magpie on his shoulder mimicked a cackling laugh.

"I'm just curious, that's all." She adjusted her grip on the beds, feeling a twinge of embarrassment. Why? The man was part of the family keeping her hostage. She had yet to figure out why.

Her fears of becoming a sex slave and of torture hadn't been realized; the only torture she had endured was Aris's comments and the housework. The latter she signed up for willingly. If anything, the men were tip-toeing around her. Klein spared her the hard work, Lai left treats on her bedside and Ryan stocked the empty shelf in her room with adventure novels. Aris was abrasive, but the grain on that grindstone grew finer with each passing day.

Lucy scaled the staircase, grumbling halfheartedly about being overworked. The west wing was still mostly new to her. She was familiar with Aris' office and his room, but anything further than that was off-limits.

The room Klein mentioned seemed silent. No dogs howls or barks greeted her as she approached, so she assumed the hounds must have gone with their owner or were playing outside. Lucy crept closer, noticing a thin line of light between the door and the door frame. Aris had forgotten to close it properly, let alone lock it. She doubted he would ever lock it, considering the blind obedience he expected from the household.

Feeling a tad rebellious, Lucy slowly opened the door with her foot, looked behind her to make sure the coast was clear, and peeked inside.

The interior was nothing like Aris' other rooms. No clutter, no mess, just a restful space with a small fireplace, wall-to-wall bookcase and a cozy leather chair with a round table next to it. On it was a pale blue book with a golden title.

He didn't strike her as someone who read anything but outdated newspapers. Lucy carefully advanced inside the room, hoping that the creaking floor wouldn't give her away to anyone downstairs.

Placing the dog beds down she picked up the book, drawn by the gold lettering, and examined the cover. The book had a bookmark sticking from it. A red silk ribbon was obscuring the words. Shifting it out of the way, the title was revealed.

'*Burning Passion on the High Seas*', by Madison Moon.

"Is this a fucking romance novel?!" Lucy gasped in disbelief, immediately opening the volume to the bookmarked spot.

The young pirate lord faced the dragon, his raven locks cascading over strong shoulders.

"I need a ship," he demanded of his master, blue orbs flashing with fear and determination.

"What do you have to offer in exchange?" Goldfang asked, his massive maw lowering to examine his servant. The dragon grinned, a row of white fangs glistening in the moonlight with a single gold tooth standing out.

The boy paused, his eyes meeting the dragon's. "Only myself..."

Lucy winced, "Now that's a cheesy romance book if I've ever seen one," but for some reason, she was unable to put it down.

The dragon shifted to his human form, a formidable man with ebony skin and glowing yellow orb-like eyes. His nude torso was glimmering in the candlelight.

He beckoned the young captain over.

"I'll call her Artemis..." The pirate let out a breath he didn't know he was holding and removed his shirt.

"No..." Lucy whispered, covering her mouth. It was the most scandalous memoir she had ever read. "Did he name his ship after this? What a fanboy," she chuckled as her eyes trailed from word to word, abandoning all caution. She drank it in, captivated by the story.

"Come here, Aris," Goldfang growled.

She stared at the page, quickly reading the passage again and again. She hadn't imagined it. "How—"

"What the hell are you doing here?"

A gruff voice snapped her back to reality, away from the steamy romance between a pirate captain and a dragon. Aris had returned home early, catching Lucy violating yet another rule on top of his privacy.

She wished he had caught her with any other novel on the shelves.

Lucy jumped, startled, holding the book against her chest; she could feel her heart pounding against the pages filled with secrets and intimacy. Her mouth opened, hoping to summon some sort of an excuse, but no words came out.

"Get out before I drag you out," he ordered coldly, but his face showed no anger. Some other emotion furrowed his dark brows, leading his gaze away from her.

Lucy nodded, forgetting she was holding the book as she tried to make her escape, but Aris grabbed her upper arm.

"You are on your last warning, girl," he growled and pulled the book away from her, shutting it with a loud SNAP.

"Hey, I'm not judging. I'm sure it gets lonely here sometimes," Lucy tried to keep her cool, but she hated being grabbed.

As if sensing her thoughts, the man released his grip, flexing his fingers into a fist. "These are not mine." He glared at her. "Go! I don't want to see you again today. Nosy little pest."

There it was again. That strange act. Lucy paused despite her better judgment. There was something soft behind those scars.

"Maybe one day I'll be important enough to have a romance written about me," she said from the safety of the hall. "Weird that your ex is the author though."

Aris didn't reply for a few heartbeats and Lucy was worried she had overstepped.

"The only reason this book is not flying out to crack your skull is because it's a signed copy."

She did her best to suppress a laugh, but the empty hall amplified the little snorting noise that escaped her. The moment to leave was well overdue.

Giggling to herself, she almost skipped downstairs, tempted to burst into Lai's room to share the gossip. Would he know, or was he oblivious to his father's secrets? Beaming with excitement, she dashed across the grand entrance hall, the sounds of her bare feet echoing under the high ceiling.

Knock-Knock.

She stopped, sliding a few more inches across the cold marble, looking at the direction of the sound.

Knock-Knock.

The front door! Someone was there.

"Klein?" Lucy called out, tip-toeing towards the entrance. She hadn't been told that they were expecting visitors, and who the hell would visit this place anyway?

"Klein? Someone is here!" She tried again, avoiding opening the door.

No response.

Another knock. Then, a spark of hope. Maybe, just maybe this was her chance. Could someone have found her? Tracked her phone? Maybe it was Xim, worried sick about her friend. She could be on the other side of that door with her father's private security, her knight in shining armor. Heart pounding against her ribcage with the intensity of a war drum, Lucy approached the front door.

"Who is it?"

"Here to see Aris!" A cheerful voice replied.

Her hopes dashed like waves against the rocks.

"Um, may I ask who is asking?"

"He and I have a meeting! Sorry, I'm very late."

Lucy scratched her temple. No one had told her about any arrangements. Well, maybe they had, but she couldn't remember. What would the logical solution be? Open the door, greet them, take a message and check with Aris, right? Unfortunately, logic didn't apply here most of the time. Still...what if it was someone important and she kept them waiting?

"Name please, so I can tell him who's here."

"*Saa*...Please tell him that Death is here to collect. Oh, don't worry. I'm not here for you, sweetness."

Lucy's eyes went wide as she desperately looked around for anyone who'd know what to do. She didn't doubt the visitor for a second. They called themselves Death, and she believed it. She wished she was surprised but in fact, nothing could surprise her anymore. Not after what she had seen here.

Death was literally at the door, and Lucy had no one to help her. She knew where Aris was, and his wrath didn't seem as scary as what could be behind the door.

"Wait there a moment."

***

"Aris!" Lucy chose to forget the established rules. It wasn't the time to play 'Upstairs, Downstairs'. "You have a visitor!" She burst into the room which she was chased out of mere minutes ago, finding her boss in the fireside chair with a book in his hand. She didn't have time to examine the cover, seeing only a blue man with a pale planet on it. Something about barbarians...

"By the gods, girl, you have a short memory." He gave her a fed up look, snapping the paperback closed. For a moment Lucy feared he might be having a stroke, but then realized it was rage that made his face spasm in that manner. "I am not taking visitors, so see them out."

"They say they're Death and that they aren't here for me," Lucy winced, swinging on the creaking door. "…you, on the other hand…"

He groaned in frustration, reluctantly putting the novel away. "Just open the door and tell them I'm out. Tell them I'm available for a meeting in–" He glanced at the calendar on the wall. A calendar for the year 1978. "...August."

"Are you sure you want to keep Death waiting?"

A coy smile curled his lips. The man seemed awfully smug. "I've been keeping them waiting for a while. A little longer won't kill them."

Lucy squinted at Aris, trying to figure out his age again. He didn't look old. He behaved like he belonged in the middle of the last millennium, but his physical body was still in pretty good shape. Tall, tan and muscular, he definitely didn't look ready to go.

"Don't give me that look, girl. Go and deal with it."

"Fine, fine, I'm not getting paid enough for this," Lucy grumbled. "Hey, when am I getting paid?"

"Go. We will discuss that later." He dismissed her with a simple wave of his hand.

With a roll of her eyes, Lucy left him to his book. Surely dealing with Death should net her hazard pay.

She approached the double doors, hesitating for just a moment longer before unlatching the heavy bolts.

"Hello?" She looked through the narrow gap, expecting the familiar image of a grim reaper to be on the other side.

"*Saa...* you must be Lucy. Truly a pleasure to meet you!" Death grinned from ear to ear, their large heart-shaped glasses sparkling in the sunlight.

That was not a reaper and they were positively not grim.

It took Lucy a good minute to take in the being standing in front of her. They were short, shorter than her, with white hair and almond eyes that beamed with friendliness. They had a gap in their front teeth when they smiled, and their smile never faded.

"Would you be able to come back in August by chance? He had to step out earlier and threatened my life if he sees me again today, so I can't look for him."

Death pondered for a moment. "I guess I can. Do remind him, though..." The entity spun around, colorful robes and countless trinkets turning them into a sun-catcher. "He can't avoid me forever. If Life comes for him...Well, Life isn't as generous."

"Wait, life?" Lucy asked.

"Oh, yes. *Saa*...Such a common misconception." Death looked at Lucy over their glasses. "You see, I never hurt anyone. If anything, I help people. Life...Life is nothing but suffering."

"Um, good point." Lucy forced a smile, slowly inching the door closed. "Anyway, I'm super busy. I'll see you in August."

"Oh, I'll see you in a couple of months."

She slammed the door shut with a deep frown, taking a moment to process that. What did they mean? Were they coming for her or visiting someone else in the house?

It's meant to be my day off!

"You followed the rules and didn't let them in. I'm impressed," Aris said from the top of the staircase, swilling the contents of a glass as he spoke. "There is hope for you yet."

CHAPTER FIFTEEN

LUCY

Breakfast the next morning went on in pleasant silence with no major incidents for a change, aside from the usual playful teasing the family used as a form of endearment. Even Aris didn't seem to have any complaints about Lucy.

Once everyone left the table, Klein motioned for Lucy to join him. She didn't mind. Klein felt the most genuine of them all, yet Lucy still couldn't figure him out. He was attentive and treated her like part of the family, but the moment they got within touching distance, he'd flinch away. She had only ever seen him be close with that strange bird, talking to the magpie into early hours of the morning.

She picked up a cloth from his serving trolley, her finger caressing his ever so slightly. His face flashed with color but instead of staying close, Klein scooped up a handful of dishes, putting some distance between them.

"I'll need some help with something," he said, looking away.

Lucy didn't know what to make of that reaction.

"Alright, what's the job?" She wiped down the table; Lai had left behind a bigger mess than a literal toddler.

"Pest control. Not the most pleasant of jobs."

Lucy shivered. She hated bugs, but it needed to be done. "You should have put an ad for a handyman instead of a nanny."

"It said 'help needed'. At no point did the ad mention a nanny," Klein smiled, loading the last of the servingware onto the trolley.

"I'm sorry, the 'Must be good with children and animals' threw me off," she grinned back, playfulness in her voice.

"I did my best not to mention the details. I'm sure you can understand why. What was the alternative? 'An overworked family member needs help to look after four toddlers and a zoo?'"

Lucy chuckled. "The pay better be worth it. You weren't kidding about the dog care."

"How did that go? Worst job in the house in my opinion."

"It was…" She trailed off, thinking about the river and Aris paying the way for her parents to cross. She would be forever in his debt for that. That and him saving her from those stairs. Maybe he wasn't so bad after all. Still an asshole but not an unbearable one like she had first thought. "It wasn't that bad."

Klein opened the pantry and loaded a canvas bag with fly spray bottles, poison and leftover cake from the night before.

"What's the cake for?"

"It's a bribe for one particularly stubborn pest."

"Don't talk about your brother that way," Lucy laughed.

"Oh, I wish for nothing more than to just..." Klein sprayed the air, probably imagining Lai's face.

"He isn't that bad, is he?"

"The amount of trash, dishes and laundry that boy generates is astronomical," Klein sighed, hanging the bag across his chest. "Grab the beekeeping hat. They get angry."

Lucy had a feeling that she was not going to enjoy this. With all the weird animals running around, she didn't want to see what could possibly scare Klein enough to wear safety gear. Without question she put on her hat, tucking the edge of the protective net inside her shirt's collar. The face cover felt redundant considering she was wearing only a t-shirt and a pair of shorts.

Klein motioned for her to follow, taking Lucy to the forest's edge through his little private garden full of medicinal herbs. She followed, making sure not to step on any of the plants, each one of them carefully tended to and labeled.

"I don't know how they multiply so fast," Klein muttered as they approached the tree line. Just beyond it, flashes of light were visible with a low hum of wings accompanying it.

No. Are they...?

The faeries were hanging in a swarm off an elegant weeping willow that trailed into the water of a small pool at its roots; all of them were furiously chattering at a mermaid in the pool below, with one especially loud little sprite showing off a remarkable litany of curses and swears.

"Are those... Faeries? Dear God, I'm in a bad Peter Pan remake." Lucy squinted as the realization hit her.

Klein sighed. "Wait until the pirates show up..."

"You mean your father isn't Captain Hook?"

"He did have a very intimate relationship with an overgrown lizard..."

Lucy snorted at that, remembering the dragon in his book.

The swarm of fae looked up as one at the noise; they blinked in perfect unison, every one of them flicking a single antennae. They didn't look anything like what Lucy used to see on the covers of children's books. There was nothing human about them. Not even humanoid. They had multiple insect-like arms and long delicate legs, using them like a grasshopper would to jump from branch to branch.

Their faces unnerved her the most, pointed and alien with large reflective eyes that tracked every movement she made with predator-like precision.

"Woah, hey." Klein lifted his hands in the air, obviously not expecting so many of them. "Hey, Fish, I got cake. Call off your friends, will you?"

Fish— the faerie at the very top of the willow switch, who had been yelling at the mermaid— flicked her wings and separated from the swarm, flitting to Klein. "Cake?"

"Lucy, would you so kindly offer our friend here the carrot cake in my bag?"

Rummaging in the satchel among a dozen fly spray cans, Lucy found a box with the promised dessert and opened a clear lid to display the offering. Although slightly squished and smeared with frosting, it produced the desired result—the little creature beamed with delight upon seeing it.

Fish dove into the cake. With a noise like a chainsaw she devoured it from the inside out, the hollowed cake collapsing around her. She belched loudly, stomach distended, licking her antennae covered in sweet cream cheese.

"Now, you've had your cake." Klein slowly reached into his bag with trembling hands and pulled out the wrapped package. "Why don't you deliver this to your queen?"

The fae glanced over to the package, sniffing at it with a squint. "Is poison."

"Yes," Klein nodded. He didn't even try to lie.

The faerie considered that carefully; for all that she was cute, she was bloodthirsty and cunning. "I take. For chocolate cake."

"It's a deal." Klein let go of the package. "Southern colonies too. They all need a cull."

Lucy watched the exchange, intrigued, trying to hold back all of her questions. Her only point of reference when it came to queens and colonies were a few videos she'd watched about saving the bees. They seemed protective of their queens, but this one was ready to kill an entire colony for dessert.

The little faerie looked over to the girl, calculating. "Cake from her too."

"She is not great at baking."

Lucy gasped, giving Klein a look. How dare he? She was perfectly adequate. Well, she thought so. Granted, a couple of days ago she burned the cupcakes. She might have also put the frosting on before chilling them but hey, they were still pretty damn good.

"Store-bought is fine," Fish insisted, business-like.

"Chocolate as well?" Lucy asked as she wondered if Klein's master plan was to kill the faeries off with diabetes.

Fish lit up greedily; clearly, this girl hadn't been taught how to handle her. "Rainbow cake. Five layers."

Lucy gave the faerie a noncommittal shrug. There was no way she could get the cake without Klein's help; she couldn't just leave for a supermarket run, and five layers was a bit of a stretch for her baking abilities.

"No. Pick one layer color and frosting." Klein caught onto Lucy's distress, offering a counter deal. "If you cooperate, Lucy will add sprinkles."

Fish scowled. "Two layers. And swim lesson."

"Swim lesson?" Lucy asked.

Fish nodded while her swarm laughed at her; she turned to hiss at them before facing Lucy. "Fish is want to swim, like mermaid. Like water. But sink."

Lucy looked at Fish, then at Klein. "You said not to make any deals."

"Fae can't tell a lie, but they can add tricky clauses to their deals so discuss it carefully," he warned.

That went against everything Lucy had learned so far. Why was he bending the rules all of a sudden? He could've at least prepared her for it.

Reaching deep into her memory, she tried to remember anything she knew about bartering. Start high and go low! Or was it the other way around?

"One layer, and I'll get you a bowl of water that you can splash in?" Lucy countered, making a face. Pretend like you don't care about the deal. That is what they did on TV. That and the 'walk away' bluff. "Take it, or we will find someone else."

The faerie looked offended, scowling at Lucy. "Is rude. Will not make deal. Will warn queen."

Klein gave Lucy a *'what the hell'* look.

"I'm not that great of a swimmer," she said defensively, shrinking a little under his gaze.

The swarm's buzzing grew louder as other fae picked up on Fish's irritation. Klein backed away, a can of fly spray in each hand, ready to retaliate if needed.

"How about a three-layer cake, and I get you something that will help you float?" Lucy quickly backpedaled on her previous offer. Being savaged by fairies wasn't on her bucket list.

The faerie glanced back at the swarm, chittering at them in a voice that sounded like bugs chirping, settling them down. "Is good offer. Will accept and poison queen for you." She paused. "Is good time to die. Has been queen for whole week. Greedy."

Lucy let out a sigh of relief. She really didn't feel like running.

Fish flicked her velvet wings, ready to take the poison to her short-lived queen. "Is good deal. Come back for more deals, girl. We always hungry."

"Damn it, Lucy." Klein sighed in relief as the swarm vanished. "We could've been ripped to shreds. You don't get to make any more deals around here. Not because of the inherent dangers. You are just rubbish at it."

"It's why I never tried to become a lawyer and in my defense, you told me not to make deals, then brought me here to make a deal."

"Oh, so it's my fault now. Okay. I hope you can bake a cake using a wood oven," Klein huffed, but a hint of smile danced on his lips.

"I can't even bake a cake using a regular oven," Lucy groaned. "Just give me a warning next time, please?"

"Didn't even know we had mermaids here...this is the effluent pond." He watched the trout shaped creature dive down into murky water. She was barely two feet in length with doll-like features and dull, moss green scales.

"The what pond?"

"I buried a pipe to drain all the filth from the house to it." Klein winced as one of the mermaids swam to the surface, chewing on something covered in slime. He shrugged, walking back to the house, Lucy following with a disgusted grimace on her face.

***

"You two look defeated." Ryan eyed them from the kitchen table. He had an open book and a bowl of cereal in front of him. Considering breakfast was a mere hour ago, he must have arrived purely for entertainment.

"Well jokes on you. We have secured a deal with the fae and it's in our favor." Lucy poked her tongue out at him.

The boy's arrogant face lit up with a cocky grin. "A deal with the fae in your favor?" he asked, examining a spoonful of sugar coated flakes. "My goodness, Klein. She is the one. The chosen one. I don't think anyone in the history of the realm ever managed it. Daddy must be happy with your find."

Lucy clenched her fists, looking for something to throw, but Klein's firm hand on her shoulder quickly grounded the rising indignation.

"At least Lucy is helping." Klein grabbed a cloth to clean up the mess his brother had made; spilled milk, stray pieces of cereal, and every cupboard door left hanging open.

Lucy watched the exchange, still confused by the dynamic in the family. Neither of them seemed particularly fond of each other. The family meals were the only time they spent together, yet even those were filled with jabs and insults.

"I don't know why Lai thinks the dinner party will be fun. You lot can't stop tormenting each other…" she muttered, taking the cloth from Klein. "It's his mess, make him do it."

Both brothers froze, the same confused look directed at Lucy. Oh no. She forgot. She was supposed to tell Klein.

"Dinner party?" He swiped the cloth back, his irritation no longer directed at Ryan but aimed at Lucy instead.

She swallowed, shrugging it off. "You know. Lai invited some people for dinner." She paused, noticing his body tense up. "The day after tomorrow."

The next few minutes were spent in grim silence, but Klein managed to get his feelings across clearly. The copper pots were slammed on the stone counter, followed by a heavy leather tome of recipes. Lucy didn't need the translation.

Are you telling me now?

SLAM!

With just a day's notice?

CLANK!

I will be baking all night!

HUFF!

"Weren't you defending her a moment ago?" Ryan chuckled, turning the page in his book. "If it was any of us you would've issued a punishment already."

Klein paused his sulking, turning back to look at Lucy as if Ryan had given him an idea. "I'm missing a number of dishes. I'll need them to make preparations," he said in a strangely calm tone. "Would you mind finding them for me tomorrow?"

The brother's exchanged a look, sharing the same knowing smile. Klein kept his composure but Ryan covered his mouth to suppress a giggle. Lucy didn't like it one bit. On one hand, seeing them get along was a pleasant change, but she knew that it meant only one thing. It wasn't a simple request.

"Um, sure." She forced a smile. "Where can I find them?"

Two voices answered in unison.

"The dragon's lair."

CHAPTER SIXTEEN

LUCY

Lucy slinked up the stairs with dread sitting heavily on chest. One job. Klein had given her one job for the entire day. He had set her up to fail, she was sure of it. Why would anyone need a whole day to collect a few plates unless it was an impossible task?

The dragon's lair. Right. Those two thought they were so funny. There were no real dragons in the sanctuary, Aris had told her as much. The next candidate to the title was obvious.

She stopped briefly in her room to splash cold water on her face, bracing herself as she looked up. The old silver-backed mirror showed the reflection of someone she knew well. The same face had stared back at her every morning before work.

Reluctant despair was the name of the expression–the product of an early fast food shift, dealing with hungry and naturally angry customers, but just like any other day a fake smile appeared, together with forced determination. She was ready to brave the beast's lair.

"I need your dishes!" Lucy barged into Lai's room like a dirty cop; no knocking, no warning. The element of surprise was on her side, or so she thought. Before even stepping a foot inside a cushion bounced off the wall, inches from her face.

"No!"

The squishy projectile was repurposed as a shield, allowing Lucy to advance inside. "Give them to me!"

"I don't have any!" Lai peeked from his pillow fort. "Did you just wake up and choose violence? Why are you picking on me? I thought we were friends!"

"It's my job of the day."

"Sucks to be you. You're now trespassed from my room."

Lucy gasped in frustration. He wasn't going to make it easy.

"Why? Are you starting a collection?"

"No. I just don't like when others rummage through my things. I don't want you throwing anything away."

"I don't care about your stuff. I just want the dishes."

"Come and get them." His icy blue eyes flashed silver from among the cushions. "I dare you."

"...or you could just give them to me?" She squinted back, getting ready for a standoff.

"I'm busy." Lai piled the pillows on top of himself. "Also lazy. If I find any, I'll leave them outside my door."

"It's gross. Do you want your precious stuff to grow moldy?"

"It's my depression garden. I love watching things grow. Mold, laundry piles, plate stacks..."

"Yeah, I'm not letting that happen. Where are they?"

Silence. Lai had decided he was done with this conversation, but Lucy could see the glow of his laptop from the cracks in his fort. Then, just to add an extra insult, the loud, startling noise of the Netflix startup screen loading up.

"Fine! I'll find them myself!"

Why is he being so precious about it?

Lucy huffed, entering the dimly lit room, looking around for anything she could reclaim. Before she could find a single cup, the laptop lid slammed shut, and the next moment Lucy was tackled to the floor, her arms restrained behind her back.

"Ahh, let me go!"

She never expected Lai to move so quickly; the usually big and slow-moving target showed surprising agility.

"Or what?"

"Let me go, or I'll…" Lucy tried to think of something but gave up, resting her chin on the ground. "I'll make you stay like this all day with me."

"Wow, you are…hopeless," Lai sighed. "Hardly a punishment if you ask me. But I guess with those limp arms of yours you never could have broken out of my grip; if you are ever captured you are screwed."

"You're starting to sound like Xim."

"Xim sounds like a reasonable person," Lai chuckled, letting her go. "Now shoo, little miss. I truly am busy."

"Not until I have the dishes." Standing back up, Lucy got into a fighting position that Xim had taught her. Not that she knew what to do if Lai accepted the glove she had thrown at him.

"Are you…Are you challenging me, sweetcheeks?"

Swallowing this strange fear, Lucy motioned for Lai to come at her with one hand.

He wouldn't really attack me, would he?

He grinned, shrugging off his silk robe, standing in front of Lucy in just loose white pants. He didn't have that chiseled physique one would expect from someone of his strength. One could even call him soft, but Lucy knew that under all that boyish tenderness was something dangerous.

Athena M. Bliss

A blush crept up her cheeks as Lucy examined his half naked form. Tanned olive skin entirely unblemished aside from the unfinished tattoo of a rose vine creeping over one side of his body and a deep burn peeking over the band of his pants. She recognized the design branded into his flesh. The tree from the family crest.

Are all of them branded?

She watched his body language for any signs that he was going to come at her. Lai did, but slowly, one step at a time. He was now within her punching distance, a smug smirk on his lips. Lucy waited for him to make the first move, but he only leaned in closer, forcing her to back away.

"What's the matter? I thought you wanted to fight?"

"Want to fight? No, but unless you are giving up the dishes I don't think I have a choice."

"Guess you're leaving empty-handed then."

"I refuse." She clenched her fists in frustration. "You wanted a nanny; let me do my job."

Clicking his tongue, Lai leaned back, considering her argument. "You can't fight, can you? I'll make a deal with you. Let me teach you a few things, and you may take the dishes if you can find them."

Lucy blinked in surprise. The deal seemed far too good to be true, but Lai didn't seem to be as dangerous to negotiate with as the faeries had been. Was it wrong of her to think he was openly simple? Yet Klein's warning echoed in her mind; make no deals. A rule she had broken already.

"What do you want in return?"

"I'll think of something later."

Not a harmless demand, something wasn't right. Her logical side argued against it, but despite her best judgment, Lucy agreed. "...Alright."

Lai wasted no time before jumping into the lesson, far too eager for Lucy's liking. Perhaps it'd been a while since he got to show or use his skills. What did he do around here anyway? Lucy was yet to see him out of bed for any other reason than food. She held her hand in front of her face, just like Xim taught her, defensive and apprehensive.

"Alright. First lesson. I call it WWYDT. Try and punch me. Right in the face." He hovered close enough for Lucy to land a hit, and she did. Expecting him to duck out of the way, she put all her strength into a solid punch that connected with a loud crunch, followed by a splatter of blood.

"Ouch, fuck!" Lai grabbed his bleeding nose, hunching over on the floor.

Lucy gasped, horrified. "You were supposed to block it!" She dropped her guard, leaning over him in panic.

"Why would you do that?" He sniffed then scooped up Lucy's feet while she was distracted and, in the blink of an eye, restrained her again.

Of course he did. Lucy groaned from her spot on the ground, face pressed against a rug that smelled faintly of lavender.

"Don't ever attack anyone expecting an attack. If your opponent is in a fighting stance, who knows how good they are." Lai squeezed his hand around Lucy's wrist. "You have to throw them off balance. Do what you need to do. Act crazy, shit yourself if you must." He let her go. "If you can get your opponent to underestimate you, then you have an advantage."

Lucy rubbed her wrist, feeling foolish to have fallen for his trick and slightly unnerved by his demeanor. He got hurt, not a light graze; his nose pissed blood, but he sat there with a masochistic grin on his face, as if the pain did not affect him.

"Alright, what's next?" Lucy asked. Did she want to know?

"If you ask me, the physical altercation is the worst-case scenario. So if you do have beef with someone, you want to kill them before it gets to that." He sniffed, wiping his face with a wet towel.

Kill them?

Lucy swallowed, regretting agreeing to the deal. The last time she had the self-defense talk, it had been a lot less extreme. She couldn't kill anyone if she tried.

"Alright, kill them before I have to fight them," she nodded as she inched away from the man, but he had other ideas, pulling Lucy towards an oriental cabinet inlaid with an intricate dragon design.

He opened one of the doors and presented her with rows of tiny jars, each with a drawing rather than a label.

"Are those... poisons?"

He nodded proudly.

"Please don't slip any of that into my food."

"Why? Do I have a reason to?"

"Not yet…" She forced a smile, standing next to him as Lai pulled out a handful of jars, showing them off with childish enthusiasm.

"White Snakeroot. One of my favorites. Oh, I killed so many with that stuff. The best part about this poison is you can pass it on secondhand, in a sense. Feed this to a cow, then let someone drink its milk, and they are dead. I'm immune to it after years of microdosing, so all I have to do is take enough to make the dose lethal, then have some naughty, unprotected fun. Stops the victim's heart, so the coroner just stamps the paper with 'natural causes'."

What was Lucy supposed to say to something like that? She wanted to know more, but the reasonable part of her brain reminded her to keep her guard up. No one admitted to murder unless they were sure that the information wouldn't leave the room. Right?

"Why are you telling me this? Are you going to use one of those on me?"

"If I was, I'd use this. Hemlock." Lai took out another bottle. "It paralyzes quickly and kills slowly. Want someone to witness everything but do nothing? This baby is perfect. It's a root, so add it to anything savory and no one will be able to tell. Tea is good too; just add a slice of lemon to increase the potency."

"You're a little sadistic, aren't you?"

"Not really. I prefer a peaceful death. Less mess, less noise. Easier to get away."

"Remind me not to get on your bad side."

"Here." Lai reached into the cabinet, taking out a small jewelry box and presenting Lucy with two pearl earrings. "Put them on. Never know when you'll need them."

"What are they?" she asked, taking out her simple hoops and replacing them with the ones he handed her. Any other day she'd politely refuse this strange gift but not now, not while sitting next to a mad man with a cabinet of deadly poisons.

"Left is hemlock, right is a cyanide pearl. Crush it between your fingers if you need to off someone else or between your teeth if you need an easy way out. Mine are in piercings elsewhere," he winked.

Okay, I have to admit, I feel like a badass wearing them.

"Thank you."

"Can't leave you completely defenseless," Lai smiled, offering Lucy a hand. "I'd like to teach you a few more things later. Unfortunately, all those skills like knife throwing and swordsmanship take years of practice despite what movies would have you believe."

"If it helps, I know how to shoot a gun well. My parents taught me when I was growing up. I'm only completely useless when I don't have a weapon."

"Fair enough. I'm not a fan of guns. So loud and unnecessary. I'm only keeping this one as a memento of an entertaining night." He dug in the cabinet, drawing out a tiny pistol that was smothered in his grasp, holding it fondly as he let Lucy have a look.

"Care to share the story?" Lucy used this distraction to begin her hunt for dishes; she had almost forgotten the reason for being there. Thankfully Lai could listen to himself talk for days on end. She had a few minutes at least to dedicate to her mission.

"Oh, it was a lovely summer. She was the captain of a city watch but sadly under an oath of celibacy. No one said she couldn't use me like a gun holster, though."

Why did I ask? Why am I imagining it?

Lucy clenched the first plate, begging for that mental image to leave. Focusing on the hunt rather than the graphic story, she found one more under the topmost cushions and the next three buried amongst dirty laundry.

"How many of these do you have?"

Lai ignored her with a partisan silence.

"Lai, how many?"

"I don't know. It's not my job to find out." He pushed a stack under the dresser with his foot.

"Are you hiding them?"

"Why are you insisting on disturbing my hoard? I have it exactly how I like it." Lai opened his laptop, giving Lucy distrustful looks every time she touched anything other than dishes. "Leave that glass. I like it there."

"You agreed to let me do my job," Lucy huffed.

"You got that in writing?"

"You mean drawing?" She picked up the forbidden glass, ready to start another fight.

"You are so rude to me."

Three more bowls joined the rapidly growing pile. "Think this would be okay enough for Klein?"

"Ah, is that the traitor who is sending his spies into my lair!?"

"Yes, stop being so dramatic!"

"Fine! Come into my home and disrespect me!" Lai produced another dozen plates and a small mountain of cups and cutlery seemingly out of nowhere.

"Thank you! Was that so hard?" Lucy frowned, balancing the stack.

She reached for the door handle, careful not to drop anything when the door was kicked open from the other side.

By Ryan.

The boy burst into Lai's room, his shirt torn and bloody and a ridiculous grin plastered over his face.

Lai scrambled to get up, fighting the mountain of cushion that trapped him in while Lucy carefully stepped over all the broken plates, knocked out from her grip by the door.

"He gored me! He gored me!" Ryan laughed pointing at the blood and bits of flesh on his stomach.

Holy shit. Holy shit. He is going to die!

"Why the hell are you so happy?" Lucy looked around for anything she could use as a bandage, but the eclectic clutter offered her anything but.

"Congrats," Lai laughed, sitting the boy down. "Guess it's finally working."

What was going on? Why weren't any of them panicking? The boy was bleeding all over the rug, yet they were exchanging congratulations like it was some big accomplishment. Lucy looked at Lai then at Ryan. Her face expecting an immediate explanation.

"The unicorn!" Ryan beamed, holding his hand against the gushing wound. "It only kills men!"

"The boy is just going through some gender euphoria." Lai pushed his brother down and removed the torn shirt, revealing a tightly bound chest underneath. "Come on. Time to practice that magic of yours. Consider it training. Use me to heal him."

Ryan frowned but didn't protest. The blood loss was taking its toll and his happiness was giving way to embarrassment.

"I don't know what Lai is talking about but I have about twelve minutes left," he sighed, relaxing in Lucy's arms.

Lucy stayed still like she would with a skittish animal, barely daring to breathe; she had never expected Ryan to be vulnerable around her. He had always seemed so cold.

The sight of so much blood made her stomach clench, almost bringing up the toast she'd had for breakfast but Lucy managed to keep it down. Her powers were something she could barely control. Flowers weren't people. Nowhere close, yet the clock was ticking. It was a ludicrous idea but it helped that Lai sounded so sure of himself…

and of her.

Taking Lai's hand Lucy placed her other one on the wound, blood pulsing under her fingers. She reached for the strings of light, but it was nothing like she had even felt before. There weren't just a few strings, there were thousands, each carrying memories and energies unfamiliar to her. Lucy grabbed one pulling it through herself and into the dying boy.

The life force didn't come alone.

The memory that flooded her mind was not her own. She was sitting on the bed, a cigarette in her hand and a cool breeze caressing her nude body. Lucy looked down, her wrists were red and sore, deep rope burns still visible. Next to her was something much worse. A naked man with his dead face looking at her with an expression of frozen horror. His mouth was gaping with a swollen blue tongue and cracked lips, his glazed over eyes staring in silent accusation.

Lucy screamed, pushing away as the memory melted into the familiar room. Lai was there instead of a strange man and he looked rather concerned.

"You didn't do it. You need to focus. Ryan is going to die if you don't," he said, offering his hand again.

"I can't. Your memories. I can see your memories when I pull. I saw a corpse." Her voice trembled.

"…and you will see another if you don't suck it up." Lai forced his hand into hers again, for a heartbeat his features flared with what seemed like muted panic. "They are my memories. You might not like what you see but they are nothing more than flashes of information. You need to use me to heal him."

His eyes sought hers but Lucy's gaze didn't stray away from the wound, only now realizing how cold Ryan's skin was. She had no more time to lose so taking a deep breath she grabbed a handful of threads and pulled, connecting them to the fading threads of the younger boy.

The memories that played at the back of her mind were something Lucy prayed she'd soon forget. Tangled limbs, strange devices and murdered lovers. However, as she focused on the light instead, the images faded and she could feel nothing but warmth followed by strained gasps.

Opening her eyes she found only a red scar where the nasty wound was mere minutes ago. Ryan was breathing steadily, his eyes bright and staring at Lucy with uncharacteristic wonder.

Lai was on the other side of the room, chugging soda to flush down his medication. Lucy had almost forgotten he reacted to magic, but it was a small sacrifice to save his brother's life.

"He actually attacked me," Ryan whispered looking up at the decorated ceiling before sitting back up. "He used to just chase me, warnings, nothing else, but today he actually attacked."

Lucy finally had enough. "Would you stop that?" She picked up Ryan by both shoulders, shaking some sense into him. "You could've died!"

She expected a snarky remark or a cold stare in return, but it was neither. Ryan hugged her, in a fleeting and tight embrace then ran out of the room leaving Lucy too stunned to speak.

"Fun never ends, huh?" Lai leaned on the door frame, scratching his swollen hand. The hives looked angry but were slowly fading away.

She needed a moment to collect her thoughts and the broken porcelain. A multitude of questions flashed in her mind. "I thought your family... the pit?"

"You think we should? I've been tempted a few times. He is insufferable."

"Be nice..." She lowered herself to the bed. "What about your father? Does he know?"

"Of course. He doesn't question it. Like I said, he is very old fashioned. Transphobia is relatively new. His crew had a few sailors like that. He only had a problem when a woman who identified as a woman was on board," Lai shrugged. "I can't tell if he is backwards or progressive some days."

"Neither can I. I'm still struggling to figure out if he is an asshole or just pretending to be one," Lucy sighed.

"Me too, Luce. Me too."

CHAPTER SEVENTEEN

AL

"I think it's your bedtime, my man," Al sighed, peeling another drunk regular off the pole in the middle of the stage. "The girls don't want to play with you anymore. Let's get you a taxi." He let the club patron lean on him for support, leading him outside and waving over an empty cab. Once he was safely on the way home the bouncer returned to the club, making sure the winding down went on without any trouble.

"Hey Candy, need a ride home tonight?" Al leaned on the bar as the girl behind it poured him a nightcap.

"I'm good. I finally got my car back today." She adjusted her glimmering gold bikini top and put her thick golden curls into a messy ponytail. "Are you off this weekend? Pretty sure you've promised to come over and help with that flat-pack." She pursed her lips in an adorable pout. Al could smell her cherry scented lip gloss from across the bar.

"I know, I'm sorry. How about Monday? I'll swing by after my shift, and we'll erect that shelf that you are perfectly capable of putting together on your own," he smiled, tossing back the shot.

Candy tugged on Al's stray strand of raven hair, hanging loose from his tight bun. "What are you implying?"

"Oh, nothing. No ulterior motives there. Just like that game level you wanted me to beat for you. The game you scored a platinum trophy on," he winked.

Just say yes and go, you idiot. You are not thinking about him still, are you?

"I'll see you on Monday then. Now shoo. Out of my club. Make sure all the girls get to their cars safely." She swatted him with a tea towel.

Al did just that, watching all the dancers leave one by one. "Goodnight, Ash. Night night Chloe. See you, Monday, Marly." He waited until all of them had departed with no creeps around, then waited for Candy to lock up. Once the lights were off and the neon sign stopped buzzing, it was finally time for Al to head home.

He lingered in the empty car park, admiring the love of his life.

A red 1969 Mustang he had restored himself with more love and dedication than he'd ever given to a lover. There was something incredibly soothing about nursing a cigarette and watching his lady in total silence. It was a welcome change from the noise, smells, and flashing lights of the club. He glanced at his watch. Only four a.m; plenty of time to get some sleep before his main job at eight that morning. One quick chore before then, a stop by the 24-hour pharmacy.

***

"That will be $640.95." A scrawny pharmacist in large round glasses placed a couple of pill bottles into a paper bag. "Need anything else?"

A bullet.

"No. I think that's enough damage for one day." Al slid two cards across the counter. "$400 on the Visa and rest on Debit, please." He tapped anxiously on the pin pad, praying for the "accepted" message. The last few months had been rough, with extra bills eating into his already stretched budget. Thankfully the transaction went through and he could breathe a sigh of relief.

Finally, at half-past four, he made it home. The apartment was flooded with light, the TV playing late-night infomercials in the living room.

"Why is everything lit up like a Christmas tree?" He sighed, turning off all the lights. "Our power bill will be huge. On a related note, why are you still awake?" He leaned over the couch, kissing his sister on top of her head.

"Couldn't sleep," she smiled at him. Lilly was sixteen, with the same warm brown skin as her brother, but with white, wavy hair falling over narrow shoulders. "Why are you so late tonight?"

"Had to stop by and get your meds. Take some now, okay?" He tossed the paper bag worth a small fortune next to her; Lilly did not look impressed. "Don't give me that look. It's good at controlling your seizures."

"They are not seizures," Lilly snapped. "Why don't you ever listen? Why doesn't anyone listen?" She snatched the bag and hurled it and its contents across the room.

Different day, same fight. He was tired of struggling with her, but he had to push on. No one else would take her in. His parents wanted to take the easy route and lock up their daughter in a mental facility. She couldn't be in any trouble if she was sedated most of the time, simple enough. His parents had done it before with Al as well. The moment he'd begun acting out as a teenager, they'd shipped him off to a military school. No one ever asked him what was wrong. He just had to be fixed.

The school did its job. He was taught how to hide and bottle anything he felt, focusing all of the pent up emotion into physical activity. Only his soft spot for his sister remained, so the moment her fate was sealed, doomed to die locked up and drugged, he took her and made his escape.

That decision cost him almost everything. Jumping the border wasn't that hard–he used his savings for fake passports and visas, but real hardship kicked in on their arrival in a new country. He had nothing, and he knew no one. Jobs were scarce, but that didn't faze him; little by little, their life improved. Never to reach the luxury of the parental estate, but enough to be comfortable.

Al took a deep breath; getting angry now would achieve nothing. "I know. We can't have this fight every time." He picked up her pills and took a couple out of the bottle, bringing it to her with a glass of water. "Do it for me. Tomorrow we are going to Lai's for dinner. You don't want to have an episode there, do you?"

Lilly scowled, taking the medication and swallowing it without further complaining. "Why are we even going there? They hate me, Aris dislikes you, and it never ends well."

"Don't be like that. It's just dinner and a weekend away from this stuffy apartment. Plus, I've heard they hired a new girl to help around. You might have a friend there at last." Al knelt on the floor in front of his sister, trying to sound excited for her. It did seem to work. Lilly perked up at the promise of a new friend.

"Do I have to wear formal clothes?"

Al nodded, fully expecting the eye roll, and he wasn't disappointed. Lilly groaned, pressing her face into a cushion, muttering dark, sullen complaints.

"What about the black dress you wore last time? It looked nice on you." He lifted his sister's chin and placed another kiss on her forehead. "Come on, let's get you to bed. I have a short shift tomorrow, I'll pick you up after. Can you get my suit ready?"

She nodded, wrapping her arms around Al's neck, allowing him to carry her to bed. "You know Lai just wants you there for his amusement."

"He's my best friend, and we've been through a lot." Al sat Lilly on her bed, taking a hairbrush from her bedside table. "I don't mind keeping him company from time to time. They do a lot for us." He ran the brush through her badly tangled hair, gently smoothing it out from the tips.

"Just don't leave me alone for too long, okay?" She turned to face her brother.

"Never," Al promised.

CHAPTER EIGHTEEN

LAI

"Oh, sugarplum, no. You can't wear that." Lai grabbed Lucy in the hallway outside her room. "You can't wear denim to a dinner party. We'd like to pretend that we're cultured tonight."

Lucy looked down at her simple denim skirt with a frown. "No one told me I had to dress up in anything fancy. What should I wear, then?"

"A dress?" Lai smoothed out his evening suit. It was the first time Lucy had seen him wear actual clothing. He was happy with the feeling of silk over his nude body most days, but it was fun to dress up once in a while. "Something dark. Black preferred. Long."

"I don't think I have one of those. Didn't exactly plan on going to a ball."

"A ball? Oh no. This is low key. I'll take you to a proper ball one day, but this is just dinner with family and friends." Lai looked her up and down. "You know, I think I might have something for you." He reached for her shirt sleeve, pulling Lucy unceremoniously along to one of the rooms between his and hers. A tiny brass key sat in the lock.

"What's this room for?" Lucy asked.

"Just storage." Lai opened the door to a large, cluttered room filled to the brim with wooden boxes and trunks. The mess was daunting. Lai knew exactly what he wanted though, pulling down a dusty wooden crate, careful not to ruin his attire. "Ah, there it is."

He pried off the lid, tossing it onto the nearest pile. The soothing scent of lily of the valley perfumed the folded clothing inside the crate. Lai had to pause to take a breath of the familiar aroma that brought back bittersweet memories. A shadow of sadness passed over his face, but he didn't let it linger. Not while Lucy was there to see.

"This one," he decided, lifting a flowing navy dress embroidered with a design of intricate scales. Holding it against himself, Lai sought Lucy's approval with a knowing grin, sure that she would be impressed.

"It's stunning," she breathed, her fingers shaking as she caressed the fine fabric, thousands of tiny white pearls gathered around the neckline and cascading down to the hem. "Your father won't mind me borrowing it?"

"He can't fit them," Lai grinned. "Let's see if I can squeeze you in." He pinched her side, teasing her.

"Stop it. It's not my fault the food tastes great."

"I'm only joking. I can't even breathe in this suit. My legs are getting zero circulation," he laughed, unlacing the back of the dress for her. "Come on. Clothes off."

Lucy slipped out of her skirt and unbuttoned her blouse. "You sure it's not too much?" She glanced over as Lai pulled the dress over her head, smoothing out the layers.

No such thing.

"Look at me. I look like a penguin. No, it's not too much. I bet even father will go as far as washing. Suck in!" Lai ordered, then pulled on the strings, tying them off. "Huh, look at that. Perfect fit."

He adjusted the flowing half cape sleeves attached to a silver braid that sat across her shoulders. Maybe it was a little too much, but what was a party without a staircase dress reveal, and if Lai couldn't be the one dropping jaws then he might as well be the one pulling the strings.

Lucy took a few steps, checking how much movement the dress allowed. "Might be a bit tricky serving in this." She tried raising her arm.

"Oh no, you are not serving tonight. Unfortunately, my godfather declined the invitation due to a scheduling conflict, but he did send wine and his personal servants. So tonight, you are a guest." Lai walked over to her, scooping up a handful of her curls, the long ago bleached part now below her shoulders. "Let's do something about this as well, shall we? Follow me."

He paused as the dog's barking downstairs announced the first guest's arrival. He recognized the roar of the engine outside, the distinct purr of the car that competed with him for Al's affections.

"I can just put it up, it's not a big deal," Lucy protested with a huff. "I don't want to be late. Your father already hates me."

"He doesn't hate you. Hate is a strong emotion, and he wouldn't waste that much energy on you. He thinks you're irritating, that's all, and he thinks that of all of us–so, welcome to the family, I guess," Lai laughed, pulling Lucy along to his room and sitting her down by the mirror.

"Thanks. You know how to make a girl feel better," Lucy muttered, staring at her reflection, studying her plump, flushed cheeks and chapped lips. "I already feel ridiculous."

"You are ridiculous. Who the hell wears a dress like that then has anything to complain about?" He sighed, picking up a comb. "This is a very important night for me. So just sit still and let me do this."

"Important for you?" Lucy asked, wincing as he dragged the comb through her hair. "Why?"

Lai didn't answer, humming a song as he carefully brushed out strands of unruly hair and braided them into an elegant design that draped over her shoulder. Satisfied with his handiwork, he tied off the braid with a deep blue silk ribbon that matched her dress.

"Almost done. Stop fidgeting." A hand-carved wooden jewelry box produced a handful of hair pins decorated with shimmering pearls, not perfectly round but raw and mostly unpolished. Lai placed them carefully one by one, connecting the pins with a string of smaller pearls. The mermaid's crown was complimented with a light layer of makeup, just enough to shimmer in the candlelight. "Ah, look at you. You wash up nice."

"I do, don't I?" Lucy smiled, dodging his playful insult.

"Well, may I be the one to accompany you downstairs, my lady?" Lai offered his arm to her with his usual dramatic flair.

She rolled her eyes at him and slid her arm over his, indulging the harmless request. "Okay, we've got to go. Just a few things before we go down there. Firstly, if anyone asks whose idea this dinner was, I'm gonna use you as my scapegoat. I'll make it up to you later." Together they walked to the grand staircase, while Lai proudly admired her makeover.

"Is there anything else?"

"Yes. Secondly, don't bring up your powers in front of my father," Lai cautioned, voice low.

"He already knows I have them. Why not?"

The man shook his head; it wasn't Aris knowing that worried him.

"Don't give him a reason to hate you more."

"You said he doesn't hate me," Lucy frowned.

"Yet."

"Yet?" She raised her eyebrows, nails digging into Lai's arm.

"Well, you are wearing my mother's dress," he smirked as her grip tightened.

"You sneaky little–!"

"Evening, everyone!" Lai announced their arrival, ignoring Lucy's panic.

The party was off to an excellent start.

CHAPTER NINETEEN

LUCY

Lucy stood frozen at the top of the stairs, withering under the loathing in Aris's eyes. Beside him Klein stared at her in a mix of intrigue and apprehension, but thankfully the tension was broken by a stranger in a dark suit.

"You must be Lucy." He approached the staircase and offered his hand in a greeting. Lucy offered hers in return, expecting a kiss over the top and startled by a firm, enthusiastic handshake instead. Lucy heard Lai scoff behind her, but she barely spared him a thought as slight lightheadedness swept over her at the man's touch. It wasn't unpleasant, just bizarre. It felt like thousands of tiny insects crawling inside her body, carrying away blood drops from her heart to her fingertips.

Then just as suddenly as it came on, the feeling rushed away when he released her hand.

He seemed nice enough, though Lucy knew better than to accept first impressions in this place. "I'm Al, and this is Lilly," he gestured to a shy teenager standing beside him.

The girl waved, half hidden behind her brother. Lucy nodded a greeting, trying not to look too surprised that they were siblings when they seemed to be worlds apart from one another. Al had dressed the part. White shirt, black suit, dark hair slicked back into a top knot with freshly faded sides. His crisp shirt collar couldn't cover a full neck tattoo and intricately designed ink decorated both hands. His sister Lilly wore dirty white sneakers, long socks, and a hoodie so large it almost reached her knees.

It took a moment for Lucy to remember her manners. They didn't seem like the kind of people who commanded the uncomfortable level of propriety. She also didn't think she would need to constantly mind her tongue around them, which was a relief.

"It's a pleasure to meet you," she smiled, relaxing just a little.

"Pleasure's all mine. What's a girl like you doing in this zoo?" He laughed as he picked two crystal flutes of champagne from a serving boy, offering one to Lucy.

It was then she noticed half a dozen almost identical young boys with gray hair and pale skin. None of them paid her any attention, too busy preparing for dinner. She couldn't tell if they were real or apparitions, gliding between family and guests with trays of starters.

Lucy swilled the drink down in a single gulp, still feeling the cold of Aris's glare on her skin, her nerves standing on end. "Just trying to make a living. Nothing else," she explained, nursing the empty glass. Was it too late to run back upstairs and change? *Note to self, drop hemlock into Lai's drink.*

Al looked skeptical. "Strange place to do it if you ask me–"

"Hey, leave her alone," Lilly interrupted, taking Lucy's hand in hers, her eyes calf-like and wide as she looked up to her. "Would you like to join me in the gardens? I do love them, especially at night. Besides, you look like you need some fresh air already." She smiled shyly.

"Please." Lucy nodded. She placed the glass on a tray carried by a young servant and followed the white-haired teenager outside.

The cool night's air was refreshing. Lilly took her to a nook with a bench surrounded by flower beds filled with fragrant white blossoms. She plucked a single flower and held it to her lips.

"Have you been here long?" she asked, watching Lucy closely.

"Less than a month," Lucy replied, lifting her dress hem as she sat on the bench, fingers caressing the grain of ancient wood. "It's not too bad so far."

"I hope they're treating you well," Lilly leaned over and slipped the flower into Lucy's hair. "I'm glad to have you here tonight. I always find these parties are so lonely."

"You come here often?" Lucy asked. She hoped it didn't sound like a pick up line.

"Not really. My brother works for a private security company; his jobs occasionally take him out of town. He doesn't like leaving me alone, so I have to stay here. I hate it. They don't trust me. Tell me I'm crazy. If you ask me, the family living here are the last ones to judge anyone's sanity," Lilly huffed, blowing a stray lock of white hair from her face.

Lucy tilted her head curiously. "They think you're crazy? Why?"

"Because my memory isn't mine." Lilly gave her a sad smile. "My memory is from a long time ago. You'd probably think I'm crazy too." She folded her hands on her lap, swaying like a flower in a gentle breeze. "Enough about me. Tell me about yourself. Who are you?"

"I needed money and this job caught my eye. That's how I ended up here."

"I wasn't asking about your financial situation," Lilly laughed. "Tell me who you are." She took Lucy's hand in her own, examining the subtle palm lines.

"Lucy Howard."

"That's just your name." Lilly sought Lucy's eyes with hers. "Who are you?"

The cogs in Lucy's head seized. The years after her parent's death had blurred into a maddening slush of grief, loneliness and struggle. Who was she? Surely not this mess of anxiety and desperation? Who was she? "I don't know," she whispered, looking down at her hands and barely recognizing them as her own.

"I'll help you," Lilly offered softly; Lucy blinked at her, unsure of what exactly she was offering to help with.

"Dinner is almost ready," Klein cleared his throat. Both of them jumped, the spell broken; Lucy felt her face turning red, embarrassed by how close she'd come to opening up entirely to a stranger.

Lucy stood, offering her hand to Lilly. "We'll chat later, okay?" She smiled as the girl nodded, and followed her back inside.

Once everyone was settled, the conversation began to flow and the atmosphere had loosened its formal grip. The wine glasses were filled, and tiny, delicate portions began to appear on their plates, served by pale boys dressed in red velvet suits. Aris had stopped glaring daggers at Lucy, for which she was thankful.

One seat had remained empty, and Lai caught Lucy glancing at the vacant place setting. He winked at her, unconcerned; the last guest was simply late.

***

The evening was a stark contrast to the everyday life at the manor.

It was the first time the family had interacted with each other beyond the usual breakfast bickering. Lucy found herself enjoying the playful jabs and sharing of stories from times past.

Aris spoke of Martha's younger days and how the friendship between the two of them had formed. Al shared the latest gossip from the outside world, and Lai kept managing to steer the conversation back towards himself. Lucy could have sworn she heard Lai and Al switch to Spanish at one point, Lai surprisingly fluent. She could recognize some words but that part of her family never bothered to teach her and school's lessons didn't help much.

"Put down that fork, Leander," Aris cut into the conversation between his son and Al. "You're still banned from using sharp cutlery."

Lucy had to know the story behind that. She was on the edge of her seat, eyes darting from Lai to Aris then back to Lai. He scoffed as he dropped the fork and picked up a spoon instead.

Was no one going to elaborate?

No, it seemed not; the family resumed the discussion and Lucy sat back, disappointed.

"You can't just mention something like that and not explain it," she grumbled as she tried to get Aris's attention.

Irritated by the demand, the man gestured to Klein. "Ask him how he lost his eye."

Her gaze moved to the eldest brother, who was fidgeting with his eye patch and looking uncomfortable with the sudden attention, then to Lai, who was already putting on a pout. There was a sudden thump and Klein winced. Lai had kicked him under the table to suppress the information.

"I was attacked by a cockatrice." Klein shifted away from his brother and the apparent abuse.

"Lai, cut it out." Lucy picked up an olive and launched it across the table. "I want to know—"

She didn't get to hear the story. Not because Klein refused to tell it but because the entire house shook from the sounds of thundering explosions above them. Startled, Lucy cried out in fright and looked around the table. No one seemed as concerned as she was. Aris was clenching his wine glass, absolutely seething. She wasn't sure why, but deep inside she was thankful he had found something else to be mad about.

"What the hell was that?" Lucy gasped.

"Who invited mother?!" Ryan slammed both fists on the table.

"Mother?" Lucy asked as the dogs ran outside, barking like lunatics at the landing airship, its shadow blocking out the moonlight.

The family followed behind them, gathering in the garden to witness the arrival.

Despite the promise she made to herself not to freak out about anything weird, Lucy had to pick her jaw up off the ground at the sight of the magnificent vessel descending from the heavens. It looked like a man-o-war, hoisted into the air by a zeppelin. The *Kikimora* demanded respect with her mere presence.

Hanging from the side of the vessel, with one hand on a rope ladder, was the most magnificent woman Lucy had ever seen. A long, red dress hugged her perfect hourglass shape, abundant cleavage

unapologetically on display. The high split showed off a pair of muscular legs in combat boots with a dagger strapped to her thigh. She was tall, perhaps an inch or two taller than Aris. When she jumped off the ship before it landed, she made the ten-foot fall look no higher than a single step.

"Sorry I'm late. I did mention in my RSVP that I had started a siege. Thankfully they surrendered in time for me to make it." She flicked a speck of rubble from her shoulder, her long raven hair falling in perfect waves.

So, this was Eleanore. Lucy swallowed the lump in her throat, suddenly feeling underdressed. Then again, she didn't know anyone who could eclipse that woman. Everything about her demanded attention, and she got it. Everyone's eyes were upon her, even Al's, brows raised in unsubtle admiration.

Eleanore strolled inside, swaying her hips as she approached the table. She did not bother with guest-like formalities. She felt at home.

"Oh, look at you. Why so glum, my little pup?" Eleanore leaned down to kiss Aris on the cheek, leaving a red lipstick stain that re-marked her territory after a long absence. "Aren't you happy to see me?" she cooed, fluffing up his hair.

"Ecstatic," Aris muttered, turning and heading back into the house.

She purred her satisfaction and followed Aris inside, taking her seat as Ryan settled beside her. "Oh, my precious baby. Looking like a real boy these days. Just got to lose those puffy cheeks of yours, and your father might actually pay for you.”

“I owe you nothing, Eleanore,” Aris answered with palpable disdain in his voice.

“Oh? You know, if the cash is tight, I do have some interest in–” She trailed off as she finally noticed Lucy. “Oh, that's a new face. A cute one at that. What are you doing here, little one?”

Lucy grit her teeth. She hated being spoken to as if she was a child. “I'm just working here.”

“Oh, good job. Nine months and you can buy yourself one of those.” She pointed at her ship. “Good value for your time if the man pays up. If.”

If? Lucy was getting worried about her lack of pay, but each time she brought it up Aris promised to deal with it.

“I'm not here for that, just to take care of the family,” she mumbled.

“Oh, are you?” Eleanore looked around the room, finding only averted gazes. “Good for you. Enjoy that. You are so precious.”

Lucy felt the sinking feeling once again. Like she didn't belong, like she was being lied to. Frantically looking at others in the room, she found that not even Klein could make eye contact. The uncomfortable silence delighted Eleanore.

A gentle touch on her thigh snapped Lucy back.

"It's okay. Don't let her get to you," Lilly whispered. "She's always like this."

Easier said than done. Lucy couldn't understand this sudden bubbling of envious rage she felt burning in her stomach. Was she threatened by this woman with the demeanor of an apex predator, dominating the table while every man shrunk in their seats? What was that like? To walk into the room and be feared? Obeyed without question? Lucy hadn't known that she wanted that, but now the desire to command everyone's attention was consuming her mind.

Slowly, Lucy tried to relax as conversation and eating gradually resumed, but her attempt to enjoy the evening was soon interrupted. A blood-curdling screech tore the air; a flapping of wings and then a pained howl from one of the hounds pierced the night. Aris lurched to his feet but Lucy was faster, running outside.

He followed close behind, shoving her out of the way. His youngest hound howled in pain on the wet grass. Above the dark horizon the silhouette of a large bird-like creature escaped, chased away from its meal by the sudden flurry of attention.

"Shhh, it's okay, Scarlet, my girl. It's okay." He knelt by his dog, gently scooping up the hellhound and cradling her to his chest. Lucy already knew that she wasn't going to make it, a large chunk of her flesh missing from the tender belly area ripped open by the griffin's talon.

"Don't let her suffer," Eleanore placed her hand on Aris's shoulder, but he didn't seem to hear her as he whispered words of comfort to his precious pet.

Lucy rubbed her fingers together; the tickle of rapidly approaching death danced on her fingertips. She considered her abilities.

I did it with Ryan. I could do it again.

Lucy stood there feeling like an utter failure as the dog slowly passed in her master's arms, one last lick wiping away a stray tear from his rough skin.

"Go on..." Lai nudged her. "You can do it."

Ryan was looking at her as well. Hell. She could do it! She had magic. She had powers. She could show them that they falsely perceived her as something fragile. She could put Eleanore in her place. A sting of guilt jabbed at her conscience. Was that why she wanted to save the animal? Not because it was the right thing to do but because Lucy needed to prove something?

So what?

Lucy took a deep breath, lowering herself next to Aris, who was paralyzed with grief. She placed one hand on the dog and another to the ground, fingers digging into the soft earth next to the roots. She felt the energy that fed the garden and the forest. Each string of life caressed her fingertips.

I'm sorry. She apologized to all of the living things that were about to pay the ultimate price, and drew from the ground using her body as a conduit.

The hound's torn flesh stitched itself back together, fibers of the skin and muscle forming before their eyes, life returning as everything around them rapidly died. The trees, flowers, and every weed turned yellow, shriveling up, forced to donate their lives to save Scarlet.

Soon the lovely overgrown garden was nothing but dirt and wilted plants as far as the eye could see; even the forest in the distance shed its leaves, bare trunk trees shivering in the rising wind. Lucy kept pulling, basking in the awe and fear in everyone's eyes.

At last the hound showed signs of life. A tiny whimper and strained breath followed by frantic licking of her master's face, stubby tail wagging furiously.

Lucy withdrew her hands; one stained green and the other so red it looked black in the low light. She stilled her breath and finally looked at Aris. Their eyes met.

"Who are you?" he asked, wide-eyed, so many questions written on his face.

Anyone I want to be.

"I'm Lucille Howard," she said quietly.

"What the man meant to say was 'thank you'." Eleanore helped Lucy up, giving Aris a stern glare. "Let's get you inside, child, you're trembling. What a performance that was. The dinner entertainment gets better every year."

She *was* trembling, her entire body filled with the leftover life force that sparked like little pricks of electricity. She didn't feel weak, though. On the contrary, her mind felt clearer, her vision better, her senses more vibrant.

It was the first time she'd had that much energy run through her; what would the side effect be like? What price would she have to pay for this reckless abuse of power? She looked around the dead garden, saddened by the state of it, the lonely white bloom in her hair serving as a reminder of what it once was.

Lucy followed Eleanore, who led her to a cozy parlor room with a smoldering fireplace. The woman's powerful hand pushed her down onto a sofa; Lucy didn't fight it.

"Need a moment to collect yourself?" Eleanore offered a glass of brandy to Lucy, which she politely declined.

"No, thank you. I probably shouldn't drink right now." A mild buzz always followed the use of her abilities, but this was something else entirely. Lucy felt like she could stay up for days, and the slight pain in her neck from sleeping wrong the previous night had vanished.

She felt renewed, yet the guilt from causing that much death ate away at her conscience.

Eleanore shrugged and emptied both glasses herself. "Something tells me it's going to be a long night with many questions. Been a while since I've seen magic this strong. Who are you, girl?"

"I'm guessing you are not asking for my name," Lucy sighed. She couldn't sit still, getting up to pace restlessly, her body tingling with residual energy.

"No. I'm curious about you. What is a gem like you doing in a place like this?" Eleanore narrowed her eyes as she watched Lucy. She wore calm like a mask–an ill fitting one.

"Why does it matter?"

"Oh, it does, my little flower. You see, you almost destroyed the most advanced piece of technology in existence just now, and it leaves me a tiny bit irked. So irresponsible of you."

Lucy looked confused, pausing in her steps; did Eleanore mean that Gaia had been affected? "I didn't do anything, the only thing I hurt was the trees and stuff," she protested, frowning.

Eleanore scoffed. "There aren't enough blades of grass in the world to fix that damage. You had to tap a lot deeper than that; you broke into Gaia, all for the life of a slobbering beast."

"Of a beloved pet," Lucy scowled, irritated at how blasé Eleanore was towards a living creature. Deep down, she couldn't help but feel that she had made up for her mistake as a child, the cold body of her kitten redeemed by the hellhound's survival.

"If you are trying to please your boss, just hoist your skirt. He's a simple man with simple pleasures. The next time you feel the need to show off, just use what the Gods gave you."

"Why the hell do you even care if something happens to Gaia?" Lucy snapped, flushed red at the very idea of sleeping with Aris. She opened her mouth to defend her innocence, but before she could get out so much as a squeak Eleanore had arisen from her seat. Lucy flinched, and hated herself for it, but Eleanore ignored her completely, opening the door they had come through.

"Lilly, stop hovering outside. Come in." She rolled her eyes as Lilly sheepishly slipped into the room.

"I was worried about Lucy." Lilly walked over to Lucy and took her hand. "I think the dinner is officially over. Lai had to retire after getting exposed to so much magic, and my brother is helping him. He's good at nullifying the effects. Aris took his dog upstairs to keep an eye on her."

"Oh shit, I forgot about Lai," Lucy gasped, covering her mouth. He had reacted badly after her small demonstration; she didn't want to imagine the pain he was in now. "Is he okay?"

"I'm sure he will be fine. I think he got in the way on purpose. Now my brother is soothing the poor baby." Lilly rolled her eyes.

"That crafty bastard."

Lilly smiled, fixing Lucy's hair. "On the bright side, Aris is now indebted to you."

"If he doesn't kill me." She sighed; she wondered if he knew that she had taken power from Gaia, and what he would have to say about it.

"Why would he? You saved his baby."

Had she? The dog showed signs of life but was she able to bring it back fully? Lucy had to find out. "I might need a moment; I'm sorry. Thank you for everything." She nodded to the other two and left them behind.

CHAPTER TWENTY

AL

Lai ran up the stairs to his room, abandoning the party and his guests. He hissed in pain as he groped for the door, but the handle refused to cooperate with his swelling hand. Painful blisters covered his neck and shoulders, magic wreaking havoc on his body.

"Would you slow down, you idiot," Al brushed Lai's hand out of the way and pushed open the door. "Come on, get inside. Let's get you sorted."

That was how they had discovered Al's abilities in the first place.

Years ago, Lai had been exposed to an artifact with a hefty dose of magic still in it, triggering an allergic reaction. He had sought the comfort of his partner's arms and had found much more. He had found relief—all of the magic draining from his body and pooling inside Al, unable to cause any more harm.

Al had been scared of it. The magic itself hadn't affected him; he'd absorbed the power, storing it inside of him like lead encasing radiation, but it had spelled the end of their relationship as he pushed Lai further and further away, unwilling to be involved in his world.

"I didn't hear you follow. I'm fine, really." Lai knelt among the cushions on his bed, trying to unbutton his uncomfortably tight shirt as it rubbed against itchy skin.

Idiot. Do we have to do this dance every time?

Al grabbed him, ripping the shirt down the front, each button popping away under pressure. He pressed both hands against the burning skin, his touch negating the magic, drawing it away like a cold compress with fever.

Lai lowered his shirt down past his shoulders, letting Al do his thing. "You don't have to, you know."

"And hear you complain about it the whole time I'm here?" Al grumbled softly. There was no venom in his voice, just concern.

Lai tried to force a laugh, wincing as it caught in his itchy throat. "Me? Complain? When have I ever?"

"I'm surprised you're not complaining right now. What the fuck was that, by the way? Do I need to get Lilly out of here? Is she safe down there?"

"Yeah, she's fine. Lucy was trying to impress father and overcooked it a little." Lai looked down at his hands, watching as the red blisters that covered his knuckles faded away.

"She must be one hell of a suck-up. Guess it's marginally better than her sucking him off," Al smirked and squeezed Lai's hand before letting go, just testing to make sure he wasn't faking feeling better.

"Wait, don't go yet." Lai grabbed for the man's wrist but pulled his hand away, most likely afraid of looking desperate. "I haven't seen you for months."

Had it truly been that long?

Al glanced toward the open door as he settled back onto the bed.

He had been trying to avoid this exact scenario. Their relationship scared him. It had never been meant to last as long as it had; it was just a quick fling, an experiment. Nothing more. But Lai was a siren's song, inescapable, luring Al to his doom.

"You know I've been working. It's kind of nice to have a few days off, though."

Lai turned around to face him, fingers tracing the black ink design on Al's forearm. "Wouldn't kill you to text back, you know."

It would. It's hard enough being here as it is.

"I'm thinking about getting another tattoo," Al muttered, changing the subject.

Lai moved closer. "You haven't finished mine yet."

"You're right. Too bad I left my equipment at Candy's place," Al said gently. He hoped Lai would take the hint.

Lai looked as though he had been stabbed in the heart, quickly masking the pain with a smile that could cut glass.

"Oh? How's she doing?" he asked, getting up to pour both of them a drink. "Last I heard she had bought the club."

"Yeah, I'm a part-time bouncer there. Decent enough money, and she lets Lilly stay with her sometimes when I work the night shift at my other job."

"Ah, no wonder we haven't seen you two as much." He poured a generous amount of amber liquor into a crystal glass and offered it to Al. "I just hope you're not working too hard. You have to remember to take time for yourself. Relax a little."

"Tell that to the pharmacy. Lilly's meds could mortgage a house."

Al took the glass and drank a considerable amount in the first swig.

Thinking about all he had to do when he got back stressed him out.

Lai swirled his drink but barely had a sip, topping up Al's glass. "I don't know how you're holding it together. I would've gone mad by now." He removed the ripped shirt entirely, pacing the room like a tiger circling a prospective mate.

Don't look. Don't look.

Little doubt remained in Al's mind. Lai had planned this, and here he was like a fool on his bed, trapped by the damned cushions, drink clouding his judgment while Lai bided his time.

"I know what you are doing."

"The door is right there."

Lai's clothes fell slowly to the floor, pooling gracefully at his feet. His strong body glowed in the low candlelight. Al could see his skin was still as soft and porcelain smooth as the last time he'd bedded him, olive skin warm and inviting, every shift of his lithe body whispering sinful promises.

"I'm surprised you're staying in shape, you barely leave your room."

Lai pursed his lips with a look of bemused satisfaction, taking it as a compliment and disarming the sting. He wouldn't let Al de-escalate.

"Perhaps you had an impact on me after all. I don't look like this just for my benefit," Lai purred, sinking down onto the bed beside Al, his naked thigh pressed against Al's suit. "I'm considering moving back to the city. Although my family would be lost without me."

"You could still lose a few pounds." Al pinched Lai's side, desperate to break his spell over him. "I'm sure Klein wouldn't know what to do with himself if you didn't live here."

"Exactly. He needs a reason to get up every morning. Want another drink?"

"I shouldn't. What is this, anyway?" Al asked, sniffing the last of his drink.

"Could be paint stripper. I'm no liquor expert, so don't ask me." He stood and topped up the glass, pouring the strong drink as if it was water. "You look like you need it."

That was an understatement.

Lai settled back down beside Al, leaning lazily against him. "I'm glad you could make it tonight. It's been lonely around here."

"You have company now. It seems like you and Lucy hit it off." Al's treacherous hands had already begun loosening his buttons. The alcohol took over from there, dismantling his shirt and tossing it aside.

"She's a breath of fresh air. I crave something a bit more familiar." Lai pressed on Al's shoulder, guiding him down to the mattress.

"You know the rules," Al whispered, catching Lai's slender wrist in his hand and pushing Lai down on his back. No amount of liquor would get him to take the submissive role—it was a boundary he had set in stone, and Lai had never been permitted to cross it.

"Wait, I have a present for you." A smile curled Lai's lips as he slipped out from under Al and into the darkness of his room; a moment passed before he returned, long enough that Al was considering leaving, before he was met with the soft hiss of satin on skin.

"Is this more to your liking?" he asked, standing in candlelight for Al to admire. His satin robe opened to reveal red lingerie and thigh high stockings — his lips the same shade of crimson, begging to be kissed.

"That looks new," Al sat back up with an eyebrow raised; any doubts of Lai's intentions vanished. He reached over to caress Lai's long hair, hair that framed androgynous features that had been painted to be more feminine just to please him.

"Thought you might approve," Lai bit his lip with a smile, leaning down to kiss him.

Al laid back with his eyes closed, anticipating what was to come. Victorious, Lai positioned himself between Al's thighs, fingers making quick work of the zipper and pushing his clothes down. He was happy enough to play dress-up if it meant that he would have Al all to himself, even if it was just for that night. With no hesitation his lips wrapped around Al's rigid cock, sucking greedily, eager to please.

Al stifled a moan, downing the last of his drink. The burning alcohol mixed with Lai's touch in a heady rush of bliss; he would never admit it to Lai, but he had missed this. He craved it during lonely nights, a forbidden lust he tried to bury.

Lai gasped, breaking away to catch his breath. Al reached down, catching him by his chin and lifting him to meet his gaze.

"I think you still have lipstick on your lips. That won't do." He pulled his lover towards him, their lips meeting in breathless urgency.

Running his hands through soft lavender hair, Al pushed him back down to finish what he started, his hips raised in demand. Lai obeyed completely, letting him take the lead; Al gently but firmly pulled Lai's head down so that he could fuck his willing mouth, forcing himself in until Lai's lips left red marks over the bronze skin below his navel.

The last barriers of resistance crumbled beneath the feathery strokes of Lai's tongue, igniting a carnal hunger that engulfed Al. He wanted so desperately to suppress that part of him but the feel of Lai's lips, his fevered skin and the gentle persuasion of the man's kisses made him impossible to resist.

Free at last of his self control, Al pushed Lai down. Grasping his lover's thighs he eased them apart, his body trembling with need in a frenzied race to fulfillment.

Giddy with lust and alcohol, Al groped for the small vial of thick oil that Lai kept on the bedside. It flowed smooth and lightly scented as he poured it over his hand, stroking it over his entire length. Al took a moment to admire the man before entering him with a determined push.

A soft cry escaped Lai's lips as the burn overshadowed the pleasure, but his body adjusted quickly, relaxing into powerful thrusts as their climax neared its apex.

"Please…" Lai begged against Al's mouth.

Aching tension built between them, rapid, shallow breaths filling the silence. With a few rolls of his hips Al hauled in a breath and tensed as molten waves of pressure rolled over him, and he filled Lai with the warmth he yearned for.

"I love you," Lai whispered between shallow breaths.

"I'm sorry."

CHAPTER TWENTY ONE

LUCY

"Lucille. A moment?" Aris called out to Lucy from the top of the staircase. "In my study, if you don't mind."

Any other time Lucy's heart would have been sinking with dread, but not tonight; Aris didn't feel as menacing as before and she didn't feel as vulnerable. She followed him in silence, neither of them daring to break it.

The office was dimly lit and empty. He paced the small space, struggling to start the conversation. Lucy didn't rush him, allowing the man time to formulate whatever it was that he needed to say. She did wonder what it would be. Was he going to thank her for saving his dog? Punish her for wrecking the garden? Interrogate her about her powers?

"You should keep that dress."

Her brows lifted in shock; that wasn't where she had expected this conversation to start. Lucy found herself speechless; she'd had answers prepared for everything but that. "I–I didn't think you liked me wearing it."

"It brought back painful memories," Aris muttered, folding his hands behind his back.

"I didn't know. Lai said—"

"Should've drowned that boy when I had the chance." He laughed softly, looking everywhere but at the woman in front of him.

"I know, I was tempted to throttle him myself." Lucy took a few steps forward, seeking his eyes. She finally had a proper chance to look at Aris after spending most of the dinner avoiding him. Still dressed in the tailored evening suit, he polished up nicely, handsome and tamed and dark with blood.

"Are you alright?" Lucy pressed. "You were holding the dog. I'm worried some of my magic might have affected you."

He paused, meeting her eyes with his at last. "Maybe it did." Aris reached for Lucy, his rough fingers resting on her bare neck, thumb gently caressing her flushed cheek.

Lucy froze, hesitantly placing her hand over his. She closed her eyes, feeling for any stray magic in him. There was... something. It wasn't hers, though. Aris's magic was old, diluted by centuries, weak and tired but still alive. She drew the threads of it closer, finding it as comforting as an embrace from an old friend.

"You are a strange creature, you know that?" Aris cupped her cheek, leaning in closer, scarred lips only inches away from hers.

"So I've been told." The energy buzzed through Lucy still, but her head was light for a different reason now. All of the doubts and worries in her head melted away as Aris closed the distance between them, pulling her into a firm kiss.

She hesitated for only a second before she deepened it. Her head spun giddily. She needed more.

What is wrong with you?

This wasn't her. The death of the garden had her craving life, and all the good that came with it. Lucy allowed herself her moment of weakness. Regrets and consequences — a problem for tomorrow.

The eager kiss seemed to be all the consent Aris needed, her lips soft and warm, seeking his even after he pulled away. He lifted Lucy in his arms and cleared the desk in one sweep. Ancient books and irreplaceable artifacts shattered on the floor, forgotten. He laid her down, pausing to admire her soft curves. Even with hunger clouding her mind, Lucy allowed him to savor the sight of her, ready and yielding.

Lucy smiled, laying back, her fingers running through Aris's dark hair. Excitement and surprising calm settled over her as she pulled him down, eager to taste his lips again. He let her take charge, their kisses increasing in intensity, quickly turning deep and passionate. She could feel his rough, calloused fingers exploring under layers of her dress, teasing her soft thighs. Lucy arched her back towards him, her own hands slipping under the thin shirt fabric, tracing old battle scars. She needed him closer, thighs parted in invitation as she lifted up her dress, allowing his hands to travel.

"You are mine..." his deep voice vibrated near her ear, low and with a subtle hint of a threat.

Yours?

A sudden wave of sobering clarity washed away the submissive girl. Was this what she actually wanted? Aris had been so cruel to her–he had almost let her die! Did the flashes of tenderness really make up for making a prisoner out of her? Allowing this to happen now felt wrong. Like she would never be able to stand up to him again; like she would never command his respect.

"No," she said, unsure how he would respond, her voice showing a little too much weakness for her liking. Even to her, she sounded uncertain.

Aris froze, his eyes seeking hers as if looking for a reason to the abrupt stop, but he didn't question her. That one word command was absolute.

"I'm getting a drink," he whispered, gently pulling away.

"I might need one too," Lucy sighed, sitting up. Her dress was a mess, but she did her best to straighten it up.

It seemed that Aris wasn't going to bother with glasses this time, uncorking a dark unlabeled bottle and taking a big swig straight out of it, then passed it over to Lucy.

"Strange night."

"Very," she agreed, offering the bottle back.

They sat in oddly comfortable silence, passing the bottle between them, each dwelling on their own thoughts.

Glancing over at Aris, Lucy found him avoiding her eyes again. Was he embarrassed? She sure as hell wasn't. If anything, she felt stronger. She wondered if he had already picked up on the shift.

"This doesn't change things. You are still a prisoner. You cannot leave, not after what you've done."

"I figured," Lucy shrugged; the word prisoner hung in the air between them, strangely weightless, holding no real power over the woman. "Kinda made that hotter, though."

"You are insane."

She got up, stretching, then adjusted her dress while he watched. "So are you."

Aris frowned as he took another deep drink, complex emotions changing his face into the countenance of a man who had lost control.

***

"You're sneaking in late," Lai laughed as Lucy approached. He was sitting on the cold marble outside his bedroom, smoking a cigarette, dressed in a sheet draped loosely around his waist. Red marks covered his neck and shoulders, evidence of an exciting night.

"Your father had lots of questions." Lucy took the cigarette from his hand and inhaled a lungful of fragrant smoke. "Looks like you had fun."

"That's why I'm cooling my ass here. A little too intense of an end to my dry spell." He smiled. "You played your part well."

"My part?" She squinted at him.

Lai took a deep breath. "Well, I wanted Al all for myself, but the only way he'd agree to be close is if he was using his ability to help me get over a massive magic exposure." He flashed her a grin, a villain about to expose his diabolical plan. "That's where you came in. You have magic, but for you to use it someone needs to get seriously hurt. There aren't many creatures here who will actively attack anyone except the unicorn, who is too unpredictable, and the resident griffins, but even they need to be provoked. They despise intruders in their airspace, so if I was to invite Eleanore and she arrived by airship, they'd be pissed. Someone would have to be outside, that's where the dogs came in. Anytime someone arrives they go out barking and howling. The griffins would take out their anger on the hounds, and you'd be forced to use your powers. So I invited everyone under the guise of a dinner party and watched it play out."

Lucy stared at Lai as though he had just confessed to being a serial killer. He couldn't prepare a morning routine. There was no way he planned all that just to get laid.

"I'm gonna go use your bathtub," she shook her head as she tried to process the avalanche of information.

"Join me in my parlor." Lai rose to his feet with a wince of discomfort.

"Start that bath for me, my diabolical friend. I need to get a change of clothes first." Lucy waved him off and entered her room, grabbing a set of pajamas from her bed. She didn't bother changing yet, heading back to Lai's room for her bath. Lai was sitting on his bed and watching Al; the other man was reclined among cushions, entertaining himself with a phone game.

"She called me her friend. Did you hear that?" Lai beamed at Lucy as she entered.

"Careful, you'll get his hopes up." Al swiped on his phone, connecting rows of jewels. "I know him all too well. Give him an inch, and he will take all eight." He laughed as Lai launched a pillow at his head, blocking it with his arm without ever looking up from his screen.

"Need help getting out of that dress?" Lai offered, launching another pillow at Al.

"Yeah, please." Lucy wasn't in the mood to get between the bickering lovers. All she wanted was freedom from the suffocating corset and the feel of hot, cleansing water on her skin. Lai's nimble fingers made quick work of the dress, dropping it down so that Lucy could step out of it, freeing herself from the layers of fabric that clung to her damp skin.

"Thanks for your help," she smiled in gratitude, slamming and locking the bathroom door behind her.

Once she was alone she sat on the edge of the bath, exploring the countless bottles of salts and oils, picking out a jar of pale purple powder that smelled like lavender and jasmine. She poured a generous amount into the bath and watched as the running water turned into a cloud of perfumed bubbles.

Lucy dimmed the lights and slipped into water hot enough to burn, letting it momentarily distract her from her thoughts. As soon as her body adjusted to the scalding heat her mind began to race again, unable to relax. She wanted to feel embarrassed about how the night had ended, but couldn't. She'd enjoyed the kisses, and it didn't feel wrong. If anything, she felt empowered for the first time since arriving in this strange little world.

Lucy lifted her hand out of the water, watching bubbles melt away to expose heat flushed skin that slowly returned to its normal color. She thought back to the moment when she had drawn the living energy from the ground. Looking back without panic, the experience felt strange. Hidden between her own thoughts were foreign memories, memories that had seeped into her mind as the life force of the garden had passed through her body, settling inside like sand filling cracks in pavement. It wasn't anything coherent; a flash of light, a high pitched sound, the feeling of seasons changing, and the satisfaction of water saturating the ground.

Did plants have memories? Could trees speak? Lucy scooped a handful of water and let it run down her bare shoulder, and the sensation resonated with the borrowed memories of rain.

"Strange night," she sighed, leaning back, enjoying the last few minutes of heat as the water cooled to an uncomfortable tepid soup. With a groan, she flopped out of the tub and dried off with one of the soft towels Lai owned by the dozen, pulling on her fresh pajamas. She found the boys gossiping on the bed, both a little drunk.

"Nightcap?" Al offered her a bottle of cheap sparkling wine. "Don't tell me you're off to bed already? Come on, spend some time with us."

Lucy glanced over the half naked man, with tattoos covering his perfectly sculpted muscles and then at Lai who looked like he wasn't quite done. Was she even considering it?

No.

Not tonight.

"Goodnight, you two. Keep it down in here."

***

A single candle burned on her bedside table when Lucy returned to her own room. She approached the flame cautiously, lured by its light like a moth.

"Sorry, my room is so cold," Lilly's voice startled her. She was lying in Lucy's bed, wrapped up in a thick blanket for warmth. She'd changed from her comfy clothes and into a white nightgown that made her look like a ghost.

Lucy sighed in relief. "It's okay. Want to take my room, and I'll use yours?" Lucy hung the damp towel over her chair.

"We can share; I don't take much space," the girl murmured, already half asleep, shifting to make enough room for Lucy to lay down.

Lucy smiled and stretched out next to her. "This reminds me of the slumber parties I had back in school."

Lilly scooted closer to leech more warmth, wrapping both arms around Lucy's waist. The poor girl was freezing. "What's a slumber party?"

"It's when friends come over to spend a night at each other's house."

"Maybe one day you can come over to my place."

"I doubt I'll be able to leave here any time soon," Lucy sighed. "Aris made it pretty clear I'm not going anywhere."

"As if he could stop you." Lilly looked up with bright pale gray eyes, heavy with sleep. "You have control over life and death. I've only ever seen one other like you."

Maybe she was right. Tonight Lucy felt unstoppable. What could Aris do if she decided to leave? He'd seen her power. She could drain him of life in an instant.

And then what? What would she do back in the city? Go back to serving doughnuts and scrubbing deep fryers. Out there, she was just another nobody struggling to get by.

Wait.

"One other?"

Lilly nodded, resting her head on Lucy's chest. "You're going to think I'm crazy. I see things. Memories from a long, long time ago, before I was reborn into this useless body. I wish I had your powers. Then I could prove to everyone I'm not sick."

Lucy held Lilly in silence. She could feel her tremble. "What memories do you have?" She asked to fill the quiet.

Lilly didn't answer for a while. Just as Lucy had thought that she was asleep, the girl began to sing. A quiet lullaby to soothe herself to sleep.

"..and as I dance on nightfall's edge,

I part the poisoned sea,

I see the moon, Her pale breast,

Her light that nurses me,

We stand alone, at crossroads sign,

My flame is doomed to die,

You light your torch, consume my soul,

And sing our last goodbye,"

She finished the song with a deep sigh. "It's torture. Imagine getting an amazing toy for Christmas. Then you open it up, but the batteries aren't included. Hell, they don't even exist."

"That sounds rough, I'm sorry." Lucy hugged Lilly tighter. The song lingered in her mind, resonating quietly, over and over again.

"You're the opposite. All power and no knowledge to back it up."

"Two halves of the same coin," Lucy laughed. She stroked Lilly's back as they drifted off to sleep, thankful for each other's warmth as the temperature sank enough to make their breath visible.

CHAPTER TWENTY TWO

LUCY

"What the hell happened to Gaia?" Lai was shivering as he slunk into the dining room, wrapped in three moth-eaten fur coats, his breath crystallizing in the air with each puff.

It should have been close to midday when Lai finally rolled out of bed. All of the clocks in the house agreed on the time, but outside the sun hung low in the sky, weak and watery. Freshly fallen snow glowed in the pale light, seeming to have forgotten that it was well into late spring. The temperature inside the manor reflected the unbalanced nature, frost covering their cutlery and delicate porcelain teacups.

"Something went terribly wrong last night." Aris tapped the glass on his antique mercury thermometer as the line steadily sank lower.

He was dressed in a heavy, fur-lined cloak that looked like it would keep him warm even in the Antarctic. His dogs whimpered, huddling up around their master; despite the burning core of their bodies the hellhounds were cowards in the face of a cold snap.

Lucy nodded in agreement with the understatement. Even wearing two sweaters, two pairs of pants and a long scarf, her teeth chattered uncontrollably. She hadn't packed for winter, struggling to keep warm with her light summer clothes. Most Texans were not built for ice and snow; she'd lost her grandmother a few years back to an unexpected freeze.

Lai shrugged, hugging his knees to his chest to keep warm. "Maybe it'll fix itself?"

"That's the fourth sunrise this morning. Gaia is busted," Al frowned, warming his hands around a rapidly cooling cup of coffee. He gave a groan of dismay as his hot drink iced over in his grip.

Lucy poured hot chocolate for Louis. "I'm sorry. It's probably because of me."

"Oh, we are certain of it," Aris sighed, putting down the thermometer. "We need to find a way to fix it. Unfortunately, I don't know how Gaia works."

"Who installed it?" Lucy raised an eyebrow. She didn't expect the head of the family to be ignorant of the inner workings of his own home.

"I don't know. It's far more advanced than anything else we've ever seen," Aris added dark liquor to his tea to stop it from freezing. "It took me two years to figure out the telephones. This isn't up my alley in the slightest."

"It took him two years to figure out rotary phones," Lai amended. "You'd waste a lifetime trying to teach him how an iPhone works."

Lucy looked over at Klein. Surely he would know the inner workings of the house.

"Don't look at me. I've been yelling at it for a couple of hours now." Klein took a seat with a hot cup of coffee for himself. "The voice controls are off. There must be a main control board somewhere."

Another dead end. Guilt set in as Lucy looked around the table, hoping someone would know how to fix this. "Ryan? What are the chances you've read the manual for this thing?"

The boy sniffed, hiding cheeks that had turned red from the cold under a scratchy woolen scarf. "I haven't, but it's not a bad idea. I can start looking through the paperwork for anything related to Gaia while the rest of you search the house and grounds for anything that resembles a control system."

"That sounds like a good plan to me," Lucy beamed proudly, pleased to have come up with the beginnings of a solution.

No one felt any particular desire to move. The air was freezing, the marble floor resembled an ice rink and every piece of hardware from door handles to taps was cold enough for skin to stick to. Even the fire burning in the hearth seemed sluggish and small.

"If this weather doesn't lift, we might need to consider camping by the stove in the kitchen. My room is colder than a witch's tit." Lai tucked the tea kettle under his coat in an attempt to preserve heat. "Shall we pick teams and start the search? This breakfast is pointless..." He lifted a plate and turned it over, his poached egg frozen solid to the surface.

Lucy gave Lai a look. "Let me guess. You and Al?"

"That would be counterproductive," Al shook his head, ignoring Lai's sulky huff. "Why don't you pick?"

"Or, we can just let the leader of the house decide?" Lucy shrugged, looking over at Aris. This might have been her fault but she wasn't about to step on her boss's frozen toes. Especially not after last night; in private she might snub him, but she wasn't going to humiliate him in front of the entire family.

"Why are you giving jobs that I have no time or patience for?" Aris placed his cup down a little bit too hard, spilling his drink onto the saucer.

"Because you should know everyone's strengths and weaknesses. Besides, there are locations I'm not allowed to go to, and frankly they would be the first places I'd check," Lucy pointed out with a frown; the desire to preserve his pride was rapidly fading away.

Aris scoffed, pushing aside his plate and leaning closer to Lucy. "That's a conveniently timed change of tone. You've done nothing but break the rules since arriving here. Why the sudden urge to follow them?"

"Is this really the time for it?" Lucy frowned. She was not sure of what she had seen in him last night; she wanted to slap him now.

"Take Lai, keep him focused. Al can go with Klein, and I'll go with–" Aris paused with a frown. "...I was going to say my dogs, but a bitch will do."

Eleanore had let herself into the family meeting and smiled as she lowered herself onto Aris's lap. It was not a friendly smile. "You should've allowed me to study Gaia when I asked. You wouldn't be in this mess if you had, you stubborn little man."

"I'm not stupid, Eleanore. I know what you'd use her for. Gaia will not be a part of your warmongering. Now, enough talk; if we wait any longer, we will die at this table."

"How will we communicate if someone finds it?" Lucy watched Eleanore caress Aris's jaw with flushed cheeks, jealous anger twisting in her gut, unexpected and unwelcome.

"Yell?" Al paced around his chair; he was shivering even under layers of clothes. "Why don't we meet up in the kitchen in a few hours? Lilly can keep the fire going 'til then."

"Sounds good," Lucy turned to Lai. "Are you done?"

"With breakfast? Yes. Sulking? No," he huffed. "Where do you want to start? Inside? Or..." they both looked outside to where the snow was waist-high with damp, clumping ice, the kind that stuck to clothing in heavy lumps before slowly melting into one's boots.

"It's probably out there, huh?" Lucy sighed.

"I don't know. You have to remember, Gaia is impressive but still only technology. I always assumed it was built into the house. But now that I think about it, it's probably weatherproof. I've never stumbled across it inside, and there's no good reason why it wouldn't be out there."

Lai couldn't have been less helpful if he tried. Lucy pondered their options. The howling wind outside didn't entice her in any way, and their clothing was far from weather appropriate. "Hmm. Attic maybe?" she offered, optimistic.

"I think the entrance to that is above the old servant quarters. Shall we start there?" Lai offered; Lucy didn't care where they started as long as it was within the safety of the manor walls, away from the painful sting of the blizzard.

"Lead the way."

***

Their route took them past their rooms in the east wing, then up to the third floor by way of a hidden staircase used by servants back when the house was in its prime. Each stair creaked in protest as they were forced out of well-deserved retirement. Countless rooms that once had housed the dozens of kitchen maids, valets and servants needed to run a house of that size offered nothing but hollow silence as each was opened in vain hope. The claustrophobic corridors and rooms squeezed closer together, the low ceilings and the dark gray paint that covered the walls adding to the grim atmosphere.

At the end of the hallway Lucy and Lai reached the last set of stairs, leading to a locked door.

"Ladies first."

"I don't suppose you have a key for this, do you?" Lucy examined the latch with a heavy padlock on it.

"No, why would I?" Lai gently pushed past her. "Who needs keys anyway?" He wrapped his fingers around the cold metal body of the lock and yanked it out, metal bracket and all; the rotting wood offered as little resistance as wet cardboard.

"Oh, you think you are so impressive. Move," Lucy opened the hatch and climbed inside, using her phone flashlight to illuminate the dark attic, glad that Lai had let her charge it in his room last night. In her heart she only acted brave to keep Lai from teasing her. Attics were terrifying in the nicest of houses; with the monsters that roamed the manors ground freely here, she could only imagine what manner of beast might lurk in the pitch black room. At least if something decided to snack on them she had Lai to hide behind, though a little voice told Lucy that Lai was more likely to use her as the shield.

"That is blinding." Lai squinted as the phone's light reflected off of an absurd amount of shiny garbage. The room was packed to the rafters with candy wrappers and priceless jewelry, old road signs and soda cans, all gathered into an enormous nest and bound with yards upon yards of copper wire. A magpie sat on the edge of the nest, shredding an industrial roll of foil with its powerful beak.

"Oh, it's you!" Lucy squeaked in surprise as she climbed the stairs.

"Oh, it's you!" The magpie copied her, mocking.

"May I have a moment of your time?" Lucy retorted in a silly voice.

The magpie hopped closer, one black eye staring at her curiously.

You may.

He squawked and mimicked a laugh—a heart chilling cackle from something inhuman.

Bright white light flooded Lucy's mind. It felt like a dream, yet she knew it was real–she could feel her body, smaller than an atom and bigger than a galaxy at the same time. Millions of eyes were connected to her, seeing every moment that ever was and ever would be, all happening in the same breath. Time flowed around her in golden strings, stitching itself into delicate and complex patterns, forming new worlds, dimensions and possibilities. She was a ghost moving in the infinite, watching history repeat itself again and again.

"Halcyon," A voice called out to her. Her million eyes all looked for the source, her human mind unable to comprehend what she saw. The being that had called to her was both incredibly ancient and impossibly young; her form shifted from one woman to three, her eyes as wide and bright as the moon.

At last, mercifully, the visions faded, impossible images replaced with a blinding headache.

"What the fuck was that?" Lucy gasped weakly, hands clenching her throbbing temples.

"You asked a god to give you a glimpse into time. Be glad your brain didn't turn into mush." Lai held her close in his arms, the look on his face underscoring the seriousness of what had just happened. It was the first time Lucy had seen him show genuine concern. Not even a hint of sarcasm.

"I didn't think he would do it! Why would he give me a moment of his time? Wait, that thing is a god?"

"Yes. The bird is Time and gods are dicks, this is how they have fun." Lai glared at the magpie. "Don't move, just let it pass. You'll be okay." He wiped a trail of blood from her ears, probably hoping she wouldn't see, but Lucy could feel the warm trickle run down her neck

"Hey, you!" Lucy scrambled back up on her feet, ignoring the searing pain. "Do you know how to fix Gaia? The machine we're in?"

"I know everything," the magpie picked up a string of golden beads and began separating them, one by one.

"How can we fix it?"

The bird laughed and flew onto a higher perch. He offered no help.

Lucy clenched her fists in frustration, choking down the urge to throw a shoe at him. "Give him something shiny." She turned to Lai, demanding he offer a sacrifice.

"What? Why me?" Lai quickly tucked his bejeweled fingers under his arms, defending his many, many rings.

"Because I don't have anything!"

"How is that my problem all of a sudden?" He huffed and reluctantly slid a silver ring off his pinky to present to the bird. The ring vanished into the hoard while the magpie cackled; Lucy had forgotten to establish the terms of the exchange, only instructing Lai to surrender the ring.

"No *Deus Ex Machina* for you," Time teased, tucking the gift between the rafters as if hiding a nut for winter. "Get it? God...in the machine?" He laughed louder, far too amused by his own humor.

Lucy scowled in irritation. Aside from the mountain of rubbish the attic seemed to house only old furniture, nothing that screamed futuristic pocket dimension controls. She looked at Lai and he hastily stuffed his bejeweled hands into his pockets; she doubted she would talk him out of another ring. "Well the bird is a dud, any other ideas?"

"Kick open all the doors and keep eliminating possibilities room by room?"

"Let's go," Lucy nodded. Kicking down the door was precisely what she needed right then; the only form of therapy the manor could offer. She climbed back down the stairs, darkly muttering about gods and puns.

Returning to the service corridor, they checked each room again. Most of them were empty, but some were furnished with the basics; a rusted boxspring and a desk, nothing else. The task had long since turned tedious, but when they reached the last door on the left Lai froze.

"Did you find something?" Lucy looked over, closing another empty room.

"No, but it stinks." Lai stared at the door handle with some apprehension. "I hope it's not another...rat."

"Let's check. Sometimes electronics stink when they burn out."

With some trepidation Lai opened the door and peered inside the room. No electronics. No furniture either. Inside of the tiny room was a five-foot-wide wheel of cheese, just sitting in the middle of the floor.

"The hell is that?"

Lai poked the wax seal on it, just as confused as Lucy,

"It's *Pecorino*."

"How long has this been here?"

"Are you planning on eating it? Let's just leave the giant cheese. I'm not ready to deal with this right now."

"Why would you have this here?" She had so many questions.

"Don't look at me. I've never seen it before. You are vastly overestimating how much we've explored since moving in."

"Think something might be inside it?"

"Yes, absolutely. The incredibly advanced mechanism of a pocket dimension is in a stinky, five hundred pound wheel of ancient *Pecorino*. You are welcome to come back with a knife. I'll even find you some crackers to go with it." Lai rolled his eyes.

"You know, you stink more than the cheese," Lucy stuck her tongue out at him before exiting the room.

Lai sniffed his armpits to check, but smelled only of scented oils. "Offer still stands."

"No, thank you. Cheese isn't exactly my thing."

"Oh? What is your thing then?" Lai opened another door, finding nothing but a room filled with filing boxes, each overflowing with old accounts.

"I'm a slut for pizza rolls," Lucy sighed dreamily, imagining the hot, cheesy snack in her mind.

"How much of a slut? Say I have a box in the freezer."

"I'll let you be a little spoon for a week."

"Ah! Tempting offer." He tapped his chin, considering it. "It's a date then."

Slipping inside another room, Lai rummaged through meticulously handwritten documents that dated back hundreds of years, looking for anything diagram-like.

With a pep in her step after the promise of pizza rolls, Lucy approached another door. As she opened it, a thick wall of darkness greeted her. It reflected no light at all, creating an illusion of a bottomless hole.

"Oh, careful. It looks like we have another void room," Lai cautioned, pulling her back a step. "Whoever set up Gaia didn't finish, so that door isn't connected to anything. There's another one downstairs; Klein uses it as garbage disposal."

"Let's just close this door." Lucy backed away, shutting the room and fishing lipstick from her pocket. *VOID.* She wrote it in dark cherry red.

"Well, you've just ruined an amazing game of hide and seek. Shall we get back to the others? See if they had any more luck?"

Lucy nodded; her fingers were going numb, and the headache from glimpsing into a god's mind was still very present. A little disappointed at the lack of progress they had made, she followed Lai back, a thought occurring to her as they walked.

"Hey, Lai?"

"Mmm?" The man replied without looking back to her.

"What's the deal with you and Barbara? The peacock?" She noted with interest how suddenly his shoulders stiffened at the mention of the animal, as though after dealing with the magpie he'd already had a gutsful of birds.

"I need to be far more drunk before we have that conversation," he muttered bitterly, and would say no more, even as Lucy pestered him all the way down.

***

The kitchen stoves were brightly lit, with a fire roaring in the hearth and a copper kettle boiling over hot coals. Only Klein and Al were back, both sitting by the fireplace in defeat.

"We've checked the west wing. I can't say it was a very thorough check though," Al winced, nursing a bruised hand, two of his knuckles bleeding. "Most of the rooms are sealed shut. We couldn't even break them down. Not that we were very keen on trying; I've never met a room that could growl before."

"We've found some cheese and a Void." Lucy walked over to the wall cabinet where she'd seen a medical kit earlier. The second world war era metal box had a small supply of bandages and cotton padding, enough to cover a minor wound. Al looked grateful despite the stinging of the warm water on his split skin.

Once the man was all patched up, Lucy sat down on the floor by the fire. Thankfully the room was warm enough to shed some layers. The search of the house had been a waste of time, and she flopped with a disappointed sigh; it was looking more and more like they would have to brave the ice and snow.

Klein cleared his throat. "I did find one interesting thing." He waved an old piece of parchment. "According to this birth record, my name is Kleisthenes." He looked like he was in utter disbelief; a wave of chuckles filled the room, lightening the mood just a fraction. "I'd thought only Lai had gotten a traditional name. Guess not."

"Did no one ever tell you that?" Lucy asked.

"Not once in my thirty years did anyone ever use my real name. Not that I blame them. How do you even pronounce that?"

"*Klees-the-niss*," Lai plopped himself on Al's lap. "What's so hard about that?"

Klein spun in his seat, shock written all over his face.

"You knew?"

"What? Father calls you that all the time."

"I thought it was just drunk slurring..." Klein sat back, staring into the dancing flames in a silent stupor.

CHAPTER TWENTY THREE

RYAN

"You know it's up to you and me, right?" Ryan wrapped Louis in a sheep skin, securing it with a belt. "The rest of them aren't exactly bright. I bet they are looking for a big red button to reset Gaia."

Louis would have nodded if he could, but the layers of warm clothing were so thick he was barely able to move, arms and legs sticking out like a starfish. Ryan muttered darkly, adding layer after layer onto himself, his fingers numb from cold, refusing to cooperate. His warmest piece of clothing was a bomber jacket he wore on his mother's ship. Great protection against the high altitude wind, not so much for the mini ice age.

He wheeled out a red toy cart from the closet in the room they shared and plopped his little brother on it.

"I do blame myself. I had ample time to study Gaia, especially since my mother pressured me to. I could've found how it all works. The house is not that big…"

"Mamas said Gaia built their mountain," Louis said, flopping back in the cart and unable to sit himself back up again.

Ryan turned around, propping his brother upright.

"The griffins know?"

"They speak to the forest."

It was hard to tell if it was a child's imagination or a legitimate clue. The forest was a no-man's-land. Untamed and unexplored. It looked friendly enough, beautiful on a summer's day, but Ryan didn't trust it. While reading in the gardens he'd sometimes see shadows move out of the corner of his eye like something always watching him. Could the forest truly house Gaia? Or was it just another stab in the dark?

"I'm not risking seeking out the griffins. Not after mother violated their airspace. They will be angry and I do not fancy getting savaged again. I do have an idea though."

Ryan pulled on a knitted beanie, tying it under his chin and plopping a big fur hat on top. He must've looked almost comical dressed in his entire wardrobe and tugging the red cart behind. He just hoped Lucy and Lai wouldn't cross his path; the teasing was guaranteed. Not that any of them looked any better.

Thankfully the hallways were empty and Ryan knew exactly where he was going. To find Gaia he had to look to the very heart of the home. Before someone cocooned the old manor in technology and before the Victorian facade was added to the medieval house.

Everything related to the family was kept in the old crypt below the house and it took Ryan mere seconds to spot the hidden door among the floorboards. He'd been there before, many times. To study mainly. Once the stone room contained the family fortune but it had dwindled away over the years. Not just money and gold; old artifacts and heirlooms too. Now as Ryan climbed the ladder down the room echoed his every step. Empty and worthless.

The treasures might be long gone but the most important things still remained. The records. A large red tome tracing every family member rested upon a marble altar. It was still open on the page where Ryan added his own and Louis' names. Gloved fingers traced up the branch past Lai and Klein, over to Aris and Zephir then up to his grandfather, whose name was scribbled out. Aris had vowed that history would forget the Dreadlord's name and he meant it, burning every record that mentioned the Pirate Lord. Little did he know that Ryan had restored all of them. History was above one man's petty grudge.

Shutting the book Ryan stored it in the iron box beneath the altar, just in case. It had survived a few thousand years, it would be a shame to lose it now. Besides, Ryan was after something else this time.

Looking over a wall rack full of yellowed scrolls, Ryan read the inscriptions in the corners. *The Third Blight. The Rebellion of 1676. Shifting Procedures. Anatomy Of A Serpent. Breeding Logs For 1740. House Blueprints.*

Ah!

He lifted the crumbling documents, fishing out the one he needed, unrolling them under the beam of light shining from the open trap door above. It had everything from the land purchase in the twelfth century to the floor plans of each house that had been built on the same spot since then. The last paper felt different, almost like a thin sheet of plastic. It looked brand new, unaffected by poor storage and moisture. The date on that blueprint was for the year 2084.

Victorious, Ryan climbed back up the ladder to his waiting little brother. It was time to go back.

***

"Found anything good?" Ryan pulled the cart with Louis and the scroll into the kitchen. The blissful heat caressed his face, easing the painful tingling from the frost.

"We found cheese." Lucy smiled at the boys, but neither of them seemed in the mood to return the gesture.

"Has anyone seen Father?" Ryan asked as he released Louis.

"He and Eleanore went to explore the grounds. If it is outside, we might have a problem," Klein leaned closer to the heat, warming up his stiff hands. "I've been over most of the grounds, but I've never seen anything that might resemble it. What if the controls aren't just a box? We might be using an outdated understanding of technology. We're looking for a button we can press. What if it's something else entirely?"

Oh, now they get it.

Ryan rolled his eyes. Most people didn't dare question the workings of their universe; even thinking about it could bring on an existential crisis. Gaia's inhabitants were much the same. They enjoyed the life it sustained, but no one cared to find out exactly how the mechanism worked. No one except Eleanore, that was. The brutal warlord saw the endless potential in Gaia's technology; a portal that could take her to any world, a hidden space that could store any treasure, and a machine that refused to obey the flow of time. If anyone managed to figure out how to fix Gaia, no one wanted it to be her.

Looking around the room, Ryan noticed faces deep in thought. Even Lucy was pressing her lips in a pout, her eyes staring into the distance, probably trying to imagine Gaia.

When Aris and Eleanore strolled in, covered in hard lumpy snow, no one said a word. The family patriarch scanned the room for any volunteers with a tangible solution. It seemed his own expedition was fruitless.

"I might have something, but this is pure speculation," Ryan raised his voice to get everyone's attention. He raised one hand, holding up a rolled-up parchment. "It's a survey of the grounds, but there is something...well, just see for yourselves." He unfurled the map onto the table, placing heavy mugs on each corner to keep it flat.

Everyone huddled over. The map was simple enough; the manor stood in the middle, with gardens surrounding it, followed by a buffer of terrain and the thick forest wall.

"Look," Ryan pointed at a perfectly round patch missing from the tree render in the north. "There is something in that forest. It's not marked or labeled, it's just a gap in the diagram for no apparent reason."

"Then we should check it out," Lucy looked around at the family.

"Yeah, I don't think so," Lai laughed. "The forest is not just a bunch of trees. It's Gaia's defense mechanism. It's ever-generating; there's no way to just cross it. If we get lost there, we're lost for good."

"Gaia is not functioning properly, so its defenses might be down," Eleanore suggested, studying the piece of paper with great curiosity. "It's getting colder by the hour. If you don't find out what is wrong, we'll either freeze here or be forced to abandon ship. If the scale is correct, it's a day's hike, maybe two. Worth a shot."

Eleanore's enthusiasm and willingness to help seemed to unnerve Aris, and Ryan couldn't blame his father. Her help never came without strings attached and always with a hefty price.

"It's decided then." Aris rolled up the map and tucked it into his belt. He gave Ryan a nod of approval, a little gesture that made the cold worth it. "Make your preparations tonight; we will leave in the morning. Bring your bedding here; if we keep the fire going it should be a comfortable night."

CHAPTER TWENTY FOUR

LUCY

As the crowd thinned out, leaving to start the preparations for the night ahead, Lucy followed suit. Aris was ahead of her on top of the grand stairway, heading to the west wing.

What are you doing? You have to get ready. Last night didn't mean anything.

She paused in the hallway, watching her warm breath swirl against the freezing air. Surely she wasn't going to follow that man. Their encounter was nothing more than a spur of the moment fling—a thoughtless act of passion that she herself had put to a stop before it could go too far.

Don't be stupid, Lucy. You're a prisoner. But her body moved before her brain could protest; mere moments later she stood outside Aris' bedroom.

Dancing light from a lit fire shone through the gap under his door. Lucy didn't knock as she let herself in.

Say something, don't just stand there.

Lucy shifted from one foot to another, inching further into the room.

Aris didn't even turn to acknowledge her; she felt like she was little more than a pest to him once more. But there was something in the way the man held himself, the careful distance he kept between them even as Lucy wavered on her convictions; she realized then that he wasn't avoiding her because of childish embarrassment. The tight jaw, the white knuckles and tense shoulders. He wasn't holding back shame, and despite his tenseness he didn't seem to be hateful towards her, not even especially angry. No. He was showing restraint. The taste of raw passion still lingered on their lips and their bodies craved the heat of it once more.

Aris stood with his back to Lucy in a cluttered room, pretending to read something on a yellowed page. Bemused, she could see that the document was blank.

Get a hold of yourself.

"What is in the forest that has everyone so worried?" Lucy asked the first question that popped into her head. Anything was better than the heavy silence.

"You should be getting ready."

"I will once I know what we are up against."

"Close the door, you're letting all the heat out." Aris added a couple more logs to the small furnace that struggled to heat the room. "There are creatures out there, beasts my family produced. We've traded in livestock for centuries, some have escaped."

Lucy frowned. "Like how you breed dogs? Monsters that escaped?"

Aris shook his head.

"My grandfather kept a few dozen girls in this house, constantly producing stock for the business. My father was the last to be born into the trade. Boys were raised until puberty, transformed, and sold as exotic pets or guards."

What the hell does that mean?

"Transformed?" Lucy pressed, moving closer to the fire. "Into pets–with magic?" She couldn't believe what she was hearing, hoping for an answer that would chase away her silly fears. "Is that what Ryan meant when he said that kids were sold? Wait, you didn't bring me here for that, did you?"

Lucy wasn't sure if she wanted to back away towards the exit or come closer and demand answers. She was afraid, but the fear was the logical response. In that moment her heart was in control and in her heart, she knew that she wasn't in any danger.

A deep frown of shame shadowed Aris' face.

"Our bloodline has certain traits that allow for this change to happen. I thought I could break the cycle. Find another way to keep this family running. I was wrong. This house, this sanctuary. It's a money pit. We've sold most of our collection just to stay afloat, but now the debts are crippling us."

"So...you decided to go back to the old ways?"

He didn't answer, turning away from her, but his head dropped in agreement.

Lucy held her breath; she knew her next words would shatter the tension like glass.

"I don't believe you."

"And what makes you say that?" He flinched, suspicious of her mercy, turning to face her.

Lucy hesitated, reaching slowly out to him. Her heart pounded in her throat. "Because I don't believe you're a monster."

He turned, watching her walk across the room, staying well back as if not trusting himself to be alone with her. She couldn't tell what he was thinking. She only hoped that she was right. "I guess I should get my things together."

Aris didn't answer as she turned to leave, waiting until her hand was on the door.

"I didn't say you could go." His voice cut through the air like a whip.

She turned back to face him. "Would you like me to stay?" she asked, hands trembling.

"You are so sure that you have me all figured out," Aris replied. He reached into a crate on his desk, fingers sliding over a thin golden collar.

Lucy swallowed hard but refused to back away. "I know you won't hurt me." It came out as a whisper, but she wasn't afraid. She did have him all figured out; she saw through his bid for control. He had let his entire inheritance fall to ruin before his half-hearted attempt at following in his fathers footsteps. If he had been capable of so much evil, it would have been done long before then.

"You know nothing about me. I own you," Aris whispered. He walked closer to her, leaning into her, his lips almost touching hers. The cold metal collar pressed tight around her neck, buckle stinging her sensitive skin. She didn't fight it; he needed this. The illusion of control.

It didn't hurt that she was excited by it too.

"Don't you dare take it off." He covered their little secret with the high collar of Lucy's sweater.

She nodded, her mouth suddenly dry.

"Good girl."

Lucy bit her tongue, a smart-ass comment dying before it could cross her lips. She was playing a dangerous game and she knew it, but she couldn't stop.

"...and what do I get for being good?" Lucy asked, taking quick, shallow breaths.

"What do you desire?" Aris whispered, kissing the side of her neck with slow and teasing bites.

She tilted her head, allowing him closer, a smile forming on her lips. "The same thing you do."

Control.

CHAPTER TWENTY FIVE

LUCY

The temperature dropped again, forcing everyone back to the warm kitchen. Bags were packed, clothing prepared and food divided. There was little enthusiasm about the trip and the decision was made to leave Eleanore, Lilly, and the kids behind.

Eleanore had made her displeasure very clear, plates and cups smashing against the far wall. When Aris ordered her to stop she insisted that it was keeping her warm.

"Lucy should probably stay too," Lai offered as he curled up by the fire on a pile of furs.

"I'm probably the only one who can help if any of you get hurt," she huffed from the comfort of her mattress, covers pulled up to her chin.

"Okay yeah fair enough, though I'd recommend not reviving anyone using the world's energy. Did enough damage there," he snickered. Lucy launched one of her shoes at her friend with a scowl. He knew damn well that this whole mess was his own fault, but somehow she had been saddled with all the blame. None of this would have happened if he wasn't such a horny little bastard.

Sleep came easily enough that night with Aris's hounds snuggled up against her, their warm bodies keeping her comfortable even after the fire went out, leaving nothing but smoldering coals.

The next morning Klein woke her up with a cup of hot tea, his breath visible even with the fire roaring back into life. "There's some hot water in the basin if you need a quick refresh. We'll be heading out soon," he said with a soft smile. "I found some fur boots, I think they're around your size."

"Good morning," Lucy whispered as she sat up. One of the dogs slid into the warm spot she had left, propping her up. With a grateful smile she reached out and took the tea from Klein. "You're way too kind to me."

"Don't want you getting frostbite," he teased affectionately, his pale face turning a light shade of pink. "Let me know if you need anything else."

She sipped her tea and looked around the room; she was one of the last to rise, the rest of the family was busily packing bags. Only the children were still sleeping, buried under a pile of fur by the fireplace. Lai was attempting to lure Al out of his sleeping bag with promises of coffee and cigarettes, to no avail. Al only bundled up tighter into the blankets.

Aris sat by the fire, talking to his dogs. He had picked three to bring on the expedition. Despite their supernatural heat, they were dressed in stylish fur trimmed jackets and booties, better dressed and prepared than Aris's actual children. The rest of the expedition team were dressed in moldering furs and moth-eaten gloves. Klein was stuffing scrunched up newspaper down the front of his coat for extra warmth.

Eleanore's mood had changed completely overnight; she had volunteered herself to stay back and keep an eye on the house as if it was her own idea, claiming that with her ship's engines seized up with ice, she was better off inside. She was a convincing actress, wearing the mask of care and concern for the family, but Lucy hadn't missed the hungry light in her eyes every time Gaia was mentioned.

Lucy tugged on the boots Klein had found, reluctant to leave the comfort of her warm bed. The boots were a touch too big but with few layers of socks the fur lining hugged her feet quite comfortably. She pulled on layer after layer of clothes, wondering how much warmth the flimsy cardigans would provide. As if reading her mind, the blizzard howled outside, eager to devour them.

"I'm not sure how practical this will be..." Lai buttoned up a luxurious mink fur coat he had found in one of the rooms. "But it's warm, and so soft. Here, stroke me," he leaned in towards Lucy. "I have more if you want one," he pointed to a whole pile of rich furs. Most of them had seen better days, but a few were still perfectly plush. Short blue arctic fox coats, long minks, and throws made of animals Lucy couldn't put a name to.

"Is it warm?" She stroked the fur of Lai's jacket.

"Yeah, I slept naked in it."

"You–" Lucy laughed and leaned forward like she was whispering a secret. "You know under all these clothes I'm naked, right?"

"Yeah, but so are the dogs under their fur. Doesn't mean I want to fuck them," he whispered back and pinched her thigh with a grin.

Her playful punch connected with Lai's chest. He tripped over Al, falling into his lap in a way that almost looked like he hadn't meant to land on the man's thighs. With a groan Al pushed Lai off of him, feeling around for his phone and shoes. Klein offered Al a pair of ancient snow boots; his canvas sneakers wouldn't save the man from frostbite for more than a minute.

"Get dressed," Lai laughed as he threw Lucy a long coat. "We're heading out."

Lucy nodded and gathered her things. She felt the weight of the collar hidden around her neck and shivered–she had almost forgotten it was there, a reminder from the night before. Her fingers reached up to it instinctively but she quickly drew them back, not wanting to attract any attention to the strange accessory.

The bags and coats were divided amongst the party and they reluctantly ventured into the freezing weather, struggling to even clear the garden past the waist-deep snow. The headwind felt like a thousand needles piercing their skin, as if the forest warned them to stay away.

***

Almost two hours had passed before they reached the edge of the woods, something that could have been achieved in less than thirty minutes on a nice sunny day. Every step felt more difficult than the one before, with heavy snow sticking in clumps to their clothing, weighing them down.

If nothing else then at least the forest looked pretty, the trees blanketed in heavy glittering fluff. They provided enough cover from the wind to ease their journey, welcoming the party into an icy wonderland. Lucy had a hard time believing all the warnings about the forest. It looked harmless, beautiful even, sparkling in the rays of yesterday's sunrise.

"I hate this," she muttered despite her awe. "It's so damn cold!"

"Thank you, Captain Obvious," Al laughed, shielding his eyes from low hanging branches. "I had to take time off work to help you sorry lot. I definitely can't afford that. If anyone should be complaining, it's me."

Lai groaned, trying to follow in Al's footsteps. "Do you think that's bad? We only have one tent."

"Don't worry, baby brother. Dog farts will keep you warm," Klein teased.

"An awful lot of complaining coming from the peanut gallery!" Aris yelled against the wind. He walked ahead of the group, making it easier for others to follow. The hounds trotted close to their master with only the tips of their ears showing from the deep snow.

***

They decided to stop for the first break around midday, finding makeshift shelter behind a collapsed tree. Morale was low, and even a thermos of hot tea didn't help much. Lucy hugged one of the hounds, warming her hands on the dog's toasty belly, thankful for the heat on her numb fingertips.

"Well, this sucks, but we're closer to fixing this mess than we were," she offered, hoping to lighten the atmosphere. "I refuse to be trapped in this forest."

"I don't think the forest cares what you refuse to do," Aris got up, signaling a start to another march through the unforgiving wilderness. They had barely gotten twenty yards before he paused, spotting a shadow lurking in the distance, stalking the group. He raised his hand, ordering everyone to halt.

"What is it?" Lai muttered, pulling a dagger from under his coat, his numb and trembling hands unable to effectively wield it.

The hounds sensed it, too, their hackles raised. Focused, glowing eyes followed the slowly moving form, growling low as a warning to the creature.

Lucy glanced up at Aris, staying close to others. She didn't want to show fear, but being stalked in the forest activated a primal response.

Instinctively, she reached for anyone's hand, finding an offer of comfort and protection in Lai's grip. "One of your relatives?" she tried to joke, but it sounded somehow familiar.

"Could be," Lai answered when his father did not. "I hear them sometimes at night, but they never come close. I assume they are runaways from the old regime."

"Whatever they are, they are not friendly and are most likely hungry." Aris took a few steps forward, his dogs following. "Come out! Stop hiding like a coward!"

A blood-curdling snarl echoed around them. The creature abandoned the safety of tree cover at last, revealing itself. It stood ten feet tall, with two enormous heads; one a lion and the other a goat, a fine golden chain around each head's neck. Its lashing tail hissed, spitting venom.

With shaking hands, Klein raised a tranquilizing gun; it wouldn't help and he knew it. The chimera was too big; it would kill them all before even noticing it had been stung. And that was only if the guns' firing mechanism wasn't frozen stiff.

The creature closed the distance between them as Aris's hounds rushed forward, charging recklessly into the fight. As their sharp teeth ripped into the beast's flesh it surrendered, lowering itself in submission.

"Girls, back!" Aris ordered. His pets obeyed their master's command without a moment of hesitation, jumping off the creature, their bloody maws dripping crimson over the perfectly white snow. The Chimera was still, its breath trembling and shallow.

"Why aren't you fighting?" Aris approached the beast, a hatchet in his hand for protection. He knelt by its side, cautious but concerned, his hand resting on a dinner-plate-sized paw.

The goat's head lifted, bleating in agony at the gray sky, the warbling cry carrying far enough to scare a flock of birds in the distance.

"Is it–?" Klein walked up to his father.

Another bleating howl escaped the goat's mouth.

Then another one.

Again and again, the Chimera cried out, wailing until everyone understood the words within the bellow of the beast.

Kill me.

"Kill me," the goat pleaded. "Kill me."

"I was afraid of this." Aris took a deep breath, placing his hand on the lion's head.

"The poor thing must have been trapped in here for decades. What are we going to do?" Klein looked up at his father, shaking his head. He already knew what would happen to it.

"You can't kill it!" Lucy cried out, squeezing Lai's hand. She was met with nothing but mournful silence. "It's your family, isn't it? They're hurt, they need help–"

Klein, not Lai, cut her off; his hand rested heavily on her shoulder.

"Lucy. Do you remember the statue you saw in the garden? The woman with two tails?" he asked, softly, with a finality in his voice that made Lucy's blood run cold.

"The mother of all monsters. Lucy, we are the monsters; we are the sons of Echidna. We know what needs to be done."

"There are worse things than death." Aris pulled a large hunting knife from his boot.

"No, you can help them, this isn't fair. Put the knife down!" She ran over, leaning her entire weight on his arm, but Aris pushed her effortlessly aside.

"Sometimes this is the kindest thing you can do. One day you will understand." He sunk the serrated blade into Chimera's rib cage, twisting it when it reached its destination. A fast, merciful kill, deep into its heart.

The creature howled, snake tail twisting in its final death throes. Its eyes locked onto Lucy's then dulled, glazing over as life left its body, finally at rest.

A few minutes passed in silence as the group watched the blood soak the frozen ground around the beast. Then with a gentle shift the form of the creature melted away, leaving behind the corpse of a young boy; the golden chain around his throat crumbled into dust.

"Rest now." Aris picked his limp body, brushing away messy black curls. "Boys, help me clear the snow. He deserves a proper send-off."

No one dared to protest, the somber atmosphere dampening spirits even further. A pyre was out of the question with the high snow and lack of dry wood. The ground was frozen solid, so a grave couldn't be dug either.

"We'll have to do this the old fashioned way." Aris picked up his ax, balancing the weapon in one hand.

Klein glanced at the sun moving around the sky in wild patterns. "Do we have time?"

"To bury family? Yes." He passed the boy to his eldest and found a tree large enough, making quick work of chopping it down.

"What's the old fashioned way?" Lucy asked, avoiding looking at the dead child in Klein's arms, her eyes swelling with tears that burned in contact with the freezing air.

"Tree trunk coffin," Klein answered, watching Aris chop out a hollow with quick, powerful swings. Chips of wood flew out in every direction, hardened wood carved out like butter.

Klein placed the child inside once the niche was big enough, and Aris covered him with a makeshift lid of bark. No words were uttered during the sobering ceremony; silence spoke to the volumes of their grief. None of them had ever met the poor soul before, or even knew his name, but every member of the family knew his story. Lucy pushed down the questions she wanted to ask. It wasn't the time for them. Instead she plucked a pine tree branch decorated with a cluster of pinecones, the closest thing she could find to a flower or a wreath, and placed it down on the lid.

The march continued once the snow began to settle on the coffin.

They had to keep moving or join the unfortunate in the freezing wasteland, a fate they wanted to avoid.

With suffocating thoughts of mortality, the rest of the day passed in an uneventful blur. Aris seemed to know where he was going, an old compass and the map as his navigation tools. Thankfully, the sunset was almost on time, darkness settling in at six in the evening.

The heavy bags were finally set down for the night with relieved sighs, and a camp was built with a single tent. The canvas shelter was big enough for everyone to fit in comfortably, but no fire could be lit. Giving away their location in a forest full of hungry creatures seemed unwise. All they had for warmth was each other and the hellhounds, the latter providing most of the heat, mixed with the stench of sulfur.

"Lai, get your hand off my ass," Lucy huffed, punching his shoulder as hard as she could in the confined space.

"It's on your thigh, and my hands are freezing, have some sympathy."

"I know they are, that's why I don't want them on me," she said, her teeth chattering. The last thing she needed was cold hands on any part of her, regardless of whose they were.

"Keep your paws to yourself, boy," Aris sent one of the dogs to sit between the two of them, the heat of its body helping to lessen the chill.

That amused Lucy; she looked over to Aris, trying not to smirk, focusing her attention on the dog. The hound pressed her warm body against Lucy's, enjoying the attention and a satisfying scratch.

Once everyone had settled Klein passed around a light supper and a thermos of barely warm tea. Tired and grumpy, the party devoured the meal of cold cuts and bread. The day's travel had exhausted everyone mentally and physically, so a full stomach and a night's rest were welcomed with as much enthusiasm as they could muster. Lucy considered asking everyone to take a shift as a sentinel, but upon seeing their exhausted faces she decided to trust the dogs to keep an ear out.

"Everyone get some sleep, tuck yourselves next to each other to preserve heat," Aris ordered as he left the tent to do one last perimeter check, returning only after fully satisfied that they were safe. He slipped inside past one of the hounds that seemed perfectly happy to keep watch outside and took the last available spot behind Lucy.

"You're freezing," she mumbled to Aris. "Try to get warm. The last thing we need is for you to catch something."

"I'm fine," he answered back but moved closer, slipping under the fur coat she used as a blanket.

"Sure you are."

"Don't test me, girl," Aris murmured, hoping not to wake anyone up. Minutes passed in silence with only the soft breathing of the exhausted and sleeping group filling the tent.

She felt his hand around her waist. Heavy and comforting and strangely safe in his embrace, Lucy quickly fell asleep.

CHAPTER TWENTY SIX

LUCY

It was light outside when the dog's barking woke everyone, alerting them of danger stalking the camp. They circled the tent, snarling at the hidden enemy, protective of their family as they watched the surrounding thick wood.

"Everyone up." Aris grabbed his ax, following his dogs outside, not bothering with his coat.

Lucy sat up, frantically rubbing sleep from her eyes. For a moment, she forgot she was in a tent in the middle of the forest, disoriented. Then the bitter cold, the hushed voices, and the memories of the previous night settled over her, stirring feelings Lucy wasn't ready to deal with yet. She quickly got dressed, buttoning up her heavy fur coat. Outside, the birds that had been welcoming the sun fell suddenly silent.

Lucy had just stumbled from the tent when a red-breasted robin landed on a branch close by. As she watched, he opened his beak, but he didn't sing. Instead, a shrill siren filled the air, all of the birds in the trees mimicking the noise, filling the forest with ominous alarm.

"What's that sound?" Lucy covered her ears as the noise sent chills down her spine.

"An alarm? That's what it sounds like to me." Al picked up a small rock, throwing it at the bird. It fell onto the ground, injured and motionless, but continued with the eerie symphony.

"Gaia, what the fuck?!" Lai stomped his foot. "Cut it out!"

The siren ended abruptly, drowning the forest in deathly silence. Countless birds watched the group, black eyes focused on the camp.

"Defense protocol suspended," A voice came from somewhere far above.

Lai took a breath of relief, looking around smugly. His gloating lasted for all of three seconds.

"Offense protocol initiated."

"That doesn't sound good," Lucy said, looking around into the forest, suddenly feeling very vulnerable.

"What's the offense protocol?" Aris asked, to no one in particular. "I didn't even know there was one. Klein? You're in this forest the most."

Klein didn't answer, his face pale with dread.

"What's going on?" Lucy asked Klein. "What's the offense protocol?"

"Hear that buzzing?" He swallowed hard, tossing his bag into the snow, ready to run. The silent forest slowly hummed into life around them. "Remember the faeries?"

"What, like Fish?"

"Yeah, like her. That's what a swarm of her sounds like." Klein looked over to his father for guidance, like a young child that expected his parent to have an answer for everything.

The fear in the group was palpable. The men knew their limits; one giant beast was a fair fight, but a thousand vicious monsters weren't something they could face and live.

"We need a decoy," Aris decided. "Everyone go. Run! Make for the clearing. I'll keep them away, get Gaia back under control and make her stop them."

The order was absolute and left no room for questions or hesitation. He expected the same level of obedience from his sons as from his dogs—the latter hesitating, refusing to abandon their master.

"Make sure no one gets left behind. Go!" He urged the hounds to follow the group, but the loyal pets disobeyed the order for the first time, pressing their warm bodies against their master's legs. They would give up their lives fighting the swarm without a moment's hesitation. "You have to protect them. Please." Aris lifted Scarlet's snout, pleading with her. Reluctantly the dog obeyed, licking Aris's hand one last time before leading her sisters into the woods.

Lucy braved the deep snow, moving as fast as her bulky clothing allowed. She tried not to listen as the swarm descended on Aris, desperately ignoring his howls of pain as he disappeared beneath the frenzied cloud of vermin. She stumbled, wanting to go back, knowing there was no way to save him.

"Get up, get up!" Lai grabbed her arm, dragging the woman behind him. "Don't stop. You can't help him."

"But, he's–" Lucy struggled against Lai's grip, turning to make her way back to Aris, her hand out to snatch at the strings of life that made up the swarm, cursing herself for not thinking of it sooner, but the only life force she could feel was his. Still strong but rapidly fading, the golden thread barely reached her fingertips.

"Don't." Lai jerked her back. "This is not the time to play hero."

Swallowing the bitter despair and disappointment, Lucy fought her way through the snow. Lai was right, she was powerless against a foe like that and being reckless would only cause Aris's sacrifice to be in vain. They were almost at the clearing.

"Girl lied to Fish."

The familiar voice caught Lucy off guard; she tripped and was pinned down in the snow by dozens of the faeries she had thought were so pretty only a few weeks ago. She struggled to roll onto her side, panting roughly in fear.

"Fish queen now," the faerie grinned, landing on Lucy's chest. "But girl not bring cake. So queen order liars death."

"I'm sorry," Lucy gasped, terror seeping into her bones, paralyzing her.

"Not sorry yet, but soon."

Steel sang inches away from Lucy's ear as a dagger flew by, skewered one of the faeries and pierced through shell-like armor. Within a breath the blade's owner retrieved it from the dead creature.

"Get up; it's gonna get messy," Lai pressed the weapon into Lucy's hand, tearing faeries away from her as Fish leapt into the air with a menacing hiss.

He unsheathed a second matching dagger, plunging it through a faerie as it clawed at his face, the dark blood of the dead fae spluttering over his hands. Lucy watched him in awe, still frozen in place with shock. Every thrust of the dagger was smooth and vicious, finding its target without fail. He made it look effortless.

Her own confidence ignited, burning like fuel, its flame fanned by grief and anger. She staggered to her feet and lunged at the swarm's queen. The creature moved through the air with startling agility, her wings barely visible as she hovered just out of the dagger's reach. Stabbing the empty air again and again, Lucy felt her strength drain. Her arms got heavier, her movements slowed, and the determined fae mocked her as she fought.

"Go, keep running." Klein put himself between her and a handful of vermin, hitting a few of them with the heavy branch he wielded like a club. Slowly they battled their way towards the clearing. The main swarm had fallen back but a few determined fairies continued their pursuit, attacking mercilessly with sharp claws that tore at clothing and exposed flesh. The hounds snatched them from the air, snapping the faeries' hollow bones with ease, while others met their end at Lai's dagger or Al's bare hands.

The desperate escape felt like it had taken hours and it almost looked like they might win the battle; the clearing was right behind them, free from snow and invitingly warm against their backs. Lucy's heart soared, then plummeted to her toes. The swarm had returned to protect their queen, filling the air with an evil buzz of insectile wings.

"Should have bought cake," Fish teased cruelly. It seemed like such a trivial thing to die over. Lucy almost laughed at how unfair it was. She took a step back, eyes closed, bracing herself.

The attack never came; Lucy opened her eyes. Fish hovered in front of her, fury and hate all over her tiny face.

"Luce–" Lai whispered from behind her, breathless and awestruck. "Lucy, look. I don't think they can come in."

Lucy looked; there was no snow trapping her legs, and no trees for the faeries to hide in. They had made it to the clearing. The furious insects clawed at her from the woods, but shrank back from the warmth of the circle. Finally, defeated, they retreated into the forest, the drone of their wings fading into silence.

The battered group stood motionless, barely daring to believe their luck. Lai finally broke the silence, glancing at his brother. "Should we divide the inheritance now or...?" he asked with a shaky grin.

"Shut up, Lai," Lucy snapped. She looked to Klein but his gaze only swept over her knotted, windblown hair, looking back at the abandoned battlefield. She didn't want to think about the man they had left behind, grief burning her chest, making it hard to breathe.

Al examined their surroundings as the brothers quietly bickered.

"Hey, guys? We've got company," he called to them as he shrugged off his heavy jacket, pointing to the far side of the clearing.

A young woman sat in the shade of a tree, knees hugged to her chest and full lips pressed in a pout. She looked human enough, but her glowing green skin flickered with sporadic pixelation. She barely acknowledged the group, her long narrow fingers plucked the grass blades in agitation as the dogs sniffed in her direction, confused by her lack of scent.

Could it be?

"Hello?" Lucy asked cautiously, handing Lai back his dagger and sliding off her fur coat, face red with sweat and covered in countless scratches. Slowly she moved towards the girl, Lai and Klein flanking as Al held the hounds in check.

"Admin username and password," the green girl demanded sullenly, narrowing her glowing yellow eyes. *'G.A.I.A'* was written on the girl's forearm in polished gold letters.

The awe in the face of the technology that didn't belong in her lifetime brought Lucy to her knees. The machine before her looked so alive yet still mechanical. Smooth screen-like skin stretched over muscle flowing with golden liquid, wires and moving parts all carefully hidden away behind clean panels on Gaia's thighs.

"Admin username and password."

Lucy looked at Lai, expecting him to have answers. Lai only shrugged; he was just as lost as she was. She turned to Klein instead. "Who set up Gaia?"

Klein shook his head. "It was set up long before we got here. I was expecting a computer terminal or something. We should've brought Ryan."

Lucy was not great with computers but she had to try. "Okay. Um. 'New User'?" she offered optimistically.

"Please provide admin username and password to create a new user," Gaia poked her tongue at her. Lucy scowled back, unimpressed with her bratty behavior.

"What's with the attitude?" she complained, poking Gaia's shoulder; her fingertip buzzed unpleasantly with pins and needles when it touched the girl.

"Why should I be nice to the person who drained my batteries? I'm exhausted, and it's all your fault."

"I'm sorry! It was an accident, I had no idea I was gonna hurt you," Lucy protested; she didn't think she deserved the entire blame for what had happened.

"Admin username and password, please," Gaia answered coldly.

"Come on, there's no need to be like that," Lucy gave her an apologetic smile. "I'm Lucy." She offered a handshake, unsure of how else to show goodwill.

Gaia ignored the gesture. "Wrong username."

Lucy groaned in defeat as Lai shrugged. "How about 'Admin, admin'?" He offered as a joke; it was the same password that he used for everything.

The green hue of her skin darkened, yellow eyes flashing in a fierce outburst of light.

"Welcome to the G.A.I.A interface," she answered with a roll of her eyes, her skin flickering angrily as it regained its regular color.

Everyone stared at Lai.

"There is no way that the person who was smart enough to make all of this would be dumb enough to leave the password on its default," Al insisted in disbelief.

Lai grinned, pleased with himself. "Are you kidding? If it was one of our family then they were definitely that dumb."

Klein shook his head wearily. "Gaia, we need the cold to stop. Initiate Spring sequence."

Gaia didn't spare Klein a glance, busy glaring at Lucy. Not that Lucy could blame her; she had every right to be upset.

"I cannot. I only have enough power to maintain this area," she finally offered. Klein nodded, pleased that she was willing to talk to him.

"What can we do to give you more energy?"

She shrugged, giving Lucy a sidelong glance. "This has never been a problem before."

"Sorry about that," Lucy muttered quietly, stepping behind Klein to avoid the constant reminder of her actions.

Gaia scanned the muddy slush around her safe area, examining the snow-heavy trees beyond. "I can tone it down a bit. I guess I lost my cool," she admitted. For a second she had the same sheepish look on her face as Lucy, and Lucy could have sworn that the air felt a bit warmer.

"Please. I really am sorry," Lucy said.

Gaia's eyes glowed brighter as the snow around them melted rapidly, the forest losing its white blanket cover, leaving behind bare trees. It was still cold, but nothing like the arctic freeze it had been. "I can't get anything to grow just yet. I'm sorry."

"Will the forest creatures still attack us?" Klein asked, shedding more of his clothing as the temperature stabilized.

"Not if I'm with you."

"Good. We need to go back for your dad," Lucy told Lai. He frowned, glancing towards the tree line. "Yeah, let's go then. It's strange that he hasn't caught up to us yet."

Lucy paused at that; she didn't want to dash Lai's hopes but she doubted there was much left of Aris. She only wanted to collect his remains, her throat catching suddenly as grief caught up with her.

She held out her hand to Gaia, a warm laser matrix tracing her fingers as the girl scanned Lucy's hand. Gaia hesitated, but after a moment's calculation she accepted the offer, placing her hand in Lucy's and pulling herself to her feet. Beneath the gold paint on her arm, Lucy noticed a logo she recognized– the intricate, stylized FW of the Farrowatcher Corporation.

***

Gaia led the group back to the spot of woods where they had been attacked; without knee-high snow the journey only took ten minutes. The swarm of faeries that had stayed to fight Aris scattered upon seeing Gaia, fleeing to the trees.

All that was left of Aris was a mountain of black fur, half buried in the melting snow and drenched with blood.

"Oh shit," Lai muttered. "This is bad." He ran to Aris, kneeling beside the man who seemed too big somehow. As he rolled Aris over Lucy cried out in shock; the black fur wasn't the coat that Aris had been wearing. It was him; at least she thought it was him, her knees giving out beneath her again as Lai checked over the massive, two headed dog that had once been his father. He knelt by one of the heads, looking tiny compared to the beast which must have been at least six feet tall, murmuring reassurances.

The dog whimpered. It tried to open its eyes, but their injuries were too grave. Lucy heard Lai stifling a sob, her heart twisting at his pain. Klein swayed on his feet, numb with shock. Neither of them had really believed that their father could be toppled.

"What is he?" Lucy whispered, trying to keep the alarm out of her voice as putrid fear climbed into her throat. No one looked at her, all of them watching Aris take his last breaths.

"Orthrus." Al flicked the smoldering end of his cigarette. "Cerberus's two headed cousin."

Lucy felt a prickle in her fingertips. Golden threads were seeping from the beast as its life leaked away; she scooped them up in her hands, holding onto them as wild hope flared in her heart. She could save him– if she could just find something to sacrifice in return, she could save him.

"No!" Lai grabbed Lucy's hand.

She fell back, glancing up angrily at him. "What? Why the hell not?!"

"Because you can't control it!" Lai held her wrist in his steel-like grip.

"I'm getting better!" she yelled. She couldn't believe that Lai would try to stop her. She refused to let Aris die. Not when she had the power to stop it. Her eyes and voice darkened as she moved toward the beast. "Let go of my hand, Lai, or you're going to get hurt."

"No," Lai repeated, pulling her away. "You can't. What are you going to drain? You'll kill one of us to bring him back."

She held back tears, powerless to save Aris. Her wrist turned red in Lai's grip as he dragged her away from him, his face contorted in a cruel grimace. She had never seen Lai like that; he had always seemed harmless and carefree. Has it all been a show? The rows of poison in his room, and the visions gleaned from his memories, she saw it clearly—Lai was a man who killed without remorse.

"This is why I'm here, Lai –to help! He takes care of this place, he's your father! Don't you want him to survive?"

"That's a different tune to what you sang when you first got here," Lai shook his head. "You are dangerous; why can't you see that? Haven't you caused enough death already?" Every word was designed to diminish her, to shrink her, until she was so small that she could slip between the dead leaves that littered the ground.

"Enough. Let go of her!" A loud slap echoed through the wood. Lai dropped her hand, clutching his red cheek; Klein's forceful hit had sent his brother reeling backward, giving Lucy space.

A fight seemed imminent as tension rose, both siblings watching each other's actions, ready to strike. Lucy noticed that Lai's posture shrank into a defensive stance; he was afraid of Klein.

"Enough! All of you!" Al growled, getting in between the quarreling brothers. "Have you lost your minds?! Kill each other when we get back! Lai, is there any way we can change Aris back to human? I don't want to try to drag that thing back to the house."

"I'm surprised he hasn't turned back already, to be honest." Klein gave Lai a warning glare as he knelt by his father, placing his hand on the dark fur and stroking it soothingly. "The change into beast takes place once the human body is dead. If you die changed as well, that's the end of the line. You revert to human for easy disposal, I guess."

As one the group deflated. Lucy refused to even attempt to understand the bizarre process, watching Aris's massive chest rise and fall with labored gasps.

"Should we set camp here? If we have a first aid kit, we can try to bandage his wounds. He is strong, you know…" She sighed, feeling utterly useless.

"You are determined to take away my inheritance today, aren't you?" Lai rolled his eyes, kicking one of Aris's massive paws.

CHAPTER TWENTY SEVEN

KLEIN

"I'll get the first aid kit; I did pack one. I doubt there will be enough bandages though," Klein offered, digging through Aris's discarded bag and pulling out a small white case. Lai and Al were trying to set up the tent, tripping over Gaia as she stubbornly refused to help. The dogs curled around Aris, keeping him warm.

"It's human-sized, mainly for minor cuts. I don't know how effective it will be."

"Thank you." Lucy forced a tired smile as she took the kit, examining its contents. A few small rolls of bandages, scissors, a needle and thread, and a few sealed pouches of saline solution for cleaning wounds.

They would do very little, but Klein knew that she needed to do something. Anything was better than feeling so powerless. Lai and he both felt that Aris would pull through, but it was the roughest shape he had ever seen his father in.

"I know these past few days have been intense, but are you alright?" Klein sat down beside Aris to help her, pushing a hellhound out of the way. "I don't doubt you have many questions. It's probably something I should have mentioned but I hoped it wouldn't come to that. You seeing this form, I mean."

"I do, but I'll get my answers later. Right now we need to help him." Lucy cleaned the cuts with the saline, trying not to cause the beast more pain. "I'm alright."

No one is alright, Lucy.

Klein didn't look so sure, watching her as he threaded a needle with waxy thread for her.

"It's been a bizarre few days," she said with a heavy sigh, not bothering to elaborate any further.

That he could agree with. The dinner, Gaia, and this whole expedition. All certainly out of norm but Klein felt like she meant something else. Guilt lingering over her soft features. She picked up a needle and, with shaking fingers, pierced the beast's skin.

The orthrus whined as she stitched squirming in discomfort.

"Hey, hold still. You're hurt."

He growled, flinching from the touches.

"Calm down. I know it's not pleasant but I have to clean your cuts. Some of them are deep."

"Good luck convincing him. You know how stubborn he is on a good day." Klein held the paw in place. "Want me to tranquilize him?"

"That might be the only way he gets some rest," Lucy sighed. "Let us help you, you grumpy old fuck."

"A couple of those should do the trick," Klein slid a few of the darts from his gun. "I use these on the griffins during health checks, but I think it will take down even someone as uncooperative as him."

Lucy stepped back to let Klein do his job. "Hey, Klein? Are the griffins...?"

"No, not as far as we know. Women can't transform," he assured her. She breathed out a sigh of relief, watching as Klein administered the dose. Aris's labored breaths slowly softened into deep, peaceful snores.

CHAPTER TWENTY EIGHT

LAI

"How is the old man?" Lai tossed a twig into the fire, watching the flames consume it.

Lucy joined him back at the camp, hugging her knees.

"Stubborn," she decided. She looked exhausted, gray and drawn, shivering despite the warmth.

"Figured as much."

A piece of a chocolate bar appeared on her knee. She gladly accepted.

"What for? Are you trying to apologize for something?" She gave him a tired look. "What about telling me what the hell your little display was about?"

Lai scooted closer, placing another piece down. He did feel guilty, a feeling he wasn't fond of, especially knowing he had no excuse for his outburst. It was a difficult topic that wreaked havoc on his life and relationships, but he'd learned to manage it as the years had passed. Mostly. He had always struggled with apologies, but he'd hurt his friend. He'd scared her. He'd scared himself.

"Didn't pack my pills," he sighed. "But it's not an excuse. I know that. I used it as a hall pass for shitty behavior for the longest time before I got help. I'm sorry for scaring you, Luce; today's been a shitshow, and I've never seen my father like that. I freaked out."

No one would have blamed her if she rejected the clumsy not-apology, but she scooped Lai into a rough hug, her arm around his neck, squeezing a little too tight. Despite the air getting cut off to his brain, Lai let out a sigh of relief, snagging back a piece of the candy offering.

"You okay?" he asked into her shoulder.

"Why wouldn't I be?" she muttered as she released him.

"You look kind of distracted. Or is that just your face?" Lai teased. He had forgiven himself, content to snuggle up next to her.

"Rude."

He poked his tongue out, watching the fire. "You know, I'm glad you're here."

"Why's that?" Lucy asked, resting her head on his shoulder.

"It's been awfully dull for the past few years. No one ever talked to each other–we'd pretended to be a family at mealtimes, but it was just playing house. No one meant what they said and no one said what they meant."

"I dunno about that. Your brother does a lot for you all, and Ryan is a perfect older brother for Lou."

"Yeah, yeah. I'm purely decorative."

"You bring a fun energy, and you help keep them in line."

"That's a new way of calling me chaotic," he laughed, playing with her hair. "Besides, I don't mind being decorative. Someone has to be. Are you sure you're okay?"

He noticed her eyes, sad and unfocused. Staring into the fire and beyond.

"Just wondering what had become of my life. In a few short weeks some strangers became like a family. I didn't think Stockholm syndrome could kick in that fast."

Oh Lucy…

He wrapped one arm around her, squeezing the woman tighter. In fact he felt something similar. Despite his better judgment, he had become attached to his new friend. She just…fit in. Slotting perfectly into the empty place in their strange family.

Stop being mushy. You know that you'll only get hurt if you get close to her.

"Wanna go poke at my father? Got your phone on you?" He got up, sobering himself up with cool air, away from the mellow heat of the campfire.

"I do. What did you have in mind?"

"Take pictures," Lai grinned. "Hunting trophy style."

"Absolutely not! He's hurt, and he might—"

"He won't. He isn't going to leave his beloved dogs…and we will laugh about it someday. Come on. Imagine him seeing those later."

"He's going to hate that, huh? I'm down," she nodded. Lai was pleased; his chaos was a distraction he was always far too happy to offer.

"Let's go." He grinned as he tugged his boots back on. "Before someone ruins our brilliant plan."

Klein and Al were quietly chatting by the tent, paying them no attention, so no one was going to interrupt their little mischief. The two-headed hound had shifted onto its side, still in deep and restful sleep. Its broad chest rose with each breath, both heads snoring in perfect unison.

"He looks so peaceful…"

"Don't go soft on me now, the man is an asshole." Lai grabbed a clump of soft fur and pulled himself up, climbing on top of the sleeping giant and striking a pose, flexing for Lucy as she snapped a few candid photos. He posed with his dagger outstretched as if riding the mighty beast into battle, then stretched out beside Aris and pulled his massive paw over himself, feigning sleep. Finally done with his juvenile fun, he examined the final shots.

"Your turn! I'll hold his mouth open. Climb in."

"You want it to look like your father is eating me?"

Lai smirked, taking the phone from her.

"Please, I'm not a damsel in distress." She knelt next to the sleeping creature, blowing smoke from a finger gun, her other hand lifting the soft jowls, displaying a row of lethal teeth as long as her finger.

"You were right, this is kinda fun." She climbed on top, careful of his cuts. Lai clumsily joined her, straddling the beast's strong neck.

"See, that ass is healing fast." He parted the thick fur, showing her a cut that had almost closed already. "So don't worry your pretty little head. He'll be fine."

Lucy almost cried with relief, hugging Aris around the neck, face buried in thick black fur. "You two aren't particularly close, huh?" she asked, eyes closed.

We could have been.

A moment of heavy silence followed before Lai offered a shrug in reply. Their relationship was complicated. Both men dwelled on their guilt and had never bothered to talk it out. "He didn't cope well after mom died. I coped worse. She and I were very close. He did all he could to save her and when he couldn't he dropped himself into a well filled with booze and self-pity. I tend to partake in more volatile methods of self destruction when dealing with grief."

"What did you do?"

"I ran away. Ended up in a pretty fucked up situation. I was nine."

"How did you survive on your own?"

"You don't want to know."

They lapsed into silence as Lai took a deep breath, waving away the unhappy thoughts. They were supposed to be having fun. "Don't worry, my tragic backstory isn't all gloom and daddy issues. I've traveled through dozens of worlds and met so many amazing people. So don't feel sorry for me, okay?"

An indignant gasp cut their fun short. "What are the two of you doing? Lai, get down from your father immediately! Lucy!"

Lucy blushed furiously, embarrassed to be caught by Klein. She slid down off of Aris's back and landed in a damp pile of leaves, muddy and ashamed.

"Please return to the camp. I need to beat some manners into my brother." Klein grabbed Lai's ear, yanking him down from the sleeping beast.

CHAPTER TWENTY NINE

AL

"What was all the commotion about?" Al asked, nursing a cigarette. He sat on a log near the tent, watching the forest, bored out of his mind. Camping was not his happy place.

"Lai got us in trouble," Lucy mumbled, red-faced.

"If I had a penny...Come grab a seat, don't be a stranger. We've barely said three words to each other." He moved over, making some room for her on the log.

She joined him, stretched out her legs. "You're right. Any questions for me?"

"Hmmm." Al looked her up and down. "What's your usual coffee order?"

"Double chocolate chip frappuccino."

"Interesting," Al nodded, as if that was all the information he needed. "I'll be seeing you pretty often if you're staying here, I'll try to remember what to bring next time."

"Thanks," she smiled. "Your sister said you're in cybersecurity? I think? Hard to remember."

"Nah, just private security. I also bounce at my friend's strip club at night and drive for Uber on weeknights."

"Sounds like you're a man of many talents. If you ever feel like doing security full time for the big bucks you could apply to Farrowatcher Corp, they only do high ticket jobs. Good benefits too, my parents used to work for them."

Al suppressed a shudder. He was with the Farrowatcher Corporation for at least one of their branches. His boss was probably tearing his voicemail apart, Al was meant to be back today. He didn't want to bore Lucy with details of his life. It wasn't exactly exciting. "How are you finding your new job?"

"It's a lot more… permanent than I'd like."

"Guess it's not what you signed up for?"

"You could say that. I haven't even been paid yet."

"You do know you're not gonna be paid, right? The manor looks the way it does for a reason." Al glanced around to make sure that no one was listening. He was fond of Lai's family, but he knew their history. He couldn't stomach the idea of Lucy being trapped there.

"Listen. I shouldn't be doing this, but if you want to get out..."

"I do. I just want to make sure I have this under control first."

She held up her hands. They looked normal, soft and pink from the cold. It was hard to believe that they were capable of giving and taking life with just a touch. Al leaned over to her, taking her hands lightly between his own; they tingled a little as her magic shrank away from his touch.

"How does that feel?"

"Woah–" Lucy swayed a little. "Like pressure behind my eyes deflated. I feel hollow and strange. Is that your magic?"

"Pretty much the exact opposite, actually. 'The null field' is what the eggheads named it." Al examined her hands in his. "Like an air filter for magic."

"Lai's lucky to have you around." She rubbed the goosebumps that ran up her arms as her power trickled back into her skin.

Al could feel the residue from the woman's magic dance in his fingertips before settling deep inside of him, pooling with every other drop of magic that had passed into his body. For just a split second he could feel the frayed strings of life around him, but the alien sensation dulled down and soon disappeared altogether.

"That's strange." He rubbed his tongue against the roof of his mouth. It felt numb, an unfamiliar aftertaste lingering.

"What's strange?"

"Your magic. It's not anything like I've ever experienced before."
He tried to explain, even though he didn't understand it entirely himself.
"Magic has a flavor to it, like wine. The older the magic, the deeper and
sweeter the taste."

Lucy shifted closer, hugging her knees against her chest. That must
not have not sounded reassuring. "What's wrong with mine? What does
it taste like?"

"Almost like vinegar. It burns a little," Al explained. That wasn't
quite right, but it was the best he could offer.

"Are you saying my magic has soured?"

"What? No." He shook his head. "It's ancient. At least, that is how
I interpret it. It also doesn't taste real. Like–you know how you can
taste the difference between real fruit juice and Kool-Aid? It's like that.
Got this kinda chemical aftertaste."

The atmosphere felt heavy as they sat in silence, a glum expression
on Lucy's face. Al felt guilty for upsetting her, clumsily shifting the
topic of the conversation.

"Man, I haven't seen Lilly so happy in ages. She's so excited to
have a friend like you," he offered in a tone that was just a little bit too
upbeat. Lucy glanced up at him, an eyebrow raised.

"A friend like me?"

"Yanno, another girl."

"Oh. Does she not spend much time with other women?"

"She doesn't have many friends," Al explained cautiously as he tiptoed around the subject. "She can get to be a bit much without her medication."

A bit much was an understatement. Some days were hard, so hard that he regretted taking her in. When her fits lasted hours he wondered if he had done the right thing by stealing her away from the asylum.

"Everyone needs some sort of medication nowadays," Lucy said with a shrug. "Lai mentioned he'd forgotten his for this trip."

"Oh, it's not like your usual cocktail of antidepressants and anxiety medication. I have that in my pre-workout protein shake," Al smiled, relieved that Lucy was so understanding. "She can be pretty intense. Lilly has these episodes where she thinks she's someone else; she gets so worked up that she ends up having seizures."

Lucy nodded. "She told me a little about them."

"Yeah? Just try to ignore it. She's a nice girl, she just needs some help." Al got up to stretch his legs, lighting up a fresh cigarette. He wasn't used to having heart to heart chats. "I'm gonna go for a stroll. Care to join me? We have a few hours before nighttime."

Lucy stood up. "Sure, why not? It'll keep me from falling asleep before dinner."

"I honestly wouldn't dare walk in this forest most days, but it seems pretty quiet right now." Al scanned the woods, not seeing anything to worry about. No faeries, at least.

"I wouldn't jinx it if I were you."

"Hm, true." He picked up a broken branch, swinging it through the air with a satisfying hiss. "Well fear not, fair lady. You're in good hands."

"Thank you, kind sir. My, what a large stick you have," Lucy gave a mock curtsy.

"Thank you. I am very proud of my large stick," he laughed, taking an animal trail that was hardly visible among fallen leaves. "We should be careful, Gaia said we wouldn't be attacked while we're near her, but I'm not sure how far that range is. I'm not that keen on being savaged by fairies either, but just sitting and waiting for something to happen is torture."

"You're telling me," Lucy agreed. She strolled alongside him in silence for a while. "So, you and Lai used to date?"

"Date is a strong word." Al shrugged. "Don't get me wrong, we are close–like really close. But he wants to be more than friends and that's not my cup of tea."

"That makes sense."

"He's a lot of fun as long as you don't get too close. He's easy to overdose on. Speaking of, did I spy you two snuggling, or was it just him being clingy?"

"Don't worry, we're just friends," Lucy promised. "He's grossly inappropriate but it's nothing but playful banter. He's almost like a brother to me."

They walked for less than ten minutes, enjoying the earthy smells of the forest and a damp breeze that carried the sounds of chirping insects and small animals scurrying in the shady undergrowth. It was silent otherwise; Al paused, frowning.

"Do you feel like someone's watching us?" He brushed a tickling strand of a spiderweb out of his face.

"Before now? No. Now that you've said that? Yes," Lucy said, looking around, carefully stepping over the thick veins of tree roots under her feet.

"Reckon we should go back?"

"Probably. Who knows what's out here."

Al examined the canopy of branches above them, skeletal fingers reaching for the sky. "There's something up in the trees–"

Before he could finish, his entire body was violently jerked back, a crossbow bolt through his shoulder pinning him against a tree trunk. Al howled in agony, reaching for the bolt to tear out the projectile buried deep in his flesh, tearing the muscle as he tried to pull it free.

"Oh, it's you two." Eleanore dropped from the branches above them. She was wearing a sturdy set of leather armor that was stained with dried blood and fitted so perfectly to her curves that it had to have been boiled into shape around her. "Where are the others?"

"Al! Are you okay?" Lucy ran to him, tugging on the wooden shaft of the crossbow bolt, trying to free him.

"Don't pull it or he'll bleed to death." Eleanore reloaded her crossbow. "Sorry, handsome. I've been looking for your group for so long I was starting to think you were all dead. Lots of things out here wanting to eat you." She grabbed the bolt, holding it in place as she pulled Al away from the tree.

He cried out in pain, skin gray and clammy with shock. "What? What do you mean? It's been two days!"

Eleanore raised an eyebrow.

"We waited for you for six days. We figured you were dead, so I left the kids and came looking. I've been lost in this bloody forest for close to ten days, according to my watch. At least the snow's melted."

"We left yesterday! We've only been gone for two days!" Lucy snapped at Eleanore as she fussed over Al, his white shirt stained with a spreading crimson blotch. "The camp's nearby. Help me get him back, I might be able to patch him up."

"I did have a first aid kit, but my camp was devoured a few nights ago." Eleanore snapped off the tip of the bolt jutting out from Al's shoulder. "Lead the way."

"This wasn't the relaxing stroll I'd hoped for," Al winced, draping his good arm around Lucy's shoulder, leaning heavily on her for support.

"Yeah, you're telling me," Lucy muttered.

CHAPTER THIRTY

LUCY

The campfire's light danced amongst trees in the distance, a beacon calling Lucy and Al back to the safety of their camp. Lai saw them approach, jumping to his feet; he looked like didn't know if he wanted to punch them or kiss them, his face as pale as if he had seen a ghost.

"Where the fuck were you guys? You were gone for three days!" He squeezed Lucy in a back breaking hug and connected a solid punch to Al's chest, his hand coming away wet and sticky with blood. "Oh shit, you're bleeding. What the hell happened?"

"Three days? We went for a twenty minute walk..." Al protested, wincing at the hit. The sound of the man explaining himself and Eleanore defending her honor faded to silence in Lucy's ears. Sitting by the fire, pale and scarred but very much alive, was Aris. Human and whole.

"Why the hell did the two of you leave the camp?" he grumbled at Lucy as tears of relief welled up in her eyes. "Bring Al over here before he passes out."

"Aris– Aris, you're okay–" she choked out, not daring to believe her eyes, a shaking hand reaching out to brush against a bright scar on his shoulder. Aris grumbled at her as she fussed.

"Don't grizzle at them, Aris." Eleanore pushed Al towards the fire and forced him to sit down. "It seems this forest has quite a few nasty tricks up its sleeve. You lot have been gone from the house for over two weeks now, and Al's twenty minute walk seems to have taken a couple of days longer than expected."

"Would you quit manhandling him?" Lucy snapped at Eleanore, annoyed that the woman was behaving as though Lucy hadn't been on the walk with Al.

"He loves it." She smirked as she ripped Al's shirt open, ignoring his grimace of pain and stripping him down while Aris heated a metal rod from their tent, the end glowing white-hot.

"Oh, no. Please, I'd rather just wait till we get back." Al looked up to Lucy for help. "I'll just stop by the hospital. It's not a big deal, I swear. Lai? Tell them, I'm not a fan of field surgery."

"It has to be done." Lai took off his belt and gestured for Al to open his mouth. "Bite down on this. Just ignore any other teeth marks on it."

Was it Lucy's imagination, or was Lai enjoying tormenting the man...?

"Oh, you traitor." Al took a deep breath, biting on the thick leather, just in time as Eleanore yanked the bolt out with a sickeningly wet squelch.

"I'm so sorry, but she was going to do it anyway," Lucy apologized, sitting down next to Al, supporting him as he swayed.

"Listen to me, boy," Aris chuckled, holding the glowing rod. "Men like you would never last on my ship. Lai spent many a night bemoaning your selfishness; consider this your just reward."

He watched Al's eyes widen with a merciless grin. "You made my baby cry."

"Now that's just cruel." Lai raised an eyebrow at his father, but made no effort to stop the teasing, holding Al still as the man squirmed in embarrassment.

"That was the idea," Aris assured as he pressed the rod into the wound, blood and skin turning black with the hiss of rapidly cooling metal. Al stiffened a scream, biting down hard as Aris repeated the process on his back.

Lucy looked away and wrinkled her nose at the smell of seared meat. Al grabbed her hand tight enough to crush bone as his flesh sizzled, bubbling up with blisters. Even Lai looked uncomfortable; the gruesome surgery clearly wasn't his style.

"Use the clean parts of his shirt to wrap it up." Eleanore placed a couple of comfrey leaves on the wound to stop the flesh from sticking to the fabric.

"Why can't it ever just be dinner?" Al groaned, spitting out the belt. "Two weeks...There's no way I haven't been fired. Candy's probably filed a missing person report by now."

A twinge of guilt plucked at Lucy's conscience. She had invited Al over, unaware of Lai's intent of causing trouble. She had never expected it to go this far.

"You can use me as a reference," Lucy offered sympathetically.

"Relation to the applicant: got lost in a magical forest with them." He forced a laugh past the aching in his shoulder. "I'm honestly more concerned about my sister. We only brought enough of her pills for a weekend stay."

"Oh. She's probably clean of it by now, huh?"

"That's what I'm afraid of." Al got up from the log, stumbling to the tent and collapsing into his bed roll while Lai hovered above him like a fly over shit. The poor man was exhausted, passing out as soon as he hit the ground.

"So. We've lost some time, it seems." Aris tossed aside the rod, wiping his hands. "I don't understand how. No point in thinking about it now, though. Pack up the camp, we're going back home."

"I suggest we leave everything here," Lai volunteered. "It's technically a day's march back and it's only gonna slow us down."

"And if it takes longer?" Lucy asked. She eyed the bags they had to carry, not too eager to haul all of it back.

"Okay then, fair enough. We'll take a few basics, like the blankets. There's not much food left anyway."

Aris nodded in agreement. "Despite how much it pains me, I agree with Lai. Pack the essentials, let's not waste anymore time."

Eleanore stood behind Aris, caressing his hair. "Alright, let's get you kids back on the road. I wouldn't have high hopes of leaving the forest too easily, though."

"We aren't expecting it to be easy." Lucy rolled her eyes at Eleanore. "Especially if you keep shooting our friends."

"Can't blame me for being trigger happy." She traced Aris' scars with her fingertips, looking back at Lucy, the picture of innocence. "Something out there has been trying to catch me for days."

"How unfortunate," Lucy replied flippantly.

That it hasn't eaten you already.

She left with Lai to empty the tent as Aris and Klein gathered the last of their meager food supplies.

"Hey, can I ask you something?" Lai asked once they were out of earshot, dropping the tent flap shut behind them.

"Yeah, shoot."

"You were alone with Al for two days." Lai couldn't meet her eyes, stuffing blankets into his bag while Al snored awkwardly between them. "Did anything happen while you were out there?"

"Yeah, he got shot with a crossbow," Lucy sighed, trying to focus on an uncooperative bedroll.

"You know what I mean."

Really? Is that your main concern right now?

"We literally had a ten minute unsupervised walk. All we talked about was his sister. I'm not going to fuck the guy you're interested in."

"Surprisingly honorable of you considering you made out with my dad," Lai huffed, stuffing his pillow into his pack.

Oh no.

"You know about that?" Lucy winced.

Lai gave up the battle with his pillow, letting it hang from the bag. "You weren't even planning on telling me? It seems I've completely misunderstood the nature of our friendship."

"Aww, don't be like that. It's not an easy thing to bring up."

"I know it seems like I don't care about this family." Lai looked at her, cold and distant. "But when someone does shit like that, it makes things fucking weird. Why did you do it? My father is a fucking mess. He's got a temper like a five second fuse on a nuclear bomb."

Lucy sighed, sitting on her bag to think. "I think it's because on the night when he almost lost his dog I saw his pain. And when he saw me in the dress, he was obviously reminded of your mother. He knows how it feels to care for someone so much that it kills you when they're gone."

"We all do," Lai pointed out. "Pity is not a good reason to jump into someone's bed. I thought you were–" He paused, taking a breath. "Just. Be careful, okay? Especially around Eleanore. She's possessive."

"I can tell. I'll be honest, I'm counting down the seconds before she shoots me in the back. Would it be too much to ask for you to be the one to poke the hot rod into my bolt wound? As my friend?"

Lai turned to look at Lucy, a hint of a smile playing on his lips. "Oh, with great pleasure."

"I knew I could count on you."

They finished packing up the essentials, leaving Al to sleep and returning to the bonfire.

"Everything we could carry is packed," Lucy declared. "I think we're good to go."

Aris nodded. "Excellent. Then there's only one problem left." He pointed to a person sized lump wrapped in a blanket by the fireplace. Lucy struggled to keep calm as she realized what she was seeing. Gaia was curled up on the ground, motionless, her glowing skin dull and flat in the weak sunlight. The family's only hope had finally run out of power.

CHAPTER THIRTY ONE

LUCY

No one was allowed a break as they raced towards home. Aris set a furious pace despite his wounds, carrying Gaia on his back, her sleeping bag tied into a sling, the petite green girl surprisingly heavy. Finally though it became too dark to brave the woods on foot and Lucy called for a halt, panting as she leaned against a tree; it was more exercise than she'd had in years.

"We should camp right here," Lai suggested. "It's as good a spot as any, look–there's a tent right there."

Lucy groaned in frustration. It was their own camp! They had been walking away from it for over eight hours, she couldn't believe Aris had led them in circles. "What the fuck, I thought you were good at navigating?" she demanded, glaring at the man.

Aris jabbed at his compass, holding it out to Lucy to see for herself. It was pointing due north, just as it had been for their entire hike. "I don't understand how this happened. We've been walking south all day, we should be miles from here by now."

Klein cleared his throat. "This forest is designed to keep us in, isn't it? That's what makes it dangerous."

Aris scowled. "I think you're right," He sighed, putting away his worthless compass. "I'd hoped with Gaia out of commission we'd be able to just walk out."

"She must have an auxiliary battery or something to keep everything from collapsing," Al said.

"If I were a super-smart computer trying to keep people in I'd just put magnets in all the trees. Mess up your compass like that instead of making us walk all damn day." Lucy dumped her bag on the ground and crawled into the tent. Her legs were aching from all the walking and Lai had been complaining for the last six hours, making the day drag on and on.

The others followed her into the tent. All of them were exhausted; Aris was gray with pain, sweat staining his clothes. He set down Gaia's sleeping bag, unzipping it to check on their newest companion and hissing a breath between his teeth. Gaia had turned from green to a dull yellow, pulsing dimly in the dark tent.

"Well, that's not good at all." Lucy took out her cellphone, checking the charge. The battery on her phone was low, the icon the same yellow as Gaia. Lucy paused and set her phone on the girl's chest, inspired; the device beeped cheerfully as it began to charge.

"Are you kidding me?" Lai sat up. "Are you draining her to charge your phone?"

Lucy quickly snatched her phone away from Gaia. "I was trying to use my phone to charge her, but I don't think wireless charging works in reverse."

"I don't want to think of what could happen if she shuts down completely," Aris muttered as he zipped her back into her pod.

"So how the Hell do we get out of here?" Lucy sighed, pushing her sweaty hair back from her face as she looked to Lai for answers.

"Beats me. Whoever made this place set up the forest as the ultimate security fence. I don't think we can get out unless we grow wings and fly out," Lai shrugged, flopping back into Al's lap and pulling a blanket from his pack.

Aris stared at him in awe. Lai scowled back suspiciously, an eyebrow raised from the comfort of Al's thighs. "What?" he demanded, fidgeting uncomfortably and looking nervous.

"What's up, Aris?" Lucy frowned, glancing at him. He looked as though a million light bulbs had lit up in his brain all at once, stunned into silence for a full minute before shaking the stars from his eyes.

"Leander, you've just saved this entire family."

"I've done what now?" Lai asked, sitting back up and scooting apprehensively closer to Al. "You'd better not be thinking what I think you're thinking. No way."

"Oh stop complaining, boy." Aris slid a long, sharp knife from his boot as Lai paled. "A few days of rest and you'll be back to yourself.

Al, if you ever want to see your sister again then I need you to hold him still."

"What are you doing? Let him go," Lucy frowned as Al hesitantly wrapped Lai in a bear hug, panic on the man's face.

"She's right, Aris," Eleanore pursed her lips, following everyone out of the tent. "He's far too young, he won't be big enough to carry us."

"I only need him as bait," Aris assured her, kneeling beside Lai as he thrashed and kicked.

"What are you doing?!" Lucy raised her voice, horror mounting as she realized too late what was happening, lunging for Aris; Eleanore caught her arm, easily holding her out of the way.

"It's our only chance." Aris grabbed Lai's face, jerking it back. With one clean cut he opened his son's throat from ear to ear, blood gushing down in a crimson waterfall, staining Al's arms dark red.

Lucy howled in protest, throwing herself towards Lai, Eleanore's sharp nails cutting pink channels into her arms. She sobbed with rage and despair as her friend choked on his own blood, pink bubbles foaming around her mouth, a look of numb surprise on his face. His eyes met hers, wide with fear.

Lai mouthed his last words to her, his lungs filling with blood.

Don't watch.

Lucy closed her eyes tight, holding back vomit, her stomach clenching and unclenching in horror. She couldn't make sense of what Aris had just done; how could murdering his son save the rest of them? She sank to the ground, pulling her hands free from Eleanore's slacking grip and covering her ears to block out Lai's choked gurgle and rattle.

As Lai finally fell silent, his breath was replaced by wet snapping and tearing. It sounded like a raw chicken being torn to shreds by hand.

"Watch." Aris lifted her chin.

Lucy struggled against his touch, teeth snapping dangerously close to his fingers as Eleanore reached past him, forcing Lucy's eyelids open. "Just look, you idiot," she ordered.

She didn't want to see her friend's corpse, fighting not to look and failing. There was something wrong with Lai. Lucy stopped struggling, confused and afraid, her heart pounding so hard it felt like it was trying to break free of her ribcage.

Where she'd expected to see Lai's body was pure carnage. A throbbing pile of tendons and bones were rearranging themselves into something new, recycling the corpse into itself. Fresh, pale flesh stretched over the bulging mass, naked and ugly. Little lumps swelled up over the thin membrane, bright pins piercing through and bursting into bloom, opening out into iridescent red feathers. Lucy watched transfixed as the bizarre change unfolded in front of her. There was no magical movie-style transformation, no glowing light, no smoke to hide the ugliness. It was raw and primal, making Lucy feel sick all over again.

"Isn't he magnificent?" Aris whispered.

Row after row of scales formed over the creature that had been Lai, covering a narrow, reptilian snout. Thin, delicate wings folded back along its feathered sides, its long tail lashing furiously as Aris approached.

"What is he?" Lucy's voice cracked and trembled; she felt numb, her blood icy in her veins.

Aris crouched beside Lai as he shrank back with a furious hiss. He barely came up to Aris's shoulder, as frail and slender as a bird–an angry bird, spitting and snapping at Aris.

"Our family's goal for hundreds of years was to breed a dragon. Lai is as close as we've ever come."

The young wyvern was smaller than a horse. Eleanore had been right, there was no way Lai would be able to lift any of them out. At least he was pretty, despite the gore show his transformation had been; red and gold scales mixed with vivid feathers to cover slender limbs with webbed claws and a tail that spotted a wide fan at the tip.

"He looks like a real dragon to me," Lucy managed weakly. "I thought you said dragons were rare. And intelligent."

"'Intelligent' is the key word. He is lacking the limbs to be officially classified as a dragon, too. There's no market for wyverns, they're too small to be scary and they're dumb as a box of bricks."

He watched as Lai shook his head, fluffing up all of his feathers and resettling them in one fluid motion. "Don't even think about it, boy. I'm not playing games tonight," he growled as the wyvern made a strange gurgling sound, two hard lumps rolling under the translucent skin of his throat. "If you spark that I'll tear your wings off."

Lai grumbled his anger and forced out a small stream of foul smelling gas from his mouth. The lumps in his throat clicked sharply, throwing up a bright spark that ignited the gas into a fireball that scorched the ground at Eleanore's feet, forcing the woman to jump back.

"Aw, he recognizes us," Lucy smirked weakly.

"I will pluck you bald, you little brat," Eleanore cursed, slapping out small burns on her clothing. Unfortunately for Lucy, the woman's leather armor resisted the flame, but the cotton wraps over Eleanore's boots burned nicely.

Lai hissed and climbed up the nearest tree with a fluid, lizard-like shimmy, hiding amongst the bare branches.

"So now that he has wings, how do we get out of here?" Lucy asked, knees wobbling as she watched him climb.

"We use him as bait to lure something that can get out of here."

"The griffins?" Lucy guessed after a moment's thought.

"Clever girl," Aris nodded his approval.

"The two lesbian griffins are going to save the day. The same griffins that attacked the hound and started all of this. I love it when things come full circle," she said dryly.

"Only if we can get them to cooperate." Aris tossed a stick at Lai. "Fly, you stupid waste of wingspan. We need to get their attention."

"Maybe we can make a deal with them for split custody."

"Not a bad idea." Aris glanced at her as Lai clumsily launched himself out of the treetop, circling above the camp. "This shouldn't take long; the girls are wildly territorial, the second they see him they'll be on us."

"Hopefully it's not two or three months before they get here," Lucy muttered. Aris frowned; Lucy wondered if he had considered that.

Thankfully it only took mere minutes for an ear splitting screech to pierce the air. Two large shadows passed over them, blocking out the sun. Lai crashed down through the treetops with a panicked squark, dropping to the ground and wrapping his wings in a tight cocoon around himself for protection.

The two half lion, half eagle giants followed him down, searching for the reckless trespasser. Course golden fur covered their powerful hind-legs, the muscles of their shoulders tense and twitching from their flight, broad, banded wings tucked tightly across their backs.

"Well, Lucy–here's your chance to negotiate," Klein said, nudging her towards the griffins. They watched her closely, beaks slightly open, the pupils of their eyes constricting and dilating as she stepped forward.

"Hi, ladies," Lucy called out to them weakly. She hoped they could understand her. Their talons were longer than her entire hand; one wrong move would see her disemboweled in seconds.

The magnificent animals settled onto their haunches as she inched closer, curiously tilting their heads to one side as she spoke.

"You two want a kid, right?" Lucy tried to sound confident. "Well, we have a proposal for you."

The griffins looked at each other then turned back to her. She had engaged their interest.

"If you'll help us get out of this forest, we'll let you have Louis every single weekend, no questions asked," Lucy offered, feeling a little guilty for not being able to ask Louis first as she gambled on his safety.

The griffins exchanged a look that was too alien for Lucy to understand. One of them shook their head and turned back to Lucy, making sure she was watching before holding up a wicked claw. She scraped at the ground; one, two, three lines in the dirt. Lucy could barely believe what she was seeing. The griffins were negotiating with her.

"Ryan is teaching him his alphabet, and there are lots of things he needs to learn. How about once a month he gets a Friday, Saturday and Sunday with you, and just Saturday and Sunday for the rest of the month?" she offered, trying to mime out what she was saying.

"Summers are as he sees fit to spend them, so if he wants to hang out with you he can, but it's his choice. If it's gonna be longer than a few days you can come to the house so we can make sure he has food and water."

The griffins fixed her with a withering glare, offended that she thought they might let Louis starve. Another silent discussion passed between the two creatures, finally followed by a graceful nod.

Lucy grinned at Klein, flushed with victory.

"Sure, just give away my brother, why don't you." He crossed his arms with a scowl. The griffins ignored his little tantrum, their feathers fluffed contentedly.

"Lou likes them, and we need help," she reminded him. "You told me to negotiate, and I did."

"He's just complaining for the sake of complaining. It's a good deal," Aris sighed. "Better than the one you made with Fish, at any rate."

The griffins stood and bowed down low, shrugging their shoulders in invitation. Lucy didn't think that they would wait for them forever.

"Ladies first?" she offered Eleanore; she didn't want to admit that she was scared to ride on the griffin's back after all the effort she had put into making it available to them.

"Go on, Aris, you heard the girl." Eleanore slapped him on the ass with a smirk. Aris didn't look amused, picking up Lucy like a child and plopping her on the griffin's broad back.

"Wait, I wasn't talking about me." She pressed her knees against the warm feathery sides, trying to find something to hold onto. "I've never– I don't know how to!" She waved at the wings as panic set in, fingers desperately grasping at the creature's silky feathers.

Eleanore climbed on behind Lucy, wrapping both arms around her. "It's okay to be afraid, little princess. Flying is hard; it's so easy to have an accident and fall to your death," she purred into her ear.

A chill ran down Lucy's spine. She could picture Eleanore shoving her off mid flight, feigning innocence as she told Aris that Lucy had slipped. She might even force out a tear or two as she comforted the man over his loss. Lucy had no doubt in her mind that Eleanore would squeeze herself quite nicely into the gap her death would leave. She twisted to get off the beast but Eleanore held her in a vice-like grip; she didn't even get to cry out a warning to Aris before the griffin spread her wings and leapt in the air, picking up Klein by his shoulders on the way up, the poor man dangling in the air like a rag doll.

"Oh shit, oh shit, oh shit," Lucy shut her eyes as her stomach plummeted to her toes. Deep breaths, in and out. Easier said than done. The thinning air made her head spin.

"So," Eleanore released her grip on her, leaning in closer to her ear as the petrified Lucy clung desperately to the griffin. "You've been sewing chaos around here. Messing up my plans. Messing with my man."

"Your man?" Lucy's teeth were chattering with fear; she didn't know what to do. She was going to die if she didn't think of something.

"My man. You have no idea how long I've spent breaking him down into a weak, malleable shell. It took me years to separate him from his family's wealth, to make him desperate." Eleanore's voice was filled with venom; she believed her own delusions. "He was this close to giving me everything I've ever wanted. Gaia, the house–I'm going to resurrect their family business, and now you're in my way."

Lucy's life flashed before her eyes. This was it. Eleanore was going to kill her. She would never see Xim again, would never get to prove herself. She would never gain mastery over her magic, mourning the feeling of power at her fingertips.

Her magic.

Lucy reached with shaking hands for Eleanore, groping down her arms to the woman's wrists, holding tight. Eleanore laughed, unconcerned.

"Do you have any idea how important Gaia is, Lucy? How much can she do in the right hands? How much I can conquer in a year?" the woman asked mockingly. "There isn't a single world that would be able to fend me off!"

The thought was terrifying. Gaia had been made to sustain and protect life, but her ability to attach onto other worlds would be catastrophic if placed in the wrong hands. Eleanore's armies could appear out of nowhere, moving like lightning, devouring everything in their path.

Lucy's voice came out as little more than a whisper; every drop of her focus was on summoning the strings of Eleanore's life into her faltering grip.

"Try fending off this," she hissed, yanking on the threads as hard as she possibly could.

Eleanore screeched in fury, ripping her arms free from Lucy's grip. As Lucy slipped from the griffin's back she caught a glimpse of Klein below in the giant's talons, his eyes widening in shock as she fell. She heard her name yelled out behind as the trees loomed up to meet her; her last conscious thoughts were regretting that Klein would have to watch her die, then nothing at all as her world turned black.

***

There was still daylight when Lucy opened her eyes again, staring up at the canopy of branches above her. She didn't dare try to move, certain that every bone in her body was shattered into a million pieces. She wished the fall had killed her; every inch of her screamed in pain. She was almost relieved when she heard twigs and leaves rustling nearby. Better to be eaten than to starve to death with a broken spine.

A brightly scaled snout bumped against her cheek, gleaming red feathers surrounding a bright, catlike eye that stared down at her from above. Lai cocked his head to watch her wake, the stones in his throat clicking in excitement and relief as she reluctantly stirred.

"Is that you, Lai?" she asked as she finally started inventory of her body, wiggling her fingers. It hurt like hell, but everything seemed to be more or less intact. Her hips shifted from side to side when she asked them to, if somewhat grudgingly. Carefully she pushed herself up onto her elbows as Lai chirped and croaked in caution, steadying herself before looking down.

Her stomach churned and twisted at the sight of her tibia jutting out of her skin like an angry broken branch, the hole too tight to bleed very much. Her legs were a patchwork of cuts and bruises, her clothes ripped to shreds by the trees that had saved her life as she had fallen through their boughs.

"Oh, my God," she gasped, looking helplessly at Lai. Lai nodded solemnly in agreement. It was bad.

"How long was I out? How the fuck am I gonna get home?" Lucy groaned, trying to remember what had happened. "That fucking bitch– Lai, Eleanore pushed me, she was planning to kill me from the start. She's trying to take Gaia!"

The wyvern rolled his eyes, his feathers puffed up. Lucy scowled at him.

"Well if you knew that already why the Hell didn't you try to warn me, huh?" she snapped at him, in no mood for his attitude. "I almost died!" She stared down at her broken leg, nausea rolling through her stomach again. "Unless you have a plan to get me out of here I still might."

Lai huffed moodily, sinking his slender body down beside her, wings flattened back. He croaked and shrugged his shoulders, one eye fixed on hers.

"...You can't be serious. There's no way you can carry me," Lucy protested. The last thing she wanted was to be in the air again, and the griffin had been far more solid and powerful than the scrawny drake was. Lai watched her patiently, clicking his throat at her and shuffling closer.

"This is a bad idea, dude. You're tiny!" Lucy groaned as she slowly pulled herself over to him; he helped her onto his back with his wing, moving gently to keep from jostling her broken bone. She was pale and sweating as she settled in between his narrow shoulder blades, eyes closed tight.

"It's fine if you just walk, Lai–" she started, her arms wrapping tight around his neck as Lai took a running start, galloping through the trees; slowly, painfully, with heavy beats of his strained wings, they rose into the air.

CHAPTER THIRTY TWO

LUCY

Lai descended onto his bedroom balcony like a brick wrapped in tissue paper, smashing through the wooden railing and collapsing to the floor, exhausted. Lucy was flung from his back and through the glass door that led to his room, her already bruised and battered body picking up cuts and shards as she was rolled across the carpet. She laid on her back in a daze, struggling to breathe through the pain and looking towards Lai.

"Next time, we walk." She groaned, slowly rolling to her side, her vision blurring into a chaotic kaleidoscope as Lai's brightly colored bedroom assaulted her aching senses.

The wyvern huffed in offense and forced himself to his feet; with a flick of his tail he hauled himself up the side of the house and onto the roof to rest in peace, settling in beside the gargoyles as they chittered curiously at their unexpected guest. Puffed up and scowling in the moonlight with the pale beams making his feathers glow, he looked like a gargoyle drag queen.

Lucy could hear footsteps running towards Lai's room, tensing in apprehension. Their rough landing had made a lot of noise, it made sense that someone had heard them. She hoped feverishly that Aris was racing to her rescue and felt guilty for the fantasy.

Klein burst through the door, staring at the messy room in shock following the trail of carnage to Lucy. "You're–you're alive–" he swayed on his feet, shutting the door behind him and dropping down beside her, checking her wounds. "Oh, gods. Lucy, your leg." His arms wrapped around her, lifting her carefully as he tried not to jostle her break. Lucy stifled a cry, eyes watering as he lowered her gently onto Lai's bed, propping her up with pillows.

Tears of pain and anger stained her cheeks. Her entire body shivered violently in shock, the bone that jutted through her leg leaking blood into the sheets.

"I'm sorry. Lucy, what the hell happened? I saw you fall, I thought you were–"

"Fuck, that hurts so bad," Lucy whispered, barely hearing him. She was almost as stunned as Klein.

"Okay, okay. Let's start with getting you patched up," he decided with a shaky breath, getting to his feet. "Um. I think I need to set the bone, Lucy. I've done it before on the animals, but it's going to hurt like Hell," he warned, patting down his pockets. He pulled out a slightly crumpled cigarette, pressing the butt between Lucy's lips. "I know this isn't exactly kosher, but I want you to smoke this. It will help with the pain," he promised.

"You've got to be kidding." Lucy would have laughed if she wasn't in agony, eyes closed as Klein lit the end of the blunt. The first inhale stung, almost making her cough, but she managed to keep it down, letting the fragrant smoke cool in her lungs.

"Better?" Klein asked as she slowly relaxed into the bed. She nodded. The drug wasn't exactly numbing the pain, but she felt removed from it, like she was watching Klein operate on someone else. Her brain kept short circuiting, breaking her awareness of her injuries into manageable bites.

Klein gave her a weak smile. "Told you it was purely medical. Now, this is going to hurt." He whispered a tiny prayer and stood up on the bed, his foot pressing unceremoniously into Lucy's groin as he took her by her calf, pulling her leg hard.

Lucy screamed. No drug could tame the pain that ripped through her body like a living beast, so powerful it knocked her from her senses. Later, she would be thankful for fainting.

***

Unconsciousness did not last for long. Lucy cried freely as she woke, hands balled into tight fists, the weak anesthetic relief burned away, leaving her horribly clear headed. "I'll kill her."

"Oh, I don't doubt it." Klein carefully cleaned her cuts and scrapes, bandaging the worst of them. "Try not to move for a while, okay?" He gently draped a sheet over her, and Lucy realized she was half naked beneath it. Klein had removed her clothes to tend to her wounds.

Lucy nodded, shakily relighting the joint and taking a fresh drag.

"I'll bring you some food, but I expect you to nap after that. You need a good, healing sleep."

"Thank you, Klein."

"Rest okay?" Klein left, returning shortly with a plate of packaged snacks. "Sorry, we've been gone a while, there's nothing fresh left." He placed another joint on the pillow next to her. "For if the pain gets bad. I'll come and check on you in a few hours."

"Please stay," Lucy whispered.

"Worried she might come to finish the job?"

"I don't care about dying. I just don't want to be alone."

Klein hesitated, his face pink. "Of course. Let me get you something to wear first, alright?" he gestured to her ruined pile of clothing. Lucy's heart skipped a beat; on top of the heap was her collar, stained with her own blood. He moved over to Lai's dresser, digging deep into the bottom until he found a linen shift that looked like it had come from a slutty Ebenezer Scrooge Halloween costume.

Lucy watched him guiltily, taking the nightgown in silence and tugging it over her head.

"I don't want to move," she muttered as she laid down and closed her eyes, focusing on anything but her leg as it throbbed with a dull ache.

Nodding in understanding, Klein sat to keep watch. He seemed determined to stay awake for as long as she needed him to, watching over Lucy, ready to act upon any sign of discomfort. Lucy fell asleep, her dreams keeping her mind from fully resting. Klein eventually stretched out on the foot of the bed and drifted off as well, trying not to take too much room.

***

"Fuck!" Lucy woke up with a start, swearing as she clutched at her leg. Klein jolted awake as she yelled.

"Hey, hey, what's wrong?" He jumped off the bed, hovering above her. "Your leg?" He moved to check her bandages as Lucy shook her head.

"I had a nightmare and moved too quickly," she explained as she sank back down into the sheets. "You never notice how much you use your muscles until moving them makes you wanna hurl."

Relief flooded his face. "You scared me," Klein muttered as he fixed the blanket over Lucy. "How is the pain? If it's really bad I can try to find you something for it."

"It's fine," she lied. "I'm just glad you didn't have to cauterize it, that looked like it sucked. Poor Al."

"I'm not entirely convinced that father had to do that, to be honest," Klein chuckled. "I think it was revenge for making Lai cry." He lifted the blanket to examine Lucy's bandage, seemingly satisfied with his handiwork.

"Well, I guess I can get behind that. But then again, Aris cut Lai's throat. God, your family is fucked up."

"I don't know, I've certainly thought of killing him at least once. Consequence-free murder would almost make braving his room for dishes worth the effort."

"Y'all need therapy."

"I thought we got on fairly well, all things considered." Klein smiled.

***

It was almost dawn when Lai slid down the drainpipe to his balcony, tiptoeing carefully over broken glass as he let himself back into his bedroom, triumphantly human and completely naked.

"You two are looking cozy." He smirked at Klein and Lucy as they stirred awake. Lucy cried out happily at the sight of him; she hadn't entirely believed he would ever be back to himself, relieved to see him hale and wholly nude.

"Pants, Lai," Klein groaned, throwing a pillow at his brother; he dodged gracefully, his parts bouncing as he moved.

"You need a bath Luce, I could smell you from the rooftop," Lai grinned, flopping onto the bed and ignoring her yell of pain.

"Yeah, I'll get right on that." She scowled at him, her relief at his survival quickly fading. He was right, but he didn't have to be so rude about it. Putting any weight on her leg was out of the question right then anyway, and she didn't want to get her bandages wet. Lai winked at her, rolling off the mattress and getting to his feet again, waltzing to the bathroom.

"I'll grab a sponge, shall I?" he called to her.

"Grab some damn pants!" Klein snapped back at him.

***

The warm sponge was heavenly on Lucy's battered skin, Lai's gentle hands easing away blood and filth, leaving her soft and clean.

"Things have been crazy ever since we got home," Klein explained, looking away as Lai scrubbed the tops of Lucy's thighs, ignoring her squeal of protest. "Eleanore and father have been at each other's throats. She wants to use her engineers to try to fix Gaia, but I don't think father trusts her."

"Good," Lucy huffed, adjusting her shift. "She tried to kill me, remember?"

Klein shuddered. "No one knew that for sure. Eleanore told us that you had panicked and slipped, and that the griffin had refused to go back for you. I think my father suspected, though. I haven't seen him look so upset since..." he fumbled clumsily for the right words. "... Since mother died."

Lai raised an eyebrow at that. "Not the best time for him to go soft on us," he pointed out, gently toweling Lucy's hair dry. "Eleanore is completely unstable. The last time they had a really big fight she opened fire on the house. We still haven't fully excavated the east wing."

Lucy shook her head. "Why did you invite her again, Lai?" she asked; Lai poked his tongue out at her.

"I need to get dressed. I think I have a plan," Lucy declared. She was feeling more like herself now that she was clean, and she was pissed. Eleanore had tried to murder her. Lucy was going to make her pay. She wiggled her fingers cautiously, relieved as strands of bright life leapt to her touch like eager pets.

"You aren't going to be able to do anything on that leg," Klein pointed out dryly. Lucy frowned. He was right, curse him. Magic or no magic, she was a sitting duck if she couldn't walk.

"Can't you heal yourself?" Lai asked curiously. Lucy blinked at him.

"I don't know. I don't want to kill someone to find out." She thought back briefly to her kitten, cold and stiff in her lap, and shuddered.

Lai and Klein exchanged a meaningful look.

"Well it's a good thing we have to die twice to stay dead," Lai pointed out with a reassuring smile, pulling Klein closer. "You've been using magic for a while now anyway, right? I'm sure you can control it if you try."

"I don't want to hurt you."

Lai's grin widened. "I'm not volunteering, I'm beat. I had to drag your heavy ass all the way here. It's his turn."

"I'm not sure if I'm okay with that either," Klein protested as Lai forced him to sit beside Lucy, pushing his hand into hers. He looked down at his fingers, then to Lucy, taking a deep breath.

"...But your magic is our only hope of fixing Gaia. I think you should do it."

"I've got a box of epipens, and Al if I need back up," Lai added cheerfully, as though Lucy was concerned about him.

Lucy squeezed Klein's hand, looking into his eyes.

"It's okay, Lucy. I know you can do this," he promised her with more confidence than he showed. Slowly she nodded. Closing her eyes, she reached carefully for his life threads, letting them slip one by one from her fingers until only a single strand remained in her grasp. Its warmth felt strange in her hand, bright and familiar. Tugging gently she led the string to her wound, letting it sink into her bandaged leg.

Klein's memories hit her like a freight train, leaving her reeling as his life's source filled her bones. His history unfurled in front of Lucy in a dizzying blur of emotions that overwhelmed her; A happy childhood on the open sea, a death, a painful mistake made by a boy who was not yet a man. Loneliness. Endless loneliness. Poison that stung her mouth and burned in her chest. A flash of silver and searing pain in her eye.

Her lower leg itched like mad for a few seconds before Klein jerked his hand away from hers with a sudden gasp. Anxiously Lucy peeled her bandages back. Where her bone had torn her skin was now only a small white scar. She slid her hand up the length of her calf, feeling along the bone. A small lump remained where each half had fused back together, not perfect and still weak, but bearable.

"I think it worked!" Lai cheered shakily, stumbling over to the medicine cabinet and administered the relief his body urgently needed, chewing a fistful of antihistamines like candy.

"Are you okay, Lai?" Lucy stood up slowly, testing her weight on her leg. He flashed her a thumbs up, so she turned to Klein.

"Are you alright?" she asked softly. He was pale and distant, taking a moment to himself before looking up to meet her worried gaze.

"Yes, it just feels weird. Like I ran a marathon." Klein focused on settling his breathing. "I might need to lie down."

"Here, let me help you."

Flinching away from her hand, Klein shut his eyes. Lucy took her hand back, trying not to let the hurt of his flinch show on her face.

"Sorry. Just give me a little bit of time to rest," Klein asked quietly, getting to his feet. "I'll be downstairs if you need me, okay?"

Lucy sat on the edge of the bed, watching as he left the room. Lai dropped down beside her and shifted to lay with his head in her lap; she caressed his messy lavender locks with soothing strokes. She looked down at him, noticing for the first time his blond regrowth peeking through the purple, a little disappointed that lilac was not his natural color.

"He'll be okay," Lai assured her, eyes closed.

"Don't lie to me."

"I never lie." He opened one eye to look at her. "I just don't usually tell the entire truth."

"That counts as lying. Do you want to be the little spoon for a bit?"

Lai nodded. Lucy sank back into the mattress, curling around him, her arms around his waist.

"I know it hurts," he whispered, pressing against her, "But he will be okay. Give him time."

She sighed, holding him close. "And what about you?" she asked, feeling the allergic heat of his body against hers.

"I'm used to it."

Lucy ran her fingers through his hair as she hummed softly under her breath. Lai tensed at the kindness, twisting to face her. Lucy gave him a small, reassuring smile as she offered up the soothing tune.

Lai groaned, resting his head under her chin. "How did you manage to turn me into mush? Ugh. Let's get you dressed." He pushed Lucy away, albeit reluctantly.

"Aww, I turned you into mush?" she teased, releasing him from her embrace.

"You are banned from the pillow fort." Lai slid out of the bed and melted to the floor. "If you're going to face off with Eleanore, you need to look the part. She's not gonna be scared of the ghost of Christmas past."

"Do you have anything that will make her shake in her boots?" Lucy rolled her eyes, following Lai to his closet. He grinned and pulled a large box off the top shelf, handing it to Lucy. She opened the lid and winced as she pulled out a latex leopard print bodysuit, staring at Lai as if he was mad. Parts of the costume were sticking to each other where Lai had forgotten to baby powder it.

"No, something professional. Something your dad would respect."

"Well, for that, you might need to grow a dick first," Lai sighed. "Strap on?"

"Not quite the look I'm going for. Try again."

"Hm," he tapped his chin in thought. "I might have something. You might not be able to fit it, but we can try."

"What is it?" Lucy squinted suspiciously; Lai's taste seemed to have peaked in the mid 1990's.

Hauling out a dusty chest, he opened the lid. First came out the daggers, then countless bottles and jars of poisons. More weapons followed before a set of fine leathers, all dyed black. A loose linen shirt and a pair of high waisted pants with a corset back, well worn and softened with use. A studded crop jacket was added to the pile, along with a pair of flat boots.

"These will make your legs look a mile long." Lai tossed her the pants. "I doubt I'll need them again."

Lucy grinned, stripping off the nightgown. That was more like it; they looked like the clothes of the heroines in her books, dangerous and deadly.

Smoothing the wrinkles out of the shirt, Lai lowered it as a thought crossed his mind. "I'm helping you fuck my father, aren't I?"

She wasn't phased by the question. "You're helping me put Eleanore in her place."

Lai raised an eyebrow, waiting for her to finish the sentence.

"...and if I have to fuck your father in the process, so be it," she admitted, slightly red in the face; she had been wondering about the missed connection the entire time they'd been lost in the woods.

"There it is."

"You've seen how territorial she is!" Lucy huffed.

"She is territorial over a nuclear dump site! There are greener pastures out there!" Lai huffed right back, hugging the shirt to his chest.

"The same nuclear dump site that controls this family," Lucy explained patiently, her hands on her hips.

"Is that what this is really about?" Lai demanded suspiciously. "Control?"

"This is about the fact that Eleanore tried to kill me, and now I want to make her pay."

"I can admire that. Not sure if it's the right time for it..." Lai paused, giving Lucy the opportunity to come clean.

"...It might also be a little bit about control," she shrugged, red cheeked. "Look, just trust me. I have a plan."

"Send Al my way. Tell him I'm dying."

"Will do." Lucy stepped into the high waisted pants, pulling the corset strings tight. It was not particularly comfortable, but she enjoyed the way it squeezed her soft middle into a curvy hourglass. "Do you think I need a dagger?" she asked, draping a belt around her hips.

"Do *you* think you need one?"

She hesitated before tucking one into the back of her waistband. "She did try to kill me."

Lai pressed his lips together. That was far from the worst thing Eleanore had ever done, but he was not about to rain on her parade.

Lucy drew the dagger from its sheath and sliced the air in front of her. "Any tips on how to use it?"

"Haven't you already had a training montage?" a familiar voice asked.

The magpie landed heavily on Lai's shoulder, seemingly from out of nowhere. "Let's see where we are in the story. We've done 'Ordeal', so this must be 'Resurrection'. If you're lucky you might live to see 'The Journey Home'."

Lucy's shoulders sank a little. "I think you missed the 'Reward' part of that formula," she mumbled, thinking back to all the stories she'd ever read.

"Everyone knows the reward is the friends you made along the way," Lai laughed, offering Time a candy wrapper. "I'd suggest you hide the blade in your boot, Sunshine. She's less likely to see it there."

CHAPTER THIRTY THREE

LUCY

Shoving down her own self-doubt Lucy double-checked herself in a mirror with a satisfied grin. Damn, she looked good. The leather fit flawlessly, smoothing out her full curves. Lai wasn't kidding about the pants making her look tall either; she lingered a moment longer just to admire herself. Who wouldn't feel unstoppable looking like that?

With her newly discovered narcissism satisfied, Lucy made her way downstairs. For the first time in her life she would truly take the reins and never rely on anyone again. They needed her to fix Gaia. Not the other way around. She felt her hands tremble with a potent excitement as she placed them on the handle to Aris's office, taking a deep breath before flinging the door wide open.

The effect was immediate and deeply satisfying. Eleanore looked as though she was being confronted by a ghost, her usually plump lips tightening into a thin white line, her nails digging deeply into her palms as her hands clenched into fists. Aris said nothing, staring at Lucy in shock, not noticing that he had knocked over a bottle of ink as he had jumped to his feet. The dark liquid seeped into the wood of the desk and dripped in thick plops to the floor, the only sound in the deafening silence.

"You're alive," Aris barely managed a whisper.

"You're alive." Eleanore barely hid her disappointment, looking Lucy over. "And you had time for a makeover. How very quaint."

Lucy ignored the barbed comment, striding into the room, her hands on her hips.

"Eleanore pushed me off the griffin, Aris. She tried to kill me."

Aris turned to Eleanore. He did not doubt Lucy for a moment, his fury blazing like the sun. Eleanore looked unfazed by the accusation, lazily examining her fingernails.

"It was an accident, little girl. You should be careful with accusations like that." She smiled up at Lucy, challenging her to prove her wrong. "Women aren't burned at the stake just because someone says they're a witch these days."

Lucy glared at her, waiting for Aris to back her up, expecting him to evict Eleanore from his house in disgust. Instead, to her horror, he slowly sat back down.

"...Aris?" Lucy whispered, taking a seat of her own.

"Our reason for this conversation was to decide what to do about Gaia." The man could not meet Lucy's eyes, staring down at the inky mess in front of him. "If your engineers can truly wake her, Eleanore, then I agree to your terms. You may take the blueprint of Gaia's technology after you restore her. In return, a crew of your men to fix the house."

Lucy swayed in shock, unable to believe what she had heard.

"Without Gaia functioning, our home is doomed one way or another," Aris explained, trying to justify himself to her.

"Perfect," Eleanore purred. She watched Lucy's despair like a cat watching a mouse in a cage, clearly enjoying her suffering. "I'll have the team take her to the airship right awa–"

"I can do it," Lucy blurted, heart pounding.

Aris and Eleanore both looked at her, one with hope, the other with loathing.

"I can power up Gaia," Lucy continued, slower, buying herself time as she spoke. "I broke my leg when I was pushed, but I fixed it. I can control the flow of my magic. I just need a source, Aris. Get me some animals. Volunteers. I won't kill them, I'll just borrow a little bit of energy from each of them. There should be plenty." She prayed desperately that her plan sounded as good as Eleanore's.

Aris turned the idea over and over in his mind, testing it and prodding it.

"Just how sure of this plan are you, Lucy?" he asked, studying her closely. Lucy swallowed, hoping he would not see through the half truth. She nodded.

He watched her lie to him and turned back to Eleanore in defeat.

"Thank you Eleanore for your generous offer. We accept."

Lucy lurched to her feet, sick to her stomach; Aris may as well have plunged a dagger through her gut. She fled the room as Eleanore smirked.

***

Lucy stormed into the garden, dazed and devastated. She would never forgive Aris for the insult. Seething and ashamed she almost walked straight into Lilly, gulping out an apology for not watching where she was walking as the girl caught herself from falling. It looked like she hadn't slept in weeks, dark puffy circles heavy under her eyes. Her collarbones protruded under the fabric of the flowing white dress, and her skin was ashen white. What had been days in the forest for Lucy had been over two months waiting for the child, away from her carer and her medication.

"Shit, when was the last time you ate?" Lucy swore, taking Lilly's hand and guiding her to a low bench, sitting her down in the same patch of garden where they had spoken for the first time; it felt like a lifetime ago.

The garden looked very different from the moment they had shared amongst the fragrant blooms. All that was left now were empty flowerbeds with dry soil and the shriveled branches of perennial plants that hoped to come back one day.

"Why are we here?" Lilly asked, seemingly startled by her own voice. She watched Lucy warily. She barely seemed to recognize the woman, which was fair enough considering how long it had been since Lilly had seen her.

"Because it's nice to get out of that stuffy old house now and again," Lucy offered, trying to sound cheerful and kind.

Lilly nodded in agreement, relaxing and dropping her head onto Lucy's shoulder. "It's so loud in there. Silly little people with their insignificant problems."

"I don't know if the problems are insignificant right now," Lucy laughed. "Are you okay?"

"Are you? You've changed." Lilly looked up. "You are burning so brightly that the flames threaten to devour you."

Lucy hesitated. She was sure that answering the strange girl's questions would feed into her delusions; it was a bad idea, unhealthy. Still, she did not think that Lilly would judge her for how she was feeling, her head swimming with her own delusions of power and control. "I feel stronger. More sure of myself. I'm tired of always going with the flow." Lucy peeled away from Lilly, shifting to the ground and digging her fingers into the dead dirt. She reached for life but found nothing reaching back.

"You can control the flow," Lilly pointed out as she slid from the bench. Her white dress drank in dirt and dust, darkening the hems and knees. "I can see it. You are a river of gold threads."

Lucy stared at her, unsure of what to say. She had never told anyone what her magic looked like. "You can see that? What else can you see?" she pressed; she wanted to know more. Maybe she could help her explore her limits.

Lilly's eyes lost focus as her head tipped backwards. "I see death. I see rebirth. I see the firebirds. I see a great dragon returning home. I see betrayal. I see us," she chanted, staring at the inky sky as though it held all of life's answers. Lilly shuddered suddenly and turned to Lucy. The tears on her face startled her.

"I think we need to go get your brother." There was a tinge of fear to Lucy's voice.

"They made us both," Lilly continued numbly. If she had heard Lucy she gave no sign of it. "Both of us, two parts of one whole. But they cannot complete us; only we can do that. We devour our own tails."

Nothing she said made sense to Lucy. Why would it? Lilly was a sick little girl and Lucy had encouraged her. Guilt washed away her pride as she got to her feet to find Al, pausing only when Lilly grabbed her hand.

"No, don't. I'm okay," she panted, trembling as she regained her senses. "Please. Don't tell him."

Lucy nodded, not wanting to risk triggering another episode. "Okay. I think we should go back inside now though, alright?"

"No, not yet." Shaking her head and taking Lucy's hand in hers, Lilly pulled her friend towards the garden. "I want to show you something."

Lilly took Lucy through the wild paths of the garden until they reached a statue that was completely covered in withered vines. She grabbed a handful of leaves, pulling them down to reveal three women standing together with torches in their hands and two large dogs by their side.

"Who are these women?" Lucy asked, confused.

"It's one woman," Lilly explained, reaching up to caress a marble hand in adoration, her eyes filling with tears again. "She was a Goddess. Like all gods of old she has been forgotten and made weak. Gods are only as powerful as their followers' faith."

"What was she the goddess of?"

"It's easier to list what wasn't part of her domain."

"So why did she lose followers?" Lucy asked, puzzled and impatient; she wanted to go and work on her scheme, but she tolerated the child's strange behavior, still anxious that Lilly might start chanting again.

"Time," Lilly frowned, taking a few steps back from the statue. "New gods are born and take over while the old guard falls into obscurity."

"That's sad."

"It's not sad. It makes me so angry, and it should make you angry as well."

"Why should it make me angry?" Lucy raised an eyebrow. The only thing making her angry at that moment was Aris.

"Because as the people stopped believing in us, we lost the power to protect ourselves when the desecraters decided to tear us away from each other. Between your power and my memories, we could be whole again."

"How can the two of us be whole if there are three of her?" Lucy muttered the first thought surfacing in her mind.

"There *are* three." Lilly grabbed Lucy, her eyes burning with crazed passion, quickly extinguished at the sound of approaching footsteps.

"What—"

"There you are," Al sighed with relief just as Lilly relaxed her grip. Her brother looked at the statue and back to them again, a worried look lingering on his face.

"Needed some fresh air," Lucy said, feeling guilty. "Did Lai get in touch with you?"

"Yeah, he's fine now," Al answered with a certain coldness in his voice. "He told me what you did, healing yourself with Klein's life. Pretty impressive."

There it was again. Another sharp stab of guilt. "Only because he offered."

"He'll offer you his life if you promise him attention." He gave Lucy one last disapproving look before turning to his sister. "Lilly, I think you might need a nap. Come on." Al offered his hand to her, but Lilly hid behind Lucy, refusing to go.

"Come on, Lilly, I'll even go with you." Lucy took a side step. The last thing she wanted was to get between the siblings.

"No. He wants me to forget!" She dug her nails into Lucy's arm, almost drawing blood.

"Lilly, you're hurting your friend." Al approached slowly, reaching into his pocket. "Let go, please."

Desperate to deescalate the situation, Lucy lowered herself to Lilly's eye level, ignoring the sting of her nails in her arm.

"Do you want me to walk you back to your room? He doesn't have to come with us."

"You don't know what she is capable of, Lucy." Al looked like he was about to grab them both and pull them inside, dragging a hand furiously through his hair.

Lucy wrapped one arm around her young friend, leading her away from Al. "You'll be fine. No need to worry, he won't hurt you." She wanted to help, feeling sorry for them both.

An uncontrollable outburst of hysterical crying shook Lilly, followed by a bout of irrational laughter. She clung to Lucy, struggling to catch her breath, her movements becoming more erratic with every second as she swayed and rocked, panic and prophecy wracking her in waves.

"For fuck's sake," Al launched forward, shoving Lucy out of the way, grabbing his sister by her jaw and stabbing a syringe into her upper arm muscle. Lilly didn't go down without a fight, sinking her teeth into his hand hard enough to break the skin.

Lucy jumped out of the way, watching helplessly as the girl's body stopped thrashing, going limp in Al's arms. She never meant for this to happen, but now she got to witness what her actions caused, and the guilt felt unbearable. "I'm sorry–"

"What did you think you were doing?!" Al snapped at Lucy once Lilly was subdued, dozing in her brother's grip.

"I was trying to calm her down a little, she had an episode and refused to go inside–"

"She doesn't calm down. It just escalates. Just... don't entertain her delusions." He lifted his sister in his arms.

"She said she wanted to show me something; I didn't know it would lead to this. She thinks she's a goddess or something."

"She is just a sick child who loves reading about myths. She is not a goddess, and talking to her about it leads to this."

"I'm sorry if I caused any trouble. It wasn't intended," Lucy promised. He loved his sister, and he knew what was best for her. She should not have interfered.

Al scowled, grinding his teeth before reluctantly accepting the apology with a nod. "I'm sorry I went off on you. This is my burden to deal with, no one else's. Come on, let's get you back inside as well."

Lucy nodded, following a few paces behind. "Would you like help? I know your shoulder must still hurt."

"She is pretty light, but thank you," he sighed, changing the subject. "How are you holding up? I forget you're technically a prisoner here."

"I think I might be getting promoted from prisoner." Lucy matched his pace. "I have an idea for how to save Gaia."

She had been brewing a plan at the back of her mind ever since she had left Aris's office; it was beginning to take shape, dangling just out of her reach.

"You're absolutely sure you want to help these people?" Al pushed. "Take away the magical creatures and this becomes a human trafficking situation."

"I'm not helping them. I'm helping myself," she answered. "Though I don't know if that makes me the hero of the story or a villain."

Al stared at her in disbelief. "A *victim*, Lucy!"

"But if I don't start now then when? I won't get another chance like this one."

"To do what exactly?" he stopped, turning to face her. "What happened to the naive girl who just wanted to make a living?"

"I want a voice."

"You have one. What you want is for others to hear it." Al looked skeptical. "This family might not be the best platform to test that voice. You'll have to prove you're more dangerous than any of them and I don't know how you'll do that."

"I don't have anything waiting for me outside of this place," Lucy insisted. "I want to see where this goes; I have magic and power and control here, Al! If I walk away from this now, then what? What could possibly happen to me here that's worse than the life I'd lead out there?"

Al looked at her, trying to read Lucy's expression. "...I can't answer that for you. Your path is your own."

"It is mine, isn't it?" Lucy looked at Lilly in pity. "Before tonight, the only time I was ever called a goddess was when someone wanted to get into my pants. Sometimes, just for a second, it's nice to believe you're bigger than your problems." She smiled at Lilly and brushed a wave of white hair from her face before leaving her and Al behind, walking into the house alone.

***

Strolling the empty hallways in silence, Lucy took a moment to think. She was at a crossroads and she needed to pick a path. Aris had refused her help, half-baked as it was, choosing to trust Eleanore's gambit over hers. The insult stung viciously. There was no doubt in Lucy's mind that Eleanore was lying, that as soon as she had her hands on Gaia she would take off and leave them in the dust. She could barely believe that Aris had been desperate enough to trust her in the first place; at least Lucy's lies had been convincing.

She paused, suddenly unsure of if she had lied at all. She was certain she could fix Gaia, just not that she could do it without accidentally killing someone.

The idea darted away from her grasp, frustrating her. There was something there at the very back of her mind, a solution she could not quite reach. It never crossed her mind that she might not be able to recharge Gaia at all. She knew what she needed to do, her grasp on the flow of life secure enough now that she was certain she could reverse what she had done. Her powers were growing stronger and for the first time in her life Lucy felt like the main character and not just some nobody struggling to survive in a hungry world. More than that, she felt as though she had finally found where she belonged; the misfits that had tried to steal her had become her foster family. Control and belonging mixed together into a heady brew, intoxicating.

She had to be careful and she knew it; if she used her magic too freely she would end up stuck in the same position as Klein. Loved but useful, a disrespected servant. Lucy had already had enough of having to work for others' profit.

No. She'd had a taste of power, and she needed more. Lucy wanted to grow her abilities, to be respected. To be feared. She wanted to walk into the room and, like Eleanore, demand instant and undivided attention.

Lilly's words echoed in Lucy's head, louder and louder.

It's not sad. It makes me so angry, and it should make you angry as well.

Between your power and my memories...

Lucy had power. She didn't want Lilly's memories; her own strength was all she needed.

She wasn't sad, she was angry. Angry that she had allowed others to take that power from her or use it against her. Angry at the people who treated her like she was weak. She had more power in her hands than they had ever had the right to use against her.

Clarity broke though the dizzying flood of thoughts and emotions like lightning through storm clouds, illuminating her path. Breathless,

Lucy stared at herself in the dusty hallway mirror; she didn't see her own reflection anymore, reaching shaking hands up to touch the glass.

A Goddess reached up to meet her fingers, welcoming her home.

CHAPTER THIRTY FOUR

LUCY

Her mind racing furiously, Lucy returned to her bedroom to think. Her door was open a crack as she approached and she felt for the strings of life around, finding a familiar energy dance on her fingertips. The master of the house was waiting inside and he wasn't pleased. His golden strand was tight with anger, vibrating like a plucked guitar string.

Lucy was ready.

"Where have you been, girl?" Aris stood by the window, looking over the dead garden. "Is now truly the time for your childish tantrums?"

"How exactly am I the childish one here?" She leaned against the door frame. "Only a kid could be naive enough to believe Eleanore actually wants to help you, Aris."

He ignored the jab. "This whole place is running out of time and you are frolicking in the garden."

"My time is mine to spend however I want." She shrugged, sitting down on her bed. "You made it perfectly clear that you don't need me to help, anyway."

"Sulk then, for all the good it does. My mind is made up on the matter."

"Then you're an idiot, and you deserve whatever she does to you," Lucy snapped back, glaring at the man. She had never thought less of him than in that moment, seeing past his facade of control for the first time.

"How dare you speak to me like that, girl." Aris clenched his fists, taking a few menacing steps towards her. "Have you lost your mind?"

"No, but you have clearly lost yours." She got up, standing her ground. "If you think I'm scared of you then you're in for a rude awakening."

"Shall we test this little theory of yours?" He hissed as his fingers wrapped around her throat, pushing Lucy against the wall.

The initial hit made her ears ring, but it did not carry any of the man's strength as he pulled back at the last second. He was bluffing. Lucy knew that for sure. This was just one last desperate attempt to regain control, and she wasn't about to let him have it. His grasp weakened for a moment as Aris watched her with a hint of confusion.

Lucy closed her eyes as her hand covered his, his life wrapped around her fingers. When she pulled he grimaced in pain, releasing her.

"Count me impressed," he cursed, rubbing feeling back into his hand. "I wouldn't mind feeding your sassy ass to my dogs. When the Hell did you get so cocky?"

"I'm not being cocky, Aris," Lucy assured him. "I can back up everything I'm saying." She reached for him, hand touching his chest as he flinched. She pushed him back towards her bed, barely able to believe what she was doing.

Aris took a few steps back, forced into obedience and not caring for the taste of it. Stubbornly he stood against the bed, refusing to lie down for her.

With her voice commanding and raspy still from his grip, Lucy pushed his chest. "Bed, now." She watched him hesitantly obey, acting like he was letting her play this game, that he still had control. "Lay down flat."

"Bossy little thing, aren't you?" He did as he was told, resting his head on his arms, his fury and shame muddled with curiosity, wanting to see what Lucy had planned for him.

Taking her hair down, Lucy moved her fingers over the ivory buttons on his shirt. Aris watched her unbutton them one by one, revealing tanned skin covered in intricate, crude tattoos and poorly healed scars. She traced the darkly inked tentacle that wrapped itself around his chest, stopping right above the waist of his pants.

He looked up at her, his expression questioning the pause.

Lucy drank in the sight of Aris's obedience, sliding onto the bed beside him, moving until she was straddling his waist. Slowly she released the first buttons of her shirt, enjoying the frustration on his face, rewarding his patience as she shrugged the clothing off to the floor. She could feel his excitement as he pressed against her, waiting for her next move, his hands sliding over her leather-clad thighs.

"Good boy," she whispered in his ear before kissing his cheek, triggering a sharp inhale as Aris resisted the urge to catch her lips with his.

You are having way too much fun with this.

Lucy smiled to herself, admiring the man beneath her. Who could blame her? The marble-like sculpted chest, warm under her hands, rose with each breath of anticipation. Something about him stirred a primal need within her. That crude, infuriating, selfish man...

"Hands up here." She forced his wrists above his head. "And don't move, or I'll start over," Lucy began at his ear, waiting for him to disobey, kissing, sucking and nibbling her way down his jawline and neck, rough stubble meeting the contrast of soft full lips.

"Bitch..." He shifted impatiently, lifting his hips again to meet the weight of her body.

With a heavy sigh, Lucy stopped her descent. "Looks like I have to start over." She shook her head, lips tracing down his neck and across his collarbones. Her fingers twisted into the curls that crowned his head as his erection pressed urgently against her warm thighs.

"I hate this game," Aris held in a moan, trying not to make any more sudden movements.

She made her way down his chest, lips trailing down lower and lower until his stomach tensed with each kiss. "I'm sure you do. Who's my good boy, Aris?" she asked mockingly as she shifted to sit up on his lap, fingers brushing against his cock through the front of his pants. She could see the conflict play out over his face, the desire to fuck her fighting with the urge to rip out her throat. His dick made the choice for him; he could regret it later, the promise of her hips too much for him to resist.

"...I am."

"Yes, you are," Lucy pulled on his pants, slowly lowering them down to his knees. Determined to drive him mad with want, she took her time, ignoring the heat of lust between her legs and deep in the pit of her stomach. Her own need for him was just as inebriating.

Drawing out each stroke and with her breath tickling the sensitive skin, Lucy placed the throbbing tip between her lips. There was no sense of urgency, just a moment to enjoy the control she had over him. She tilted her head with a soft gasp, her tongue exploring the texture of his cock.

His moans were raw, real, and she loved it, but she wasn't ready for the moment to be over, not yet. He had humiliated her. She would return the favor.

She broke away, ignoring his whine of protest as she got to her feet. She rolled her eyes at him–how had she ever been afraid of him?– and loosened the strings of her pants, sliding them to the ground with her boots, gloriously naked. With one hand behind her back she returned to him, pushing him down.

His body connected with hers, and Aris' entire length filled her. She shivered as he bucked beneath, her stomach tight in anticipation; she could feel herself teetering on the brink of climax, giddy with power, her breath hitching as she broke their kiss and pressed her body against his, his sweat slick against her breasts, her hands fumbling with the clasp of the collar he'd made her wear; that she had smuggled into the bed as she'd stripped. Lucy let out a choked cry as Aris shuddered and tensed beneath her; she could feel his heat spilling inside, making her ache, her body tightening around his cock as she came.

She sat up with a gasp, biting her lip as she slid the warm around chain his throat and pulled it tight.

"Mine," she panted, cheeks flushed blood red. Aris lay dazed beneath her, his hands gripping her thighs as he softened inside of her.

"Yours," he agreed breathlessly; he didn't try to fight, letting her fasten the collar against his skin.

"I want Eleanore," Lucy demanded, pulling the collar just a little too tight. The bauble of an idea had manifested at last.

"I can't give you something that isn't mine," Aris winced, shoving her hand away. "She's our only hope of fixing Gaia."

Oh no. She wouldn't take no for an answer. She reached over the side of the bed, fumbling for the knife she'd hidden in her boot. The thin blade pressed against Aris's skin, just above the golden collar, the sharp edge biting into his flesh.

"Not anymore." Lucy flashed him a wicked grin. "Set up a meeting for me with her. It's time she learned just who wears the pants in this family."

***

Pleased with herself, Lucy gathered the discarded clothing. Among the piles of leather armor was the yellowed linen of Aris' shirt, a trophy she had decided to keep. She needed to wash if she was going to confront Eleanore; she tucked the shirt under her arm and slipped into Lai's room.

Lai seemed to be feeling better, snoozing on top of his pile of cushions, a dragon with a misguided hoard. Lucy didn't bother to wake him as she turned on the shower, letting him nap as she washed off sweat and sex.

She dried herself off quickly and pulled Aris's shirt over her leathers, crawling into bed next to Lai.

"Feels like you want me to ask why you're wearing my father's clothes," Lai mumbled sleepily, making some room for her. "Are you going to fill me in on the details, or will I be forced to try to imagine daddy-dearest in the throes of passion?"

"What do you want to know?"

"Let's start with everything. From the top."

"I got your dad to agree to take me seriously." Lucy rolled on her back, staring at the gems decorating the ceiling.

"I've gotta be honest, I'll have to see it to believe it."

"I put a collar on him."

Lai froze at that, sitting up to give Lucy his full attention. "Fuck, okay. This is getting interesting. What's the game plan then?"

"Kill his batshit ex to get this place back up and running." It was such a simple plan that Lucy was almost embarrassed that it had taken so long to formulate. The devil was in the details, though.

"You're gonna sacrifice Eleanore? Okay, I know she messed with you, but," Lai paused, clicking his tongue. "Don't you think that might be taking it too far now? I don't know if you're magical enough to undo a murder."

"She took it too far when she tried to kill me," Lucy pointed out.

That seemed to soothe Lai's ruffled feathers.

"As long as it's personal and not over a man."

"Never. I don't fight over men," Lucy said simply. "I'll fight for one maybe, but not over one."

"Men are trash," Lai sighed. "But you and I both like to dumpster dive from time to time it seems."

Lucy ignored the jab, poking Lai affectionately in the ribs. He laughed, rolling onto his back and stretching. "Seriously, though. What's the long game here?"

"To figure out what the fuck is wrong with me, learn to control it, and minimize the damage your dad does."

"Is he really all that scary?"

"Lai," Lucy sighed, "you know what I mean. Kidnapping random people is bad for...well, the people."

"I honestly have no idea what you're talking about," Lai fibbed. "You're thriving here! Look at how much you've changed. Stronger, braver..."

Lucy picked up a velvet cushion and smacked it into his smug face. It wasn't as satisfying as she hoped it would be, but it did shut him up. She only hoped he wouldn't retaliate. A pillow fight with Lai felt potentially lethal. Lucy did not doubt that Lai knew a dozen ways to kill someone with a cushion.

"I'm going to do it, you know. I've made up my mind."

Lai pulled the cushion away, watching Lucy as his fingers teased the golden tassels. He said nothing, which was so unlike him that she almost began to question her decision as his icy eyes stared through her.

"It's the only way," Lucy mumbled with a sudden need to justify herself before sliding down from the bed. "Wish me luck."

CHAPTER THIRTY FIVE

LAI

Lai watched her go, but he didn't like the path she took. A difficult path filled with nothing but heartache and loneliness. He'd seen others like her never return. Blind in believing that she had only one choice, Lucy had chosen to leave behind a part of her: Lai knew she would regret it only when it was too late.

Rolling off the four-foot-high pile of cushions, Lai landed on his feet. "Sorry, sunshine," he muttered, shaking his head. "Can't let you do this. You're better than that."

The silk robe was thrown aside for a pair of simple pants and a dark T-shirt. He didn't have much time to think his plan through, so the usual method of 'make it up as you go' would have to suffice. He had one goal in mind; he had to stop Lucy from making the mistake that would destroy her life.

Despite the urgency, he paused to check himself in the mirror, not particularly fond of what he saw. Pale regrowth almost inch long, dark bags under his eyes — sloppy, really.

"This retirement doesn't suit you," Lai addressed himself, gathering his hair into a high ponytail. "You're a mess. Yes, you. Don't look so offended." He pointed at his reflection. "It's okay; once I sort this out, we'll hit the spa. Just you and I."

His reflection looked doubtful.

You? Sort it out? When have you ever sorted anything out?

Anything you touch escalates into a bigger mess.

"You are so dramatic," Lai winked and blew a kiss to himself, about to leave the room in search of Lucy's target when the reflection shifted from the mirror and into a bird shape on top of the dresser.

"I'm not dramatic," the magpie cawed, flapping his wings. "I am Time. I see what was, what is and what—"

Lai threw a towel and the bird glided down to the desk, all puffed up in indignation.

"Before I was so rudely interrupted. I would not recommend stopping Lucy. Her actions are guided by the pre-written timeline. Do you think it's mere coincidence that she and Lilly have met?"

If Lai hated one thing, it was to be a puppet in someone else's games. He had been played with as a pawn on the board before. Used and sacrificed again and again. The little speech from the deity did the opposite of convincing him.

"I'm not going to let her take the bait then. If your kind think they can dangle a carrot in front of the girl for their gain—"

"She is our kind."

"That can't be true…"

"Someone is always pulling the strings, Lai. Don't get in the way. You'll get hurt." With that, the god had vanished–but not before stealing a shiny brooch from one of the tapestries.

***

Lai found Eleanore outside of her ship, talking to the second in command. The skeleton crew who had been trapped by the frost were restless, eager to leave after the unplanned and extended stay. They would have been gone by now if the *Kikimora* wasn't so affected by the temperature, delicate for a warship.

The conversation lowered in volume as Lai approached. He would have been be lying if he'd tried to convince himself that didn't unnerve him. What did they have to hide?

Coming up to his once-upon-a-time stepmother, he glared at the men behind her.

"Mind if we chat? Alone, preferably."

Eleanore exchanged looks with her crew before giving them a nod. Something about their faces unsettled Lai. The men looked at him with something that seemed like pity.

"You need to go," he muttered to the woman once they were out of earshot, hoping no one from his family was around to witness the betrayal. He hated the woman as much as the next man, but she was Ryan's and Louis' mother at the end of the day and despite her outbursts she had done a lot for the family in the past. "It's a matter of life and death."

Eleanore snorted, unimpressed by his melodrama. "Your father has given me permission to repair Gaia, darling. Why on earth would you want me to leave now?"

Lai rolled his eyes, shifting from one hip to another. "My father is reconsidering the deal," he bluffed; it was not hard to figure out why Eleanore was being given permission at long last to tinker with Gaia. "He thinks Lucy can do it for half the price and she is out for blood."

"You think he would have the guts? You never were too bright," Eleanore huffed.

Lai smiled. He was used to that insult. His intelligence was always the first target of any jabs, simply because no one could ever fault his appearance. Well, if she wanted to get personal, his tongue was as sharp as his blades.

"He's got a younger bitch now, leading him on a leash. You don't think that bastard would feed you to the wolves? You are so full of yourself. Just go, because Lucy is occupied with his dick and thoughts of revenge."

"Everyone is giving her far too much credit. Just a stupid little girl, meddling in our affairs. She was brought here as a breeding bitch and she is no more than that, despite her magic tricks."

Lai tapped his nails against the side of the ship. The tension rose; all he needed was to fan the flames until Eleanore exploded.

"Weren't you just a breeding bitch before? Oh wait. You–you're past your use-by date now. Father doesn't need you anymore."

A loud slap rang as Eleanore had enough, leaving a red handprint on Lai's face. He stumbled back with a laugh, not ready to retreat just yet. "You know I'm right. He's killed for less than pussy. Those days of the two of you raiding together—That's done. This place is all he has. He doesn't even have enough money to pay her, so she's fucking her boss for free. What do you think you can offer that would hold a candle to that?"

Eleanore crossed her arms, looking at the family manor with hatred clouding her eyes.

"Fine, I'll go." She gave Lai a snake-like grin, reaching over to caress his cheek, one sharp nail tracing a line from his eye to the bottom lip. "Let me just say my goodbyes. Oh, and be a darling? Bring Ryan and Lou outside, I want to give them a hug before I go."

Lai swallowed, flinching away from her touch.

That had been far too easy.

CHAPTER THIRTY SIX

LUCY

Lucy paced the parlor room, somewhat annoyed with her punctual self. Of course she was early, like a good little girl. She knew that Aris wouldn't be here on time — He would stroll in ten minutes late like he owned the place. She smiled a little at the notion. Aris may not have realized it fully yet but she knew the manor was hers now.

She was starting to get irritated when Aris finally entered the room, slamming the door shut behind him and turning the key in the lock. He looked frazzled, his mind elsewhere.

"I have been thinking. When you told me you could fix Gaia, did you mean it?" he asked her, doubtful and anxious. He must've known, deep down, that Eleanore was not going to repair Gaia for him but he clung to the hope still. If Lucy killed her without a plan, everything was lost.

She watched him pace. *Could I do it?*

Yes. The transfer of power was easy; it was the murder she was less sure of. She nodded.

"Alright. I wash my hands here." He opened the door again. "You want control? It's yours. Fix Gaia. I don't care how. We will settle the accounts after. If I don't have to see Eleanore again, well, that is only a bonus in my books."

"How much do you owe her?"

Aris' scarred lips pressed into a thin line. It was all the information Lucy needed.

"Are you going to get rid of me when payday comes?" She leaned on the mantle, playing with drips of wax from an old candlestick. Aris glared at her, angry but too tame to argue.

"Be a darling and bring Gaia here, quickly," Lucy ordered, following him to the door. "I have a few of my own accounts to settle."

***

Lucy stepped into the kitchen, expecting Klein to be busily cooking or cleaning, disappointed to find the room empty and quiet. She placed the kettle on the stove, filling it with water; thankfully the embers of the fire were hot enough to boil it. She would have been in trouble otherwise. Somehow in all her time spent at the manor she never had to start that fire. Perhaps Klein went easy on her. Where was he, anyway?

While the water boiled, she checked the small servant's room that linked to the kitchen. She was still surprised that Klein chose to live there. There were plenty of empty rooms on the upper floors, but the man downgraded himself to a servant even at night.

There he was. Asleep. Still fully dressed and wearing shoes.

That can't be comfortable. Lucy tip-toed in, the creaking floor giving her away–but Klein didn't stir. She unlaced and removed his footwear, placing it neatly by the bed and covering Klein with a blanket. The little gesture was all she could offer in exchange for his kindness earlier.

Stop watching him sleep, you creep.

Lucy did not take her own advice, instead sitting down on the bed next to Klein. She didn't want to leave just yet, comforted by his presence. Would he be disappointed if he knew what she was about to do?

The faint whistle of the boiling kettle called Lucy away from her thoughts, and she rushed back before the damned thing woke him. The last thing she wanted was to interrupt his well-deserved rest.

Scouring the cabinets, she found all she needed, a silver tray, a couple of teacups, sugar, milk, and a pot that she filled with tea leaves and boiling water. Lucy arranged everything neatly. Her entire plan was laid out in front of her.

I hope that bitch likes tea.

***

"Are you lost, little girl?" Eleanore glanced up from the leather fireside chair.

Lucy's eye twitched, watching the woman cross her legs, the simple gesture beyond infuriating. It wasn't just her disrespectful manner. Everyone in the family knew that only the head of household sat in that gross, ancient, stained chair. Eleanore wasn't just making herself comfortable; she was making a point.

Across from her, on top of the coffee table, laid Gaia. The flickering of her slowly shutting down body added an unsettling glow to the room. Not yellow anymore but warm orange, the color of a sunset.

"I thought we might have a civil conversation. Is tea okay?" Lucy placed the food and pot on the side table, tugging on her ear lobe nervously.

"Ah, did he finally put you back in your place? Be a darling then." Eleanore waved her hand for Lucy to pour. "No sugar. You could probably stand to avoid it too."

Lucy removed her hand from her ear and allowed her hair to fall back in place, hiding her missing earring, the pearl pressed between her fingers. She knew that Eleanore wouldn't trust her outright so she made a show of pouring a cup for herself as well, adding four teaspoons of sugar and taking a big sip.

"How long do you think she has left?" Lucy glanced at Gaia as she poured the tea for Eleanore. With a little force the poisons' shell crumbled into the teacup and dissolved without a trace. "It's incredible how life-like she is."

"A week at the most." Eleanore couldn't be any less concerned over the drink preparation, not taking her eyes off the machine in front of them. "Will Aris be joining us, or is this an ambush?"

"Milk?" Lucy offered.

"Just lemon."

Placing a slice into the fragrant brew, Lucy handed the cup to Eleanore.

"If Aris wasn't such a stubborn ass, I could get some livestock and transfer the energy from them." Lucy composed her face carefully as she watched the woman take a few sips, pinkie out. How could Eleanore be so calm, sitting next to her almost-victim? She truly didn't consider Lucy a threat. Just some girl. A servant.

"That man wouldn't ever let you sacrifice an innocent animal."

"No, he's too much of a softy for that," she agreed. "But a war criminal, on the other hand..." Lucy raised an eyebrow at Eleanore, a smile curling her full lips.

A long pause followed as she processed what Lucy had said, far too late. She had underestimated her, expecting a frontal assault, not thinking that Lucy could possibly be smart enough to lay a trap.

"You little bitch..." Eleanore dropped the cup as her fingers seized up. The hot liquid burned her knees, but she was unable to move.

Reaching deep inside her conscience Lucy looked for any traces of regret but found only smug satisfaction. Was it really that easy to poison another human being? Why didn't she feel anything for Eleanore? There was nothing there, no compassion.

She felt powerful. In control.

With Eleanore's life at her fingertips, Lucy took a sip from her cup before standing up and placing one of her hands on Gaia and the other on the woman.

"You tried to kill the wrong girl."

With a deep breath, Lucy felt for the energy emanating from Eleanore, the threads of life connected to the wire-like strings leading into Gaia. Fingertips buzzing, she began the transfer, but the flow was sluggish, as if Eleanore was still fighting her even in paralysis. Her eyes darted from side to side in furious panic as her body refused to obey.

"Just let go–" Lucy hissed, pulling harder on the threads, forcing them into Gaia. As the color drained from Eleanore's face, Gaia's glow shone brighter, the dull sunset flicker pulsing with her healthy green hue as her functions resumed. Lucy could feel the difference. The air was warmer and the sun shone brighter. Even the garden seemed to awaken as birdsong grew louder outside.

A few more pulls and she would have her first kill. The control of life and death was hers.

Is this what it feels like to be a god?

Lucy felt her fingers tremble as the energy that passed through her finally sped up. The last of Eleanore's life clung to her dying body, desperate to remain. It was laced with memories, memories that forced themselves on Lucy, playing out as if they belonged to her.

She saw a young woman. Lost and desperate to survive. Parent-less, broke and alone. She saw a world so much like her own, familiar yet alien. The same towns and cities with different faces populating them, surrounding Eleanore as she moved like a ghost through the streets, powerless.

That same young woman arriving at the house.

A promise.

An offer.

It all played out in front of Lucy exactly like her own story. She saw Aris. Younger, with fewer scars. Powerful and tempting.

His embrace, so familiar. His scent.

Lucy inhaled deeply, almost tasting the aroma of rum and cinnamon, her hands drawing Eleanore's energy, desperate to experience more.

Then came the pain, the heartache. A child she hadn't wanted to begin with. She had ambitions and she had to make something of herself. That was not the life she had chosen.

She wanted power; she wanted control.

It all turned into a blur. Lucy felt her head spin, confused; the thread passing from her hands and into Gaia was not coming from Eleanore anymore. It unraveled slowly from Lucy's own chest, moving through her. Why? Lucy tried to break the hold, focusing on Eleanore, trying to find her strings, seeking out the life that was not her own.

She realized then that she could not tell the strings apart, hers and Eleanore's. The energy had the same taste, same smell, same memories— so much like her own, familiar, but exotic.

They were one and the same. Lucy was Eleanore. Eleanore was Lucy.

…and Lucy was killing herself.

The threads tangled and twisted, draining both women as the energy-hungry machine replenished her empty circuits. Lucy cried out, but the sound seemed distant; her body felt far away and out of her control. Her vision went dark, the room drowning in a shadow.

Then she heard it. The roaring of engines. It wasn't her sight fading.

The *Kikimora.* Eleanore's flagship rose above the ground, its cannons turning towards the house. Lucy could see the dark void of the barrel staring right at her, with only a thin panel of glass separating them. Then a flash, a pop, and the world went silent.

The cannonball missed her, but the force of the impact threw Lucy across the room like a rag doll, collapsing the parlor wall between her and Eleanore. Memories faded, and what little energy she had left kept her breathing but barely moving.

With her ears ringing, Lucy could not hear the subsequent dozen explosions that followed, but—

CHAPTER THIRTY SEVEN

LUCY

She had died. She had. Lucy could still feel the blood filling her lungs, the pain of her broken body crushed under stone. But there she stood, upright, unharmed, with only a headache and a few scrapes from the initial blast. She reached for her earlobe, but the second pearl was missing. Eyes darting around the room for any clues, Lucy spotted the only explanation. A magpie perched on a fallen chandelier, prying apart the golden ring holding a string of crystals together. Next to him stood one other. For the first time, Death wore a frown under their white bangs.

The magpie looked up at her, his prize in his beak.

You are wasting time.

Right. She was. For a moment Lucy considered finishing off what she started with Eleanore, but a second chance at life added much needed clarity. Her petty revenge would strip her of her new family and her humanity. She had to make sure that the kids got out safe first.

Nodding a thank-you to the two deities she darted towards the staircase, but her rescue efforts were not off to a strong start. Another cannonball hit the wall, mere inches away from her head. Knocked off of her feet, dust and debris filled the air as Lucy stared at a gaping hole in the brick.

With an ear splitting crash another projectile flew through the open window and took out most of the wall behind her, cutting her off, forcing Lucy to run towards the kitchens.

"You okay? What's happening?" Klein pulled her into relative safety behind the walk-in freezer door, the thick steel protecting the room from most of the damage. She could almost cry. God, she was such an idiot! She could barely believe she had risked never seeing him again just for her stupid payback. Tears burned her cheeks, mixing with the layer of dust that settled on her skin.

"Are you hurt?" he asked, cupping her face and searching quickly for cuts.

Shaking her head, Lucy pressed her face against his chest. She just needed a moment. A moment to feel safe as her world fell apart around her.

"We have to get Lou and Ryan out," she sobbed as his hands offered the human comfort she had almost abandoned.

Klein peeked out into the hallway, looking at the staircase that had suffered damage already, the marble handrail missing in two places and the steps threatening to collapse. "I'll get them, you go. Meet me by the front gate. Can you drive?"

"I'm sorry, but I can't let you do that alone," Lucy pulled away, wiping her face. There wasn't any time to argue, and Klein knew it. He didn't press further, instead taking her hand in his. Using his body as a shield, he escorted Lucy out.

Running through the corridors of the collapsing building, Lucy was thankful for the leathers she wore. The armor saved her skin from the dangerous wreckage protruding from the collapsed walls. Glass embedded in the upholstery of the mangled furniture and shattered door frames with sharp splintered edges made the hallway look like the maw of a beast.

Klein wasn't as lucky. His shirt was torn and covered in smeared blood stains from dozens of cuts. Still he pushed on, squeezing through a narrow gap formed between a door that had been blown off its hinges and a fallen marble column.

"Klein!" Ryan's voice echoed from behind the pillar, trembling and accompanied by the cries of the youngest sibling. Lai was with them as well, cursing loudly as chunks of ceiling collapsed nearby.

"Come on, climb over!" Klein scrambled onto the pillar's side and thrust his hand into the gap behind it, reaching for his brothers.

"Here, take Lou! I need to get my books!" Ryan insisted, holding Louis up for Klein to reach.

"Not the time! You need to come now!" Klein snapped, tucking Louis under his arm and grabbing for Ryan.

"He's right Ryan, books can be replaced," Lai agreed.

"My journals," Ryan begged desperately. "Please, Lai."

Lai groaned, heading into the mangled room behind him. "Take those two," he called out. "I'll meet you guys outside!"

Lucy swore as Lai vanished into the dark. The manor could bury them at any moment and he had decided to play the cool big brother. Selfish.

Ryan hesitated before scrambling up the pillar and taking Klein's hand; the three of them dropped back down to the ground as Lucy rushed to embrace the children, checking to see if they had been hurt. A few bumps and cuts, scuffed knees and palms; nothing major. She silently thanked the magpie. All she had to do now was get them out.

The mad dash to safety turned into a blur of dust and the deafening noise of a crumbling family home. Lucy could smell fire as black smoke rose through the cracks in the floor. Mere moments later the tongues of blueish flame licked at the carpet under their feet. The first floor was burning, and only her prayers were holding the damaged beams in place.

The wall of smoke thickened ahead of them, obscuring their vision, and Lucy cried out as Ryan slipped from her hand and down towards the inferno below, stumbling into a hole in the floor.

"Klein, help!" she screamed as she grabbed onto the boy, her knees digging into the burning carpet. Klein turned back to help as the hallway ahead collapsed, cutting off their escape.

Reaching for both of them, strong hands pulled Lucy and Ryan away from the edge, shaken but unhurt.

"I got you." Klein handed Louis over to Lucy and scooped up his brother. "Let's go back to the room we've just passed. Try the window."

Wasting no time Lucy held the child to her chest, running back. They had mere minutes before the smoke from below suffocated them, or worse, the whole floor collapsed. Over the roar of the fire she heard a voice; Aris was yelling their names from outside, guiding them towards escape.

Klein kicked in the door, breaking the rusted lock and rushing towards the window. The glass had been shattered long ago and the empty frame delivered a welcomed breath of fresh air. Lucy could hear Aris, his voice trembling with worry.

"We're here!" Lucy called back, climbing onto the window sill with Louis in her arms. She swallowed heavily; they were two floors up. Jumping was out of the question.

"I'll catch him, let go!" Aris raised his arms, but the height made Lucy's head spin. How could she let go of a child?

Behind them the floor crackled ominously, the heat rapidly rising. It was do or die. Holding her breath she allowed Lou to drop from her arms; better a quick death than slowly burning.

The child's scream cut short as his father snatched him from the air, carefully placing the youngest on the grass—an effortless catch.

"Ryan! Quickly!" Lucy helped him climb up. "Don't worry. He will catch you."

Sensing the hesitation, she offered a slight push. Time was fickle about whose side he was on.

Ryan howled curses but was soon safely in his father's arms.

Aris raised his arms again, and Lucy felt her stomach drop. She had to jump, too. Eyes squeezed shut she leapt forward, falling blindly to the ground below.

Her fall was cut short by the warm safety of a firm embrace. The cinnamon scent calmed her frayed nerves, and the gentle squeeze promised that everything would be okay.

Lucy opened her eyes. Nothing was going to be okay. The manor was going up in smoke. A dozen airships blocked off the sky, and countless soldiers were rushing towards them.

They had to run. Klein landed beside them, scooping up Lou. She couldn't even look back at the place she had wanted to call home. It was all her fault.

Please, gods, don't let this be real. Her cracked and bleeding lips chanted a prayer that fell on deaf ears as she followed the men to the front gate.

The sounds of destruction faded into the rhythmic crunch of gravel below their feet. The wrought iron gate that had greeted her not so long ago stood open, urging her to leave. Just outside of it Al's car waited for them, the red paint standing out among the gray dust like a beacon of safety.

"We can't stay here." Al fastened Lilly into her seat, pulling her belt tight as she dozed. "You lot need to go – now. I can take two more people, but the rest will have to ride with Lai. He'll be here any second now."

"Get the kids out of here first," Lucy said.

"Where are we going to go?" Ryan protested, but no one had an answer. He was pushed inside the car, tears streaming down his pale face.

"Hey, hey. Don't cry," Al reassured the boys, helping them to strap in. "We'll meet at my place. Assuming I haven't been evicted yet." He forced a laugh that broke off into a cry of protest. "Oh, hey! No! No dogs!"

Two of the hounds snuck into the back seat, curling up around Ryan and Louis. Al looked more pained for his upholstery than anything else as the dogs trampled mud into the fine leather.

"Oh, suck it up. I swear you and Lai deserve each other, both of you are drama queens." Aris slammed the door shut, ignoring Al's flinch at the rough handling of the car. "Where is he, anyway?"

A pop as loud as the cannonballs announced the arrival of the last rescue vehicle. Lai's 1984 Toyota Corolla pulled alongside the group, almost hitting Aris, brakes screeching in protest.

"I'd rather die here than drive with Lai." Klein shook his head, taking a few steps back. He reached for the Mustang's door handle but felt nothing but air. Al was speeding away from the battlefield with a deafening roar of his engine.

"We don't have much of a choice. He can't be that bad, can he?" Lucy took Klein's hand in hers, examining the car before her. Surely it was not road legal. The ancient hatchback was missing both lights at the front and was decorated with dozens of dings and dents. It should have been written off decades ago, but here it was, the last ride out of hell.

The remainder of them, dogs included, piled up into the cramped interior amongst the ton of takeout wrappers and empty bottles. Klein, Aris and the hounds took the back, kindly leaving the passenger seat for Lucy.

"Buckle in. It's going to be a bumpy ride," Lai warned them, changing gears with a makeshift stick that had been repurposed from a Christmas candy-cane decoration. The car whined and jerked forward, rolling out of the gates and down the lonely dirt track that Lucy had navigated mere weeks ago in hopes of a brighter future. She looked over to Lai, and was surprised to see him grinning as he watched the flaming wreckage in the grubby rearview mirror.

"Bye, Barbara!" he cried, his eyes over-bright with tears.

How could she have ever imagined the ending, running away with their tails between their legs, abandoning what was left of the manor to another version of herself? Lucy was almost back where she had started. Broke and homeless, at least this time she had her new family, and far more control over her powers.

She was a goddess, holding tight onto a flimsy grab-handle, rolling down a bumpy forest track, back to her old life.

Acknowledgments

First and foremost. A huge thank you to my husband and my constant supporter. Marly, you are the reason it got this far, without your encouragement this book would've died at first draft. Thank you for the days you've spent muttering darkly, weeding out a million typos. Thank you for fighting me over parts that needed to be cut. Thank you for all your hard work formatting and taking over the publishing process. Here it is in writing. You were right. I was wrong (Don't get used to it).

Next is Alex. Without you I wouldn't have this story, I wouldn't have Lucy. Thank you for visiting this crazy family and letting me show them to the world through your eyes. Thank you for the late night RP sessions helping me get through the stubborn chapters. I hope our adventures do not end.

C.C Davie; just when I thought I had reached the finish line you showed me how much of the race I still had to run! I can't thank you enough. I never would have been able to polish this to a glow without your input, feedback, and guidance. Thank you so much.

To my TikTok and Twitter followers and mutuals; Thank you for the likes, comments, and for engaging with my silly little promos. You kept me going, and I treasure every single like/comment like I'm the dragon with the misguided hoard.

A million thank yous to my Alpha and Beta readers. You lot were the real stars. You had to read the worst writing, littered with typos and still leave amazing feedback that helped me to evolve this story. I'll be forever grateful for your time and wisdom.

Brittney Zamora. Sorry your character is just dead in a tomb but you deserve to be here. Jan 23, 2012 is when you and I met on Gaia Online and started this family. Wouldn't be here without our time together.

Thank you to the Margaret King Spencer Writers Encouragement Trust for your support in getting my manuscript polished. You were the push I needed when I started to doubt.

Kendyll. Thank you, from the bottom of my heart. For keeping the hope alive and believing in my silly book. Thank you for the editorial help. That letter improved the book tenfold.

Purson. I hope that deal was worth it to you because it's invaluable to me. Thanks for the cat as well. He is the best.

And most importantly. Me. Me, me, me. ME! Drunk me, Sober me, crying me…all of the versions of myself that worked on this book. I did it! Against all odds, I did it!

About The Author
Athena M. Bliss

Athena lives in Gisborne, New Zealand with her beloved husband Marly, two dogs, a couple of cats, a lizard, some fish, and their daughter. She enjoys drawing, writing, story telling, D&D, and Magic: The Gathering. She is a member and a strong supporter of the LGBTQ+ community and hopes to pay for her husband's top surgery with the proceeds from the sale of her books.

Made in the USA
Thornton, CO
08/20/23 20:12:57

dad61f0e-6190-4cf7-a7e8-97f35888feeaR02